# DEWEY DECIMATED

# Dewey Decimated

CHARLES A. GOODRUM

PERENNIAL LIBRARY

Harper & Row, Publishers, New York
Cambridge, Philadelphia, San Francisco
London, Mexico City, São Paulo, Singapore, Sydney

This book was originally published in 1977 by Crown Publishers, Inc.

DEWEY DECIMATED. Copyright © 1977 by Charles A. Goodrum. All rights reserved. Printed in the United States of America. No part of this book may be used or reproduced in any manner whatsoever without written permission except in the case of brief quotations embodied in critical articles and reviews. For information address Harper & Row, Publishers, Inc., 10 East 53rd Street, New York, N.Y. 10022. Published simultaneously in Canada by Fitzhenry & Whiteside Limited, Toronto.

First PERENNIAL LIBRARY edition published in 1988.

*Designer: Kim Llewellyn*

Library of Congress Cataloging-in-Publication Data

Goodrum, Charles A.
    Dewey decimated.

I. Title.
PS3557.O59D49   1988      813'.54      88-45027
ISBN 0-06-080933-7 (pbk.)

88  89  90  91  92   WB/OPM   10  9  8  7  6  5  4  3  2  1

# DEWEY DECIMATED

# 1

It started to fall apart on the Ides of March. Until that time there had been the daily pulling and hauling with minor crises on the hour, but apparently without pattern or purpose. On this repellent day, with Washington at its rawest, seediest, and most disagreeable, the hairline cracks suddenly began to run the same way and within hours great chunks of the Werner-Bok's ordered world were dropping into the basement.

Betty Crighton Jones had been increasingly bemused by the mess she'd gotten herself into. On the one hand, for want of any other skill, she'd caromed through journalism school and come out clutching the master's with the world of print before her. On the other, she had been terrified by the savagery of the newspaper scene—magazines were dying right and left, and all that seemed to endure was "public relations." This carried such a stigma among her peers that she was on the verge of occupational hysteria when the position of press officer at the world's richest library appeared and she seized it like an acrophobe on a fire escape. It seemed reasonably safe; it kept her standing among her cultured friends, and it sounded as though it might be better than working. At twenty-five she had taken herself from Columbia's campus to her nation's capital and signed on.

It proved to be an unlikely form of con job. Half her time was spent keeping the Library's name out of the paper, and the other half was dedicated to getting it in. She'd quickly found that anything that dealt with the public and distracted the professionals from their bibliographic endeavors became "public relations." This included an average of three bomb scares a week. She'd noted with pride that this was on a par with the National Gallery of Art (the Werner-Bok's neighbor to the right), and thirty-three-and-a-third percent higher than the Smithsonian's Museum of Natural History, the neighbor to the left. She'd found it comforting to know that her own institution was getting as much attention as its peers.

She'd dealt with daily letters complaining about sexism in the card catalog, and fenced with the little old lady who had just changed 210 cards labelled "Father Divine" to "Jesus, God Almighty" until the nurse arrived. The cards had been neatly lettered with a ballpoint pen, and might not have been noticed for years if the visitor hadn't tried to move them from the Fs to the Js.

Indeed it was a religious matter that began the trouble—or at least it appeared to be religion. Earlier in the week, New York's leading news magazine had received a letter claiming that the Werner-Bok's Dead Sea Scrolls were counterfeit. Since the magazine had based a somewhat awed cover story on their acquisition, the editors were a little testy over the possibility that they had been had.

They dispatched a balding, middle-aged reporter to

investigate and Crighton had defused this one more by appealing to the emissary's grosser chauvinism than by her professional skills, and she was left irritated with herself and the whole incident. She was thus edgier than usual when the *Washington Post* had called on the previous afternoon to say they had a strange letter about the Library's Gutenberg Bible. It was now nine o'clock the following morning and the resulting reporter had just materialized in the doorway of her basement office.

"Hello! Come in and sit down," she said. She got him in a chair beside her desk and seated herself in front of him, leaning forward and projecting her image of the cool, sophisticated professional. She would have been distressed to know he took a fast look and thought: alert, well-scrubbed-girl-next-door with unusually good legs.

"Yeah. I brought it with me." He handed her a piece of paper.

"I'm sorry the Director isn't here," she said, "but we're staging a monster concert tonight and he's off somewhere with last-minute details." She lied; he was upstairs waiting for the report on how it went. Crighton looked at the letter and said, "Oops! It seems to be typed on our own stationery!" Casual, throwaway line; nothing to be taken seriously.

The letter was addressed to the local paper and read:

> *If you are in the market for a colorful story you should examine this Library's Gutenberg Bible. It cost the executors of the trust a quarter of a million dollars but the binding is worth more than the contents. What's worse, they're about to throw good money after bad.*

No signature or date.

---

3

"Ummm," she said, "that's a weird one. Apparently some nut. Do you know any more about it than this?"

"No. I was hoping you could tell *me*."

"I can't imagine. We do have a Gutenberg. It has its own case up in the Great Hall and I think it's belonged to the Library since the twenties. There's no question of its authenticity."

"I've forgotten—what's so great about a Gutenberg Bible?"

"Ever seen one?"

"No."

"Well, it's the first book ever printed—'set in movable type,' as they say. It blows the librarians' minds just looking at it. It *is* pretty impressive. You'd think the world's first try at printing would look fairly beat up and antique. In fact, the letters are as delicate and the ink is as black as if it'd been done yesterday. In quivering truth, if it had been done yesterday, it wouldn't be holding up as well as it is! It's huge, of course. It's supposed to have taken somebody over three years to put together. They had only enough type to do a page at a time."

"'Somebody'? Wasn't it Gutenberg?"

"They don't seem to know. There's nothing in the volume that says who did it. They're sure it was done in Mainz at the time Gutenberg was inventing the process and they know he was interested in it."

"How do they know?"

"It's in his letters—but they don't really know whether he did it himself or even if it was done in his shop."

"But it *was* the first book ever printed?"

"They seem to agree on that."

"What's with the cover being worth more than the contents?"

———

"I can't imagine. I've seen the covers. In fact, I've held them in my own hands when we've had pictures taken, but they're nothing special. Gutenbergs are usually bound in four volumes but ours has just two. It's all there, the volumes are just thicker than usual."

"Could there be something inside the covers— under the leather or whatever they're made of—that could be valuable?"

"I doubt it. I must admit when I read this I thought he meant the worth of the contents—some kind of antireligious freak. I got the picture of somebody who didn't believe in the Bible at all and was tense about the money ours cost and how large everyone takes it." Crighton read the note again and laid it on the desk. She raised her chin and, using both hands, scooped her hair away from her temples, hooking it behind her ears.

"And the 'good money after bad'? Are you buying something else he doesn't like?"

"Not that anybody's told me."

"Would they tell you? Shouldn't I be talking to someone in authority?"

Her pulse skipped a beat. She frequently thought she should have learned how to be a press officer somewhere not quite so deadly as Washington. The local press corps still dreamed of flushing out another Watergate. She wasn't paranoid, she was convinced, they really were after your throat.

"I think I would be aware of it," she said flatly.

"Could I bring in someone to check it out?"

"I doubt it." She tried the cold tone mixed with a hint of irritation. "We have no reason other than this crank letter to question its legitimacy. We don't usually open the collections to appraisers."

"So you really don't think there's a story here?"

"I'm afraid not. This really makes no sense at all.

The book has been up there for fifty years. It's not likely to be worth a flap in our time."

To her surprise, he relaxed and returned his pad to the side pocket.

"Yeah. That's what my editor thought. He figured it was the lunatic fringe but I was supposed to give it a try."

Crighton eased up with relief.

"I don't suppose I could sell you on a Sunday spread about the treasures of the Werner-Bok? How about a snappy four-color..."

The reporter was on his feet in one swift movement.

"No, no! No thanks. I . . . my editor assumed I'd be talking to your head man and I was supposed to tell him something. Would you pass on that Elsbree said, 'Either get your typing paper under control or find out who's trying to screw you'? I think they know each other."

Crighton rose and acknowledged the advice. After one more try to interest him in the evening concert, they exchanged clichés and the reporter treadled backward out the door and into the hall.

Once he was gone, Crighton reread the letter left behind on her desk and thought: that was much too easy. Had he really bought it and was giving up or was he lulling her into the well-known false sense of s.? It was hard to know. If there hadn't been the Scrolls one the week before, she'd have ignored it herself.

She moved the letter to her hold box and ran her mind through the requirements of the day. They structured better backward. The opening concert of the Kreutzer String Ensemble was the big finish. Five hundred of the Washington elite were to assemble in the Great Hall come eight-thirty (it was free but the guest list had been carefully selected), where they would listen to an evening of the finest chamber music. Washington's classical music station would feed it live into the FM network and if she had had her druthers she'd be hearing it at home with her shoes off, but she was supposed to be omnipresent at times like these. In the meantime she mentally ticked off: all press releases written and gone, bios ready, radio types upstairs hanging mikes even now—in fact all that lingered was the *Times-Herald* color stuff, and that bit about the Ides of March. She decided to take care of the *Times-Herald* first, with a loop past the Director on the way home. She resented the ease with which he'd used her as a stalking horse and she felt a little anxiety might be good for his soul.

At that moment, Murchison DeVeer had twelve hours to live.

Murchison DeVeer was the head of the Manuscripts Division which in turn was half of the Rare Books and Manuscripts Department. The two units shared a magnificent room on the second floor, rear center of the Library. The room itself was known as the Chapter House and was a grand-scale reproduction of a medieval meeting room eclectically plagiarized from three Plantagenet monasteries. It stood two and a half floors high with carved oak ceiling and hammer beams. It had linen-fold panels, Norman stained glass, a slate floor, and the place even smelled of unvarnished wood and candle wax. The ambience was overwhelming and doubly amazing since this huge, carved box was supported three sides and bottom by layers of steel book decks and twentieth-century security devices.

Crighton struggled through the heavy entry door, tiptoed down the twelfth century, turned right at the issue desk, and on reaching the wall pulled back what appeared to be a sheet of ancient oak to let herself onto the Manuscripts deck. The wooden panel was backed by three inches of steel and fireproofing and from the rear looked like the inside of a bank vault. One side William of Malmesbury, the other Kurt Vonnegut. The deck aisle had bookstacks to the right, but on the left there was a series of steel and glass double carrels which held the Manuscripts Division staff. Crighton whipped into the first one and was practically on top of DeVeer's desk before she realized he already had a visitor.

"Dr. DeVeer, I'm sorry," she said. "You're busy. I'll come back when you're free."

DeVeer was tall, imperious, and in Crighton's mental directory, a stuffed shirt. He looked at her for a two-beat pause and said: "I am rarely free, whatever that means, and having interrupted this conversation there seems no reason why you should come back to interrupt another. What do you want, Miss Jones?"

Crighton's color rose and she took a lungful of air. "The *Times-Herald* critic asked me about the holographs they're using at the concert tonight. Can you give me a little background on these, please? He wants to use it in tomorrow's review."

"Do you know what holograph means?"

"I'm not exactly sure, no."

"Do you have a dictionary in the press office?"

"Yes—yes, I do."

"But of course you didn't think to look in it. A holograph copy is a copy written in the handwriting of an author or a composer. Since the orchestra is playing from music, you may assume that we are speaking of a composer in this case."

Crighton's resentment was showing and DeVeer permitted himself a slight smile.

"The second half of tonight's concert is devoted to Beethoven. We have considerable Beethoven in the original and one of tonight's selections will be played from original Beethoven holographs."

"Which piece will it be?" Crighton asked.

"The A-minor sextet."

"Has it been performed before?"

"You obviously know very little about music. It has been performed several thousand times before— which is just as well since the copies are quite faint and would be very difficult to read under the conditions in which they'll be used. The musicians have long since memorized the music, but they will dutifully turn the pages and both the audience and the ensemble will presumably get some great aesthetic reward from the experience."

"Do you doubt it, Dr. DeVeer?" Alan Welles asked from his corner. Welles was Assistant Chief of the Rare Books side and one of the good guys on Crighton's list.

"No," DeVeer replied. "I would imagine that if I were a musician I too might. As it happens, these sheets are among the few complete Beethoven items we have. Most of our collection is unpublished fragments and I find myself considerably more sympathetic to them than to materials that any fool can secure anywhere."

"You picture your collections as working materials, not a 'treasure-house'?"

"Either you believe your own propaganda, Mr. Welles, or you've been reading Miss Jones's treacle. I do indeed. Why one dime of money should be spent by a public-oriented institution for 'rare' editions of materials which are totally accessible to the stupidest high school student is beyond me."

He looked pointedly at Crighton. "The administration seems far more interested in buying things you can get into the papers than it is in accumulating the research materials for which a research library is designed."

---

9

"Does the administration know how you feel about this?" Welles asked.

"I have made it abundantly clear. I have only recently, however, discovered some outrageous activities going on which I find shocking. That your precious Director should tolerate this thing immediately under his nose strikes me as a highly significant index of his capacity for his position. Either he is implicated or he is stupid."

Welles gave a rueful smile and Crighton felt as if she were listening in on the bitching in the men's room.

At this moment Sydney Speidel, a tall, stooping man with a Prussian haircut (and DeVeer's own assistant), appeared at the door. He had his hands clasped behind him and he leaned into the room from the corridor.

"'*And if thou tell the heavy story right,*' eh?" he quoted. Crighton wondered if he'd been eavesdropping and was referring to what had just been said or if the phrase was left over from another conversation. She assumed the line was Marlowe. He sprinkled Marlowe quotes like raisins.

"I just wanted to say you were right about . . . uh . . . your earlier guess," Speidel added. "Everything points to it. Let me know what you want me to do. Sorry."

He disappeared. DeVeer had not acknowledged his presence in any way.

"I've got to go, too," Crighton said. "If you could tell me quickly about the holographs, I'll get back to my . . . treacle." She had barely gotten it out when she regretted it. He was one up again. "When did the Library get the material?"

"It was part of a gift from an Austrian paint manufacturer in Pittsburgh. If you must slough off words, you can say that the copies are very valuable, that the original gift of thirty or forty Beethoven pieces was worth over a hundred thousand dollars when it was acquired and that they are among the treasures of the Werner-Bok collections. That's what you were going to say anyway, wasn't it?"

"Thank you, Dr. DeVeer," she said, rose, and fled.

When she reached the door to the Chapter House she shuddered with fury and thought: "You pompous son of a bitch. I hope you fry in hell." She pushed on the door and stepped back into the civilized world.

By four o'clock Crighton had reported the Gutenberg interview to the Director, met with two reporters from *Music World*, explained the intermission feature to the Voice of America program director, and been hit with the shock of the Ides of March obligation still untouched. She seized her desk phone and called the chief of the Rare Books Division.

"Dr. Rose? I do really beg your pardon! Have you been waiting for me? I am sorry. I got completely tied up."

"I thought you'd forgotten me," he said.

"No, no. Look, could you bring down one of the better Shakespeare folios? I could meet you at the case in the Great Hall."

"I've been holding one on my desk for you—I think the Wheatley copy is the most appropriate for your purpose. I'll come at once."

The Exhibit of the Week case was directly in front of the main entrance, and by the time Crighton reached it from her basement office, Rose was coming across the mosaic from the elevator. He was a large, slightly shuffling man with gray hair, gray moustache, and with gray plastic for his glasses frames.

"Good afternoon, Miss Jones," he said. "Do I have the key or do you?"

"I hope you do. I don't."

——

"I was afraid of that."

He started to lay the heavy folio on top of the case, thought better of it, and carefully balanced it on the side rails while he fumbled through his pockets for the key. Having found it, he handed it to Crighton, and picked up the Shakespeare again. Crighton unlocked the case and propped it open on two hinged side rods.

The previous week's exhibit had been tied to Charlemagne's birthday, using that questionable date as an excuse to display the Library's Cassino Codex. Although the Codex was noted for its vellum illuminations, it had been displayed closed so the beaten gold covers and set jewels could show. The volume weighed over twenty pounds and Crighton reached in to remove it to make room for the Shakespeare folio.

"What shall I do with it?" she asked as she struggled to pick it up.

"Just lay it on the floor. It was chained to a marble desk for four hundred years. Another ten minutes won't hurt it."

"It seems like sacrilege."

The book had been lying on a sheet of purple velvet to dramatize the metal, and Crighton seized this with one hand, got the cloth on the mosaic and the book on the cloth without doing any damage that she could see.

"Is this Ides of March bit for real?" she asked.

"It was the Director's idea. It's like the Codex—just an excuse to display the rarities."

"Ummmm. Are you going to put the Shakespeare on something?"

"No. I think the bare wood is quite appropriate."

Rose spread the huge volume and centered it in the case. He first turned to the *Tragedy of Julius Caesar* and then leafed until he found the famous passage, which he touched with his finger.

"'Beware the ides of March,'" Crighton read. "And this is supposed to be the first time it appeared in print?" She produced a green plastic arrow she had brought along and aimed it carefully on the page. "Could Shakespeare have seen this very volume?"

"No. He died in '16. The folios were printed in '23."

"Dr. Rose, where do you stand on the who-really-wrote-Shakespeare argument?"

"Well, I was saying just the other day that it may not have been Shakespeare at all but another man with the same name."

Crighton, who had been locking up the case, did a slow double take and came up to look at Rose. She had always thought of him as a sort of mussed, walruslike uncle, with more of the absent-minded scholar about him than anyone else on the staff. It had not occurred to her he might have a sense of humor. After a long look, she was still not sure. He might simply have been passing on some information.

She handed the key to Rose, and leaned down to pick up the Codex—revealing a display of nylon which, if it was not appreciated by the scholar, got the full attention of a young man who had just entered the Hall from the Mall steps. By the time she had straightened up again, he had worked his way through a small forest of mahogany signs pointing to the Social Science, the Fine Arts, and the Rare Books reading rooms and had arrived at her side. An older, much fatter patron was coming up from the opposite direction. The fat man headed straight for the book she held against her chest.

"Wait a moment, ma'am," he said. "That is magnificent. Is it real gold?"

"Very much so," Rose replied.

"What is it?"

"A ninth-century version of Mark and parts of John.

---

The covers are from the 1200s."

"What's it worth?"

"I have no idea," Rose replied as if it had never crossed his mind before.

"Do you know its provenance? Did it belong to anyone special?"

"Well, it came from Monte Cassino when the Germans broke up their collection—is that what you mean?"

"No, no. I have found that books that have been handled by famous people have a presence about them. My students say they have the 'vibes' of their owners. It's quite real."

This brought the conversation to a full stop. A book, to Rose, was an object of art to be studied as a thing. To Crighton it was an object of awe—to think somebody actually wrote all those words! The metaphysical approach was new to both of them. Rose thought he must have misunderstood, Crighton was embarrassed for the visitor, and the younger man—who was now looking at the book and down Crighton's blouse at the same time—smiled with open contempt. The fat man was not the least abashed.

"It's true," he said. "You can feel it about the Gettysburg drafts at the Library of Congress. I've touched the Bible that Mary Queen of Scots held against her breast when she was beheaded—it's in the Huntington in L.A. You get an overpowering . . ."

To Rose's horror, he realized he had not misunderstood at all. "Miss Jones! I really must see the Director before he goes home. Could you return the Codex for me? Just leave it with Miss Brewer."

"No strain."

"Thank you," he said, and rushed away.

Crighton tried a less volatile topic. "Are you looking for something special?"

"I am indeed," the fat man replied pleasantly. "I've come to see your *Tamerlane*. I was at a convention in Baltimore and it seemed a shame to be so close without coming down to hold it. I've never touched one in first edition. I teach Poe at Dennon College."

The silence was too obvious.

"You know what a *Tamerlane* is, of course?"

The young people exchanged glances. "I think you've got us. Is there any news in it? I'm the firm's press officer."

"Great heavens, girl! There are only seven known copies in the world and you have one of them. Parke-Bernet Galleries recently sold one for a hundred and twenty-five thousand dollars!"

"That's disgusting," the younger man said irritably. "How big is it?"

"About fifty pages."

"My God. Has whatever is in it been reprinted?"

"Of course. It's the first poems Poe ever wrote. The poor soul was starving to death—almost literally—at the University of Virginia. He got an apprentice printer to set the pieces in type and the two teen-agers titled it *Tamerlane and Other Poems by a Bostonian*. Apparently the pseudonym was supposed to give it a little dignity. They printed only fifty copies, but it's the first Poe there is and many of us believe it to be beyond price."

"But you can read it in paperback?"

"Oh, yes."

"There you are. This first edition business is outrageous. It's the contents that matter."

Crighton's mind raced to something Robert Benchley had said: I can't see why more people don't buy my books—they're *all* first editions!

The fat man was replying intently. "No, sir. I suspect you don't appreciate it because you've never tried it. There is something quite electric about a really rare book. Almost literally. I'm sure you'd feel it about this *Tamerlane*. Wait a minute! I could show you. Do you have time to go with me? Where do they keep the rare books here?"

Crighton and the young man looked at each other and laughed.

"Why not?" the young man said to the professor. "I'm working in their manuscripts and they're in with the rare books." He looked at Crighton. "I suppose that's where you're taking that gold thing?"

Crighton nodded. "Sure, come on. We'll show you the way."

Crighton took a second look at the younger man and thought, not bad. Never saw him before in my life. I wonder how long he's been up there? I'm getting as bad as the librarians—the people and the books are getting blurred.

To her relief the fat man remained quiet while they got him into the elevator, down the second-floor corridor, and through the Gothic doors of the Chapter House. Once within the room's hushed gloom the younger man said, "My name's Carson. Why don't you go on and get his ... whatever. I'll stay with him and sign 'im in."

The professor whispered, "I have a letter from the Director ..."

Crighton left them stooping over the guard's table by the door while she carried the Codex the length of the room to the issue desk. Elsie Brewer, tall, gray, severe, and in her sixties, presided over this piece of furniture—located where the altar should have been.

"Good afternoon, Miss Jones. May I help you?"

"I hope so. Here's Dr. Rose's Codex. He'll be by to get it in a minute. What I need is a *Tamerlane*. We got a *Tamerlane*?"

"What is a *Tamerlane?*"

"A book."

"Oh? Who is the author, please?"

"You've never heard of it either?"

"Well, I haven't memorized everything we own! I'll have to check the catalog."

"Apparently it's under Poe, Edgar Allan."

"I'll see."

She disappeared and Crighton turned to see how the men were coming. Although the glow from the stained glass made a greenish haze on the side aisles, the tables in the center of the room were in semidarkness. There were large bronze lamps at regular intervals and the half dozen readers in the room each became silent silhouettes in front of a circle of light. By the time the sign-in was finished and the men arrived, Brewer had returned carrying a small box. She saw the younger man and brightened visibly.

"Mr. Carson! Ready to start again? Here are your things."

"We don't deserve you, Miss Brewer. You're all that's left of an ordered world."

She gave him a bleak look and handed him a buckram-bound diary. The box she gave to Crighton, who passed it to the fat man. He immediately registered delight, led them to one of the lighted lamps, and motioned them to sit on either side of him.

The box which he held was a beautifully bound slipcase. It may have meant nothing to Crighton, but it clearly meant something to somebody. It was smaller than an ordinary book, richly covered with deep wine leather, and tooled and gilded with great restraint. The surface glowed like velvet, making the tiny golden letters of the title appear suspended in space. The older man cradled it in both hands for a moment, savoring the pleasure of anticipation.

17

He then laid the box on the table and wiped his hands across his shirt. He picked it up again, seizing a ribbon tab which extended from one side. Holding it between his thumb and forefinger he carefully drew out the inner tray. The *Tamerlane* lay revealed on the green silk lining.

Whoops! Crighton thought. Anticlimax Department! The contrast between the opulent box and the decayed contents was abrupt. That Is Really Nothing, she thought.

The book was cardboard bound, and amateurishly printed on cheap, graying paper. It looked its age. The fat man was staring at it intently.

He tilted the tray forward and let the volume drop into his hand. Laying the tray on the table, he opened the book, examined the endpapers, the title page, the poems inside. The contents were as pitiful as the cover. The pages were worn, few of them coming to a square corner, and the print had faded down to a pale gray nearly matching the paper.

Crighton looked at the professor to see if it was coming up to his expectations. Rather to her surprise, she found a mixture of irritation and confusion in the older man's eyes. He finished turning the pages and then hunched over the table, holding the book close to the lamp. He singled out one page in particular, and held it against the light. It appeared to have worn in different thicknesses. Parts of it were very thin, others seemed to have a second sheet stuck to them. When he returned it to the desk, the page again looked like all the others.

"Is something the matter with it?" Carson asked.

"Ummm. I don't know. It does seem a bit odd."

The older man turned back to the title page and held it up. It too was piebald, but not so dramatically as the other.

"Very strange. I had no idea their copy was in such poor condition. If it were any place but here..." His eyes narrowed and he turned to the endsheets which appeared to be firmly—even freshly—pasted to the covers. They were as dirty, rough, and coarse as the rest and seemed to complete the degenerate air the book projected.

The fat man suddenly snapped the volume together and dropped it into the tray.

"Well. Most unusual." The puzzled irritation was now plainly evident. "I really don't understand it. This was a part of the Finsen collection they acquired in the twenties. So much of the Finsen was mint, I assumed this was too, but..." He looked at Carson. "Well, we won't look for the vibrations I was talking about!"

He smiled wryly and struggled to his feet, holding the slipcase with casual contempt. They watched him move down the aisle, hand it to the woman, hesitate as if to say something, and then shake his head and start back. When he drew abreast he held out his hand.

"Thank you for your help and good luck on... whatever you're doing." He made a gesture toward Carson's diary. "And thank you for your hospitality, ma'am." He nodded and left.

Crighton looked at the young man. "What do you suppose?"

"Beats me. Weird bit."

They parted, and Crighton headed for her office.

Murchison DeVeer was down to his last six hours.

# 2

By eight o'clock that evening, Crighton was slumped on an overstuffed couch in the staff lounge, tired but reasonably pleased with herself. The intervening hours had been spent getting final details resolved, the musicians welcomed (with the help of the Music Division staff), and a half dozen music critics introduced to as many violinists for interviews. At seven-thirty the critics had taken off in one direction and the ensemble had moved off in the other—up the back stairs from the temporary dressing room in the Acquistions Department, headed for the Great Hall overhead.

With everyone out of sight, Crighton repaired her makeup and dug around in her purse for her discount house transistor. She snapped it on and tuned it in time to hear the announcer say,

". . . now give you Dr. Nelson Brooks, the director of the Werner-Bok Library."

"Thank you, Mr. Hamlin," came Brooks's voice. Crighton was pleased; he sounded every bit as professional as the media type. "Welcome to the first in the spring season of the Werner-Bok concerts. Once again we welcome the world-famed group which has so often thrilled us in the past, the Kreutzer String Ensemble. The Ensemble is under the baton of Joseph Bartel as it has been for so many years, and Dr. Bartel will announce his own numbers. Later, during the intermission, we hope you will enjoy an interview with the distinguished bibliophile David Rosenthal. Now let me welcome you again to the Werner-Bok concerts, and without further delay I give you Dr. Bartel." A reverberating roar broke out as the applause bounced back and forth off marble walls, and Crighton switched off the gadget.

In many ways, the concerts were the most satisfying part of her job. They were warmly accepted by the Washington cultural community, and they made everybody happy: the public got some splendid free music, the Director got some inexpensive publicity, and the staff got to show off the building. During the final hours before a performance, five hundred chairs were set up across the mosaic, a wooden platform was struggled into place, and appropriate palms and plants were scattered around the podium. The Great Hall was surrounded by marble arches lifting gallery upon gallery to the apotheosis of something on the ceiling vault three and a half stories above and it made for spectacular acoustics. As Crighton had written home at Christmas, "It worked like a big humongous shower stall, and the carols brought tears to your eyes!"

With the concert introductions complete, she hurried up the elevator to the lounge to join the rest of the staff listening on a high-fidelity set. Orchestra seats were too coveted to be wasted on employees, so the staff heard it on radio at the same time it was fed to the rest of the country. Most of them, like Crighton, would have preferred to be at home in comfort, but the Director wished everyone "to share it like a family." The lounge was at the left of the Chapter House room, and Crighton slipped in and flopped onto an empty couch without calling too much attention to herself.

She was drifting in letdown and fatigue when she realized that Speidel was hovering over her.

"Ah, Miss Jones," he said. "Lovely, isn't it?"

"Ummm," she said, without enthusiasm.

"I, ah, hope you didn't take Dr. DeVeer's remarks too seriously this morning." He *had* been eavesdropping, she thought. "He's very loyal to the Library, you know, and he has the greatest respect for the Director."

"Really? I seem to have missed that."

"Oh, no, he just feels the mission of the Manuscripts Division is so important that anything that impairs it is of great concern. I hope you . . . haven't mentioned this to Dr. Brooks. Couldn't we just keep it our secret?" He gave her a conspiratorial wink.

Before she could reply, she found he was looking over her head, staring at whoever was behind the couch she was sitting on. She twisted around to find Miss Brewer several feet away but with her voice rising so the two could hear it distinctly. Brewer was very red in the face, talking directly at Dr. Rose, who was juggling a coffee cup and trying to look past her toward the door.

"Will you please pay some attention to this," she was saying. "I really think he's become irrational."

Rose looked down at his cup, then back toward the door and said: "He has resented me for ten years. You know as well as I do this is nothing new. I don't believe he takes me seriously enough to do anything even if it crossed his mind."

"But that's what I'm trying to tell you," Brewer was

pleading. "He *is* taking it seriously. And Speidel says he's not going to tolerate it any longer and he is going to do something. This isn't his usual supercilious way. He says he's going to *do* something once and for all."

"Yes, well I guess we'll just have to see what it is." Rose started toward the door with Brewer keeping close step beside him.

"No! Don't wait for him to start it. You really must assert yourself here. You have several alternatives..."

They drifted beyond earshot and Crighton expected Speidel to resume their conversation. Instead he straightened up and said, "Has Dr. Brooks been here yet?"

"Not that I've seen."

"I'm afraid that DeVeer has forgotten we're all assembled. For the good of the division I think I'd better find him before the Director takes the roll. Nice to talk to you." He moved quickly from the room with a characteristic lope which had reminded Crighton on first sight of Groucho Marx rolling after Mrs. Dumont. It now hit her she had been missing the image completely. There was nothing funny about Speidel. He was more like a cupped radar antenna turning back and forth, listening, listening. A thoroughly unpleasant specimen, she concluded.

She had lost herself in general distraction trying to figure out who the "he's" had been in Brewer's warning when Speidel returned with DeVeer close behind. DeVeer stood dramatically in the door and surveyed the room. The sound of the concert came from the corridor behind him a fraction of a second after the same chord came from the hi-fi, making the real seem to be the echo of the electronic.

DeVeer examined each conversational group with great deliberation. His targets would catch his eye, look hurriedly away, and DeVeer would move his attention to the next. Crighton shrank with the thought that the two men might join her, but DeVeer suddenly strode to an empty chair apart from any staff member and fixed his attention on the music. Speidel drew another chair beside DeVeer's. The room relaxed perceptibly and occasional conversations resumed. For the first time, Crighton realized she was not alone in her resentment of the man.

Moments later the Director himself slipped through the door. Brooks was forceful and direct, immaculately dressed, in his late fifties. He appeared to see himself in the role of a college president, professional and clearly in charge. He too surveyed the room and then walked directly to Crighton.

"Good evening. I need to talk to you."

He pulled a straight-back chair away from the wall and sat facing her. Apparently the soft couch threatened his style.

"There's been another of those goddam letters."

"Oh, no! Where to this time?"

"The 'Morning Show.'"

"Television?"

"I'm afraid so. I suppose it was logical. First the magazine, then the paper, now the networks."

"What was the theme this time?"

"Same thing. Worthless fraud. Waste of money. They hit the Wycliffe on this one."

"That's another Bible, isn't it? Is it valuable, too?"

"Very. You can count the known copies on one hand. But that's not the point. We have got to get this stopped. I do not intend to spend the rest of my life wondering what every phone call is going to bring in next. There's too much at stake right now. I've called Edward George in New Haven to see if he can get to the bottom of it. George was librarian at Yale when I was an undergraduate, and I have a high regard for his tactical skills—and his scholarship. He'll be down around eleven tomorrow. I will want you to act as his cicerone. Please meet him at National and as soon as he's checked into a hotel bring him here. Mrs. Ferrar has all the details. Do you have anything important scheduled?"

"Nothing that can't be moved."

"Good. I've got to get back downstairs. I'll see you tomorrow." He rose abruptly. "It's asinine and outrageous and I will not tolerate it."

He marched angrily to the door, and as he opened it to pass into the hall he ran heavily against the elderly guard from the Chapter House. Brooks did a slight dance to get around him and disappeared without an apology. The guard recovered himself and held the door while he peered into the room, looking for someone. He finally identified Speidel and DeVeer and scuttled across the floor toward them. He leaned down to talk into DeVeer's ear and DeVeer leaned away in distaste. The guard said something and DeVeer rose, projecting a martyred expression. He said too loudly, "I should have thought this might have occurred to him earlier."

The guard shrugged his shoulders and DeVeer said: "Very well, I'll get them for him. I presume he's in the sound room." The guard nodded and followed him out the door.

Speidel, who had been listening carefully, was left half in and half out of his chair. He looked at the door, obviously wishing to follow but apparently thinking better of it, and sat back down. At this moment the hi-fi rose to a loud chord and faded into silence followed by a roar of applause that could be heard through the walls as well as from the speakers.

"Thank you, ladies and gentlemen," the radio spoke with a slight accent. "With your gracious permission there will now be a fifteen-minute intermission. For those who have joined us at home tonight, we would like to bring you our featured interview which will be conducted by Alan Welles of the Library's Rare Book Division."

His voice faded a moment too soon and Welles's was brought up a bit too quickly, suggesting a clumsy hand at the controls.

"And I in turn would like to introduce you to one of the nation's leading rare book dealers, an almost legendary figure in the world of incunabula and first editions—and, I'm delighted to say, an old friend of mine." Welles's voice came across with cultured ease and a fleck of humor. "David Rosenthal, bibliophile par excellence."

"Gently, Alan. I am nervous enough today."

"Not at all. Now let's see . . . I suspect we should get right to what fascinates most people most about rare books: money. I'm sure you've had your share of finds, David. What was your most successful coup?"

"Oh, now Alan, you give the wrong impression. There is a great deal more to our business than money!"

"I quite agree, but what do you talk about at the monthly Caxton meeting? Aren't all your friends bragging about their latest piece of luck?"

"Maybe yes. All right, I have had my share of surprises. I suppose I am most pleased by the discovery of my first *Bay Psalm Book*. Wait a moment, that might give the wrong impression. I have seen only two *Bay Psalm Books* in my life, but the first happened way back in the thirties when I was new to the business. I had been on a buying trip in Scotland and I was visiting the seaport towns when I stumbled onto a disreputable-looking shop near the docks in Glasgow. The place turned out to have a really remarkable collection of eighteenth-century volumes of exploration, geography, and discovery, you know. I bought twenty or thirty titles and the proprietor took them off and wrapped them with heavy paper and cord and I took them away with me.

"It was not until they were opened for customs in Southampton that I discovered he had substituted a collection of worthless sermons and hymnbooks for the volumes I had paid for. I was furious and was on the verge of dropping the whole lot in the trash when I realized that one of the miserable things was an honest-to-goodness Massachusetts *Bay Psalm Book*. I later sold it for forty thousand dollars and the copy has changed hands at least twice since then. It's now back in England where it should never have been in the first place by any kind of logic."

"That's splendid, David. That's just the kind of thing we all cling to as some day happening to us. But let me ask you, how can a book possibly be worth that kind of money?"

"Ah, my friend, much of it is the excitement of having something as unusual as this item. But let us be honest, much of it too is the lust of acquisition. People collect everything: stamps or matchbooks or election buttons. A *Bay Psalm Book* is both fascinating for its contents and it is exceedingly rare. There are only eleven known to exist—and half of these are incomplete. It is, of course, the first book to have been printed in North America. Undoubtedly the person who has paid eighty or ninety thousand dollars has gotten that much satisfaction out of knowing that he has something only five other people in the world have—it was one of the perfect copies, of course."

"Good for him! But how do you justify a library having such an item?"

Crighton thought, oh no! The Director knocks himself out begging donations for those things. He'll have a heart attack!

"... share the joy with many in a museum. For the scholar a fine volume is like a great painting, he ..."

Suddenly Speidel jumped to his feet and either out of shock at the radio or uncontrollable curiosity about DeVeer, loped out the door. It closed slowly behind him and Crighton realized she had seen Carson looking through the shrinking crack. He appeared so intent she wondered what could have attracted his attention. Her curiosity was too much for her and she went out the door to find Carson leaning against the opposite wall of the hall. He was clearly pleased to see her.

"Do you want something?" she asked.

"Just you."

"No, I mean seriously."

"So do I. We didn't get a chance to meet properly. What's your name?" She noted he was on the large side, somewhat stooped over, with very dark hair and a perpetual frown as if he were taking things much too seriously.

"Crighton Jones. How did you know I was in there?"

"Mine's Steve Carson. I kept seeing the staff go in and out. I hoped you'd be among them."

They moved out of the traffic flow. The rumble of five hundred voices rolled up from the marble hall.

"Well, at least you're direct! What are you doing here? In the library?"

"Knocking off a thesis. With any luck it should give me the doctorate and a Pulitzer. I expect the publishers to trample each other to get their hands on it."

"Good for you. What's your period?"

"Ante-bellum prairie frontier. Your library's a gold mine."

"The Werner-Bok? For western history? I had no idea."

"Oh yes. I've come all the way from Madison, Wisconsin—at great expense to the Ford Foundation—to look at your holdings. I suppose you think I should be out on the plains?"

"Something like that."

"Nonsense. You make the common mistake. They didn't write each other out there. They wrote the old folks back in Lancaster and Richmond. They were the ones who wanted to know what was happening in the West. All the best descriptions are in letters to relatives—back here. Fortunately, my fellow historians share your confusion, so I'm one up on 'em. If I do no more than claw through your shelves, I've got it made."

"I remember, you had some sort of a diary in there. Whose was it?"

"Just an ordinary farmer—a homesteader, but a really remarkable character. Christ, those guys had guts! Have you got a minute? Let me show you what he said the night after he'd been burned out . . ."

Crighton had a nagging feeling she should be in listening to the interview in case she got any follow-up questions in the morning, but the man seemed so eager that she nodded and followed him into the Chapter House room. It seemed less real than ever. There was a single reader working beside the opposite wall. The fake windows glowed from hidden bulbs behind the stained glass, but the room seemed even darker than before. There was no sign of Brewer or a replacement, and the guard's station by the door was empty except for a half-done crossword puzzle suggesting he was but shortly gone. The room was utterly silent.

Carson, leading the way, had almost reached his

diary and note cards when the door to the Manuscripts side burst open and slammed back against the paneling with a splintering crash. Fluorescent light from the deck streamed into the room and Speidel burst through shouting.

"Help! Oh, help, please! DeVeer is down there—hurt—he's bleeding to death. Please get help."

Crighton froze and Carson said intently, "What are you saying? Where is he?" Moving fast across the room, he grabbed Speidel and held him by the shoulders. "Where?"

"In the stacks. Deck Two. At the foot of the stairs." Speidel was gasping, out of breath, his face florid and wet with sweat.

Carson turned to Crighton. "You get a doctor. I'll go down. What happened to him?" he asked Speidel.

"He fell down a whole flight of stairs. It's horrible!"

Crighton said: "No, you'll need me. Dr. Speidel, you go back to the lounge and get help. We'll go down."

As the two ran on to the deck, Crighton noticed a lighted office to the left, and bare bulbs glowing down the center aisle. The rest of the deck was dark. Carson ran ahead, looking for a way down.

"Where are the stairs?"

"No. Use the elevator. Here. It's faster." It was waiting and the door was open. Crighton ran in and Carson joined her as she pushed the button for two.

With grotesque deliberation the door slowly closed and for a breathless moment nothing happened at all. The car finally began to move and seemed to lower itself hand over hand. When it had dropped seven floors it stopped, went silent, and the door slowly opened. Carson slipped through the crack and looked toward one end of the deck and then the other. Again only the center lights were on. Nothing and nobody in sight.

"Goddam it, where are the stairs?"

"Behind the elevator."

He had started down the aisle, but grabbed a shelf and pulled himself around, reaching the steps behind with a rush. Crighton ran to his side and they both came to a full stop and seized cold steel to steady themselves.

DeVeer was on the floor, kneeling, oddly crouched forward, his head split dead center by a thin, steel support at the back of the elevator shaft. It was as if in a fit of fury he had charged straight down the staircase and driven himself directly into the metal beam. The beam was buried in his skull, and a startlingly brilliant pool of blood was widening at the base of the metal sheets surrounding the elevator.

There was no hurry. Time had run out for Murchison DeVeer. He was very dead.

# 3

The following morning was a gray blur for Crighton
Jones. It had been three o'clock before the same questions had been asked by the Director and the ambulance men and the coroner right through the library
guards, the staff, and the char force. When she did get
home, groggy with fatigue, it had taken another hour
to fall asleep, whereupon, after three hours of thrashing through half dreams, it was time to get up again.

She had started the day aching, red-eyed, and fear-
ful of her ability to cope. She was acutely aware that
she was the institution's prime contact with both the
press and the scholarly world, and she would be expected to tell the story of DeVeer's demise with dignity and grace. She had therefore reported directly to
the Director for support and instructions, and instead
left more shaken than when she had arrived.

"Miss Jones," Brooks had said, "I will make this
brief. Your phone will be ringing shortly and you
should be there to cover it. You will be in a difficult

situation today. I expect you to handle this with skill and . . . maturity."

Crighton shrank inside. The thought would not have occurred to him unless he had had some doubt.

"The DeVeer situation is most unfortunate. DeVeer was, quite frankly, a mixed blessing. He brought us great prestige and, in his own field, was very skilled, but he made everyone he worked with smaller and less effective in theirs."

Crighton was surprised Brooks had known this.

"Needless to say, you will not allude to his personality in your reporting. I assume you will prepare a detailed biography for handouts, and work up a story on the accident itself. At the moment, I am more interested in the latter. I want this played down to the lowest key. The emphasis throughout should be on his *untimely death*, not on the *shocking accident*. Do you understand the difference?"

Crighton nodded.

"Even more important, I do not wish any of the media to interview his fellow staff members about him. This could only confuse the situation. Do you think you can prevent this?"

"I'll try. Yes, I think I can."

"All right. Remember, the main idea is to take the dramatics out. Play it down. Make them think this is not really news at all. Do you have any questions?"

"No. Only—what should I say if someone wants to talk to you? Will you be available, or would you prefer—?"

Brooks hesitated. "Let me see. Yes. I will give you a letter expressing my deep shock at the loss to the library and the world of letters. They can use that. I might even be able to work in something about the prestige of our subject specialists. We may make some profit out of this yet. In any event, don't bother me unless they start pressing you about the accident itself. Let me handle that if you run into trouble."

Brooks looked reflective for a moment and said: "I think that's all. You should get to your phone as quickly as possible."

Crighton fled to her office and the whirling details of her job spun through the morning. Obits, press calls, reporters, and pickup messengers overlapped like shingles. By ten-thirty she was slipping ever further behind when the phone rang yet one more time. It was the Director's secretary.

"You haven't forgotten you're supposed to meet that man at the airport, have you?"

"Even with the DeVeer thing?"

"There has been no change of plans."

"My God! All right, I'll go."

She dashed to the underground garage, struggled through traffic, and fought the complexity of National Airport. By eleven she was breathlessly walking down endless, water-stained corridors, trying to reach the shuttle waiting room.

It proved to be farther from the main terminal than she would have believed. But then, what the hell wasn't at an airport, she thought. Has any plane ever come in at Gates One and Two? If she had anything to do with it, it was bound to be Thirty-six at least, and usually Fifty-something. Damn.

The lounge finally appeared at the farthest end of the tunnel and she fell into one of its hard plastic seats facing the door. If you were supposed to meet the eleven o'clock shuttle from New York, surely that meant the one that *arrived* at eleven, didn't it? It wouldn't have been the one that left *there* at eleven? And what happened if it was held up on the field for an hour and a half? Did it then become the twelve-thirty shuttle? At which end? Damn and double damn.

She slid down in the seat and squeezed her temples with the heels of her hands. It was now eleven-o'clock-and-then-some and either the man was about due through the door or he was just leaving La Guardia. She hoped it was the latter.

The next arriving plane came at eleven thirty. Forty-odd people shot purposefully out of the door and down the tunnel, and one, an expensively tailored, grandfatherly type, was left looking around expectantly in the emptying room. Crighton rose and approached him.

"Dr. George?" she asked tentatively.

"Yes, indeed. You're from the Werner-Bok? How kind of you to meet me."

"We wouldn't have it any other way. I'm Crighton Jones, the press officer. Dr. Brooks sends you greetings and I'm supposed to deliver you to him as soon as you get checked into wherever it is you're staying."

"We can postpone the checking in. I've belonged to the Minerva Club here for forty years and I think I've been in it about that many times. I seize any excuse to get my money's worth. I called them last night and they assured me they will have a room waiting whenever I arrive. Let's go straight to the Library and let me see what has Nelson so excited."

They were staring at the luggage table which was erupting suitcases from its crater.

"You've known the Director before, of course," Crighton said.

"Hah! I got him into the business. I was librarian at Yale when he was a student there and I talked him into my trade. I've never dared ask him if he'd known then what he knows now. . ." He finished the sentence with a gesture.

"Did you promise him a quiet life of reading and reflection?"

George chuckled. "No, I couldn't have done that with a straight face even then. The average library administrator hasn't held an open book in his hands for twenty years. Between unions, boards, grievances, buildings, budgets..." He waved his hands in mock despair. "Ah, there. Those are my bags. No, no, I've got them. How do we get into town?"

"I've got the Library car. You wait by the door and I'll be back in five minutes."

They went together to the terminal and George made a genuine effort to accompany her farther but she would have none of it. After waiting a full fifteen minutes more, he decided if it was that far she had indeed known best. She finally appeared, driving carefully to the curb in a large, very black, very shiny sedan. An unimaginative logo on the side showed a lamp of knowledge hovering over an open book. This must be the place, George thought irreverently. He placed the bags on the floor in back and climbed in beside the girl.

"All right! Let's see the monuments again, I'm an inveterate tourist. Have you ever taken that shuttle from New York?"

"Yes, I was at Columbia and I get back fairly often."

"Have you noticed something? That plane takes off right across Manhattan and then flies over land for a solid hour and suddenly you're in Washington—and in between there is not one single town! How can you fly over the greatest megalopolis in the world and there not be five houses together?"

Crighton smiled. "You're right. I've wondered where Baltimore went myself."

"'Crighton,'" he said reflectively. "Different. Is it a family name?"

"Not really. My mother named me Betty and my father was afraid I'd disappear into a sea of Betty Joneses so he put the Crighton in the middle. I managed to slip out of the Betty about the ninth grade and never looked back."

"Logical," he said. "Well handled."

They were approaching the Jefferson Memorial and George was peering across the river.

"Do you know what Nelson wants me for?"

"I think I do, but I'd better let him tell it. Oh, we had a tragedy last night. Did you know Murchison DeVeer?"

"I've heard him at conventions. Why?"

"He fell down a flight of stairs in the stacks and killed himself. It was horrible."

"Great heavens, I would think so! Were you there?"

"Yes. His assistant found him, but I'm afraid a reader and I were the next to arrive."

"How did it happen?"

"Someone seems to have left a long, thin pamphlet hanging off a step and they think he stepped on it. It was about the color of the linoleum and he must have thought it was solid and it threw him forward. He fell straight down and . . . the stack elevators have steel T beams, I've learned they're called, at the back to support the metal walls, and he . . . hit his head on the thin part that sticks out . . . the stalk of the T . . . it. . . ." She abandoned it. The picture of him kneeling with it imbedded in his head was too awful to describe, no matter how clear it was in her own mind.

"That's terrible. As Cotton Mather said, 'We live on the razor's edge.'"

Crighton shuddered. The quote was apter than he knew, she thought.

"Forgive me for driving so slowly," she said, "but I'm terrified of this car. I drive an Audi with hopes of making a Porsche some day. This thing feels like a barge."

"You're doing beautifully and it gives me a chance to see the city again. It is a handsome place."

They proceeded down Constitution past the Smithsonian's Museum of History and Technology, then the Natural History, and turned into the garage under the Werner-Bok. Five minutes later George was in the Director's office, Crighton was headed for the subbasement, and the two men were left together.

"Ed," Brooks said, "bless you for coming. I need your help and I need it bad!" Brooks came around a huge, glass-topped desk and motioned George into a leather chair. The Director's office ran to brown leather, English sporting prints, and a generally corporate atmosphere. "But first—you look great! What've you been doing with yourself?"

"Just what I've wanted to." George seated himself comfortably and waved a hand. "They gave me an embarrassingly generous farewell. The president offered me an emeritus title if I'd head up the automation study, but I kept thinking of all the dead wood I'd prayed to retire in my own time and I couldn't be sure I wasn't one of them!"

"You know damn well you weren't. I talked with Rogers at midwinter and he said they were pleading with you to stay on at least till they decide what's to go into the computer. There aren't five men in the profession that have your breadth of experience."

"Ah, you touch the sensitive point. Is it possible the reason I have such breadth is that I've just lasted longer than anyone else? I feel better than I ever have. I spent a month in London right after I left the university, and then flew to Berkeley for that seminar. I've written two articles and I'm on the third revision of the book—and you know as well as I do that a man of seventy can't be doing any of this properly. It's what I suspected all along. You lose your perspective. Your sense of your capacity is as faulty as your age."

"I won't dignify that with a reply."

"You shouldn't. I was only voicing my first self-doubt in fifty years. Enough." He held up his hand. "Let's see if I'm still competent. What's the problem? You were so cryptic on the phone I thought your line was tapped." George had meant it as a joke, but Brooks did not smile.

"Dammit, Ed, I wish I knew. There's something goddam funny going on here." Brooks stepped back toward his desk and leaned against it, anger from past frustrations beginning to show in his cheeks. "We have one of the greatest institutions in Western scholarship here, and I'm not going to have it jeopardized by some psychotic crackpot who thinks he can pull the house down just to get even with somebody. If I knew who he was and who he was mad at I'd fire 'em both.

"At first I thought it was just lousy luck this had to hit right now. Now I'm convinced the son of a bitch picked this time with the full knowledge of the damage he could do. I need you to spot him for me and then so help my soul I'll ruin him professionally if it's the last thing I ever do."

"Gently, Ed. *What* has he done?"

Brooks reached behind him for a file folder lying in the center of his blotter pad.

"It seems to've started with some nut mail. *Newsweek* got this one." He extracted the top sheet and handed it to George. It read:

> *Did you know that the Aramaic Scrolls you made such a fuss about in your January issue cost $30,000 and can be duplicated for chicken feed if you know where to look? Do you know what*

*counterfeit is worth? Before you make a fool of yourself again, you would do well to look into this matter.*

George returned the sheet and said, "I remember the cover story."

"Exactly. Big write-up in their Religion section. Very decent publicity. It's already brought in a number of really distinguished gifts: we've gotten some Kierkegaard material and one of the Southern churches is giving us their eighteenth-century records. But the point is, if there were anything to it, the magazine would look like a fool, so they sent down a reporter whom we managed to disabuse, but it was a near thing."

"'We'?"

"Well, that girl that brought you here did the talking, but I told her what to say. Since then there have been two more. As you'll see, one ties to the Gutenberg and the latest to a very rare Wycliffe we've got."

He handed him the remaining two. George read them carefully and returned them.

"They don't sound particularly convincing. Either the writer didn't know any real details or didn't want to give any—just wanted to get attention. Have you fired anyone lately?"

"I checked with Personnel as soon as the second letter came in. They ran the thing backward and forward and came up with nothing. There was the usual small-time bitching but we couldn't find anyone who'd want to get even with the Library—or me—as an institution!"

"Is there any chance there really *is* something wrong with these pieces?"

"No, no!" Brooks said irritably. "The ringer is the

*choice* of the books he's using." He pointed to the letters.

"Every one of those is a rare book, of course, but we've got millions of dollars' worth of rare books. There aren't a half dozen libraries in America that can approach our collection here. But the thing is, most of our rare book materials have been *given* to us by private individuals. The stuff is usually willed to the 'use of scholarship' on the death of private collectors—with suitable tax write-offs, of course. Only a small proportion of our rare book holdings has actually been purchased by the Library. But every one of these *has*—the Gutenberg, the Wycliffe, and the Dead Sea Scrolls—but we never make this distinction in our publicity. Only our own staff and parts of the rare book trade would have any way of knowing which of our holdings cost us money."

"Incidentally, *did* your Gutenberg cost whatever it was he claimed?"

"Damn near it. But that's the thing. Nobody knows that. It was bought in Europe back in the twenties and there seems to've been a bit of tax juggling over it and the price was never revealed. The Werner-Bok was created by joining the private collections of Alfred Werner and Augustus Bok and endowing them with large chunks of steel and banking stock. Three other collections were added right after the First World War, but several of the original founders were still alive when the Gutenberg was acquired. They seem to've used the Library Corporation to protect some personal funds in the '29 Crash, but it's all open and aboveboard now. The founders are long gone."

"How much does the endowment bring in?"

"In the past, salaries and book funds came to about a million a year."

"Great Scott! You private types don't fool around."

"What are you talking about? Harvard is running six million these days. The Folger spends a fortune just on Elizabethans."

"All right. All right."

"No, it's not all right. It's the goddam money that's causing the trouble. Here's the problem. As you well know, the foundations are cancelling grant programs right and left and we've been running on grants for the past twenty years. Over half of our total budget comes from the fool things now. Every department I've got has two or three going and every one of them is coming up for renewal in the next few weeks. It's the end of the foundation fiscal year and all their directors have been told to cut to the bone. They're desperately looking for some grounds—any grounds—to kill these things off. We've had a rich game going on our vast dignity and tradition, but if the word gets out that we don't know what we're doing, they could wipe us out in a week. We couldn't even cover salaries.

"Everybody assumes that since we're on the Mall we belong to the government. We don't, of course. We're just like the Corcoran or the Morgan or the Folger. Every dime comes out of the founders' endowments—plus what we can raise by using this money as matching funds with the foundations. Our own endowments have shrunk beyond belief and if the outside cash dries up we're in desperate trouble. This letter mess simply must be stopped before it gets public and the money types hear about it."

"All right, all right—you've convinced me! So how do we proceed?"

"Well, what do *you* think? It's an odd situation. If we assume that the knowledge of the materials comes from the inside, who would want to embarrass the Library right now when everything is so tenuous and threatened? Nobody. Is someone trying to get one up on somebody else—you're down, so I'm ahead? Maybe, but it doesn't seem likely. If the person is rational, he'll know that a smear on any part of the library will jeopardize his own department's chances."

"Do you have any soft spots? Any areas with morale problems? Friction?"

Brooks nodded. "Yes, there is one. There is great tension and backbiting between the Rare Book and Manuscripts units. Oddly enough, all their employees are good or better. Each section—in its own field—has outstanding, nationally known people. But if there's anything screwed up, it could be there."

"I understand you had a tragic accident last night. Wasn't DeVeer in one of those units?"

"Yes. He was head of Manuscripts. A very mixed blessing."

"Him or his death?"

"Both."

"Could he have been your troublemaker? With him gone, could it stop?"

"Hardly. He was a pain in the neck, but he wouldn't stoop to this. But I'm afraid his division would be a good place to start."

"Very well. It sounds promising."

"If this meets with your approval, I'd like to pass the word that the distinguished librarian, Edward George, is preparing a history of the great library collections in America and we have been given the honor of a chapter. I will instruct the staff to give you all possible assistance. I want you to snoop."

George chuckled. "What happens if I find your bad seed? What do you do with him?"

"I'll crowd the son of a bitch till I find out what's really behind this. I'll wring a written explanation out of him for insurance against the trustees, and then I'll bust him so wide he can't get a job in a bookmobile.

No man has the right to jeopardize the dedicated efforts of an entire institution for his own purposes."

"Ummm," said George. After a pause he asked, "And how long do I have?"

"Two weeks at the outside. Maybe less. The grantsmen can start appearing any day now."

"Do I just barge around or do you want me introduced?"

"Neither, I think. I've asked Miss Jones, the girl who met you, to act as your guide. She always accompanies the media in interviews so she should validate your alibi and she might actually be of some use to you. Use her any way you wish."

"A very attractive young lady. She makes a nice impression."

"I hired her to give us a little livelier image. She'll be unloaded as soon as we get through the renewal mess."

"Isn't she working out?"

"Oh, sure. She's doing fine, considering her lack of experience. Just no sense wasting bait after the fish's caught."

George frowned. "Does she know she's so temporal?"

"Probably not. I never spelled it out and she never asked."

George shook his head irritably. "Very well. Unless you wrote the notes yourself, it's a waste of time standing here. I'll be back when—or if—I learn something."

He was eager to start. A distasteful explanation had suddenly occurred to him which he wished to test as quickly as possible.

# 4

"Thank you, Mrs. Ferrar. I'm back among friends now. I can take it from here," said Edward George. The Director's secretary had delivered him to Crighton's office and he detached himself with a cordial nod of dismissal. Mrs. Ferrar started back down the hall and George stepped into the room.

"Miss Jones! I understand you're to be my guide and...I beg your pardon!" Crighton had jumped so violently at his voice that she had sprayed a deck of envelopes across the floor.

"Sorry about that." He stopped her apology. "You're not tense, just terribly alert. Relax, take your shoes off. May I join you?"

He seated himself by her desk and continued talking gently to slow the tempo of her thoughts.

"You remind me of myself a hundred years ago when I got my first library. I hadn't been there six months when someone discovered the man I'd hired to do my book purchasing was getting kickbacks from the wholesalers! My first reaction was one of awe that he'd figured out how to make more money than I—and then I realized that, as the head of the place, I was going to get the blame. Graft and corruption! I was terrified.

"For the next week, I spent most of my time jumping at phone calls and hoping I'd be out. I nearly paralyzed myself thinking up alibis to save myself. What I'm getting at, young lady, is: don't get things out of proportion. I learned from that shattering experience that the only way to cope with a crisis is to take it a minute at a time. If you solve each specific question when it comes in, if you answer just one phone call at a time, you can handle it. Just don't let yourself think about what the next three days will be like, and you'll make it."

"You do have my number!" she said, collecting the envelopes. "I do go into flaps and I keep knowing I can't do what's expected. But how do you keep from thinking ahead, if only to prepare yourself?"

"The fallacy, young lady, is that you can never anticipate what's going to go wrong, so there's no sense trying to get ready for it. You merely distract yourself so you can't deal with what does come. Remember: one thing at a time. Good afternoon, come in."

Steve Carson had entered the door. "Sorry. I'll come back later," he said, starting to retreat.

"No, that won't do you any good," George continued briskly. He hoped this arrogant familiarity was the right treatment for the girl. He was determined to keep her so distracted she would have no time to think about herself. "Miss Jones and I have just been assigned to each other for the rest of our natural lives so the chance of your seeing her without me is slight. I'm Edward George. What can we do for you?"

Crighton had a faintly spinning sensation.

"Dr. George," she said. "This is Steve Carson. He's

a reader who's working in Manuscripts and . . . uh, we found Dr. DeVeer's body together."

George was immediately contrite. "Forgive my tasteless familiarity. It was obviously inappropriate."

"No, sir." Carson eased himself onto a low bookcase. "Don't feel that way. I can't speak for Crighton, but the whole thing has such an air of unreality I find myself almost frighteningly detached about it. In fact, that's why I'm here. I've found I've been applying the historical method so long I can't turn it off. I was sitting up there making Burkhardtian hypotheses about the accident as if it had taken place in Bismarck's time, and frankly, I don't like it. It doesn't hang together at all."

"What doesn't?" George asked.

"The disaster. The killing bit. Look, Crighton, are you up to going down there again? I want to see if what I think I saw matches the way you remember it."

The look of white shock in her face was enough for George, who said instantly, "Ah, Mr. Carson! I'm afraid Miss Jones is almost overwhelmed at the moment. Is it possible this could be postponed for a day —tomorrow, maybe?"

"I don't know," Carson replied slowly. "I feel like I ought to be telling someone—someone in charge— some kind of an authority figure, I guess."

George laughed quietly. "I think I'm about as authorized as you can get this side of the grave. Seriously, I am here at the invitation of the Director—who is also a close personal friend. Would it be any help to explain your—whatever it is— to me?" George wondered if his offer was to protect the girl or to satisfy his own curiosity.

Carson looked at Crighton and she nodded. "Dr. George would be most appropriate. Then as soon as I finish this stuff, I could . . ." She let it hang. She didn't know what she was up to.

"Fine. Let's go." George was on his feet. "You lead the way."

They started down the basement corridor, the behind-the-scenes activity of a great library showing through open doors as they passed order and billing specialists, processors, periodical recorders, personnel and payroll. At the center of the building they turned into a center corridor and passed beneath the Great Hall until they reached the elevator. A car was waiting and they took it to the second floor, exchanging small talk as they walked. When they approached the cathedral doors of the Chapter House, cross-braced and bolt-studded, Carson said, "Everything but the theses and a drunken juggler."

George smiled and acknowledged the image. Carson struggled the wrought iron handle back and they went in, promptly surrounded by the dark hush and that feeling of being sealed away from reality. The guard was hunched motionless beside his little pool of light, guarding the table as if nothing had changed.

"Morning, Mr. Wright. You okay?"

The old man looked up and shook his head. "Hmmm? Oh, Mr. Carson. I wish I was. Do you know, I was the last person to see him alive? If it hadn't been for me calling him out of there he wouldn't have been down on those stairs. It's like I did it to him."

It was obvious what was in his thoughts. "Did you go down with him?" Carson asked.

"No. I just came back in here and sat down till they asked me to look for Dr. Brooks."

"What did DeVeer go down for, anyway?"

"Mr. Welles called and told me to go and get him and have him bring up some woman's letters . . . Hazy . . . Esther Hazy."

"Did Welles tell you where to find them?"

"No. Just said to ask Dr. DeVeer to bring them to him. He was in that radio booth, I guess. He sounded sort of funny."

"Uh . . . you weren't at your desk when that bird came in yelling about DeVeer—Speidel. What happened to you?"

"I was out looking for Dr. Brooks like he told me to."

"Like who told you to?"

"Mr. Welles. He called back and told me to tell the Director he was going to take the radio talk man straight to the airport afterwards and not to bother to come and talk to him."

"Did he . . ."

Heads were turning throughout the room and George inserted himself into the dialogue. "Wait, I'm afraid we're bothering the readers, Steve. We'd best move on. You take care of yourself, sir, and don't worry about it."

"Yeah, hang loose, Pop," Carson said.

"Well, you can't help but wonder . . . if I hadn't called him out . . ."

The two men proceeded down the center aisle with Carson leading the way. Two readers gave them indignant stares as they passed, confirming that though he'd tried to keep his voice down, Carson's attempts to overcome Wright's deafness were enough to carry into the room.

When they reached the issue desk, Miss Brewer was in her usual place, but the traditional may-I-help-you smile was gone. She looked white and worried.

"Morning, Miss Brewer. If it's okay, I'll exploit that stack pass you gave me."

She was immediately alert. "Where are you going?"

Carson was all innocence. "This is Dr. George, a

friend of Dr. Brooks, and I want to show him the scene of last night's accident. We'll only be a minute."

Brewer looked as if she desperately wished to bar the door, but was unable to think of the necessary pretense. The men walked away leaving her even whiter and more distressed than before. Carson held the door for George and the two proceeded down the deck to the elevator. Except for the sound of a typewriter coming from one of the closed carrels, there was no one in evidence.

Carson suddenly stopped and looked carefully around the deck. "There wasn't a sound last night. Absolutely nothing. I don't believe any lights were on either, except those right down the middle. Wait a minute, maybe one of the offices . . . but the stairs may not have been lit except for light from the center aisle. If that were so, the pamphlet on the step would be valid."

"Has anyone said it wasn't?" George asked curiously.

"That's what I want to talk to you about."

They entered the elevator and Carson punched the button for Two.

"As I waited down there last night, the shock of seeing him all bunched up sort of unhinged me, I guess, and I didn't really think about what it all meant until the very end, but just before the ambulance types came, I got to brooding on that 'tripped over a pamphlet' bit. What I mean is: if you think about what would happen if you were walking down a bunch of stairs and missed a step, would you really end up on your knees with your head neatly centered on that support? I got to wondering . . ."

The car stopped and they stepped into the corridor of the second deck. Carson was struck with the sameness of the scene as it had appeared the night before. Being sealed, interior decks, the light was precisely as it had been. The same musty smell of books, linoleum, painted metal, and artificial ventilation surrounded them. They turned behind the elevator shaft, and the repetition of the place and movements left Carson half expecting to find DeVeer's body still charged against the support. It was not there, and there was no evidence of anything unusual ever having occurred.

George snapped on the shelving lights on either side of the stairs and the area was flooded with a flat white glare from the fluorescent tubes. Compared to the earlier gloom, the stairs and the floor at their feet were now lit like an operating room.

George asked, "If he didn't stumble and fall, how do you think he got that way?"

"Well, dammit, that's the weird thing. I tried a bunch of hypotheses and they're all unsatisfactory. Given: the stairs were dark, he stepped on the pamphlet thinking it was a stair step, he fell forward and hit the support. Maybe. But wouldn't he have put his arms up to protect himself? Why didn't he?

"Given: something was happening at the bottom of the stairs. He dashed down to try to stop it or to try to help someone or to grab something. Now he'd have enough drive to stumble, possibly to stay on his feet, but he'd be looking forward, and he'd automatically protect himself from butting into that thing even if it was in the gloom. But why would he be moving that fast? He just didn't act that way. Did you know him?"

"Only at a distance."

"He was a sanctimonious son of a bitch to us in the public. He knew his materials and his sources but he always managed to imply we were getting his vast intelligence as a favor. He stalked around like a blooded aristocrat.

"So, final given: someone was after him and he was trying to get away. Now he'd be too preoccupied to see either the book or the support. He'd be running hard enough to plunge down. He could stumble at the last minute and hit the floor on his knees and snap his head down against the upright. It's the only sequence that makes sense."

George followed DeVeer's course down the stairs with his eyes, trying to reconstruct each of Carson's suggestions.

"Ummh. You make an interesting case. Actually, you realize, any of your ideas could very well be right, it's only that the odds against them decrease. I mean it *is* possible that he was walking slowly down the stairs, filled with resentment at being asked to do someone else a favor. It is possible to have tripped in the dark, tried to catch himself, and finally impaled himself here. But it involves several unlikely circumstances. Each of your suggestions merely combines fewer unlikelihoods."

"I guess I'm too impressed with officialdom, but what keeps me from being surer that something was wrong is that the coroner wasn't bothered."

"How's that?" George asked.

"Well, apparently when anybody dies anyplace but his bed—maybe even there—somebody from the Coroner's Office has to case the situation. That's what held us up so long last night. There seems to be so much slaughter going on in Washington after dark that it took them two hours to work us in.

"This bureaucrat finally turned up, asked the proper questions, and released the body to the ambulance types to deliver to a mortuary. If there had been anything odd, surely he'd have caught it."

"No, not necessarily. That doesn't mean much," George replied. "I have seen some of the strangest things happen in libraries in my time and, simply because they were in libraries, the normal reactions were suspended. I have seen materials lost in incredible quantities, I have seen mental breakdowns go undetected for months, I have seen all manner of social collapse that would have been reacted to at once in the world outside, but the ordered serenity of a library seems to shield them from the most obvious challenge. I'm afraid that that coroner, having entered our sacred precincts, could have found poor DeVeer murdered and..." He left the sentence hanging in the air.

Carson looked at the older man intently.

"Was that a Freudian slip or has it crossed your mind, too?"

George did not respond for a moment, and then he said: "No, quite frankly I had not questioned the idea that he fell until you brought it up. I don't think I had, that is. The psychologists have us so confused about what our minds are doing that I find it difficult to assert anything with confidence. I think I was satisfied that the accident was ordinary. However, I did wonder what you were thinking when you questioned the guard so closely, and Nelson had mentioned a few things which implied a few activities out of the norm around here. Possibly this had stirred my subconscious. But the question is, what is rational—real—here?"

"Right. But I can't seem to get on solid ground. The coroner type said 'accidental death' and the cops said there'd be no autopsy. But what if he had been pushed and they did run an autopsy. What would they learn? It seems pretty obvious it was the brace that killed him! I can't decide what's bugging me."

"I wonder if there is anything in the fact that no one questioned the fall at the time? I gather you found a pamphlet lying on a step or something that explained it to your satisfaction. Incidentally, where is the pamphlet? Did they take it with them last night?"

"No. I think I saw somebody pick it up and lay it somewhere."

Carson glanced around and quickly found it lying flat on some manuscript boxes shelved behind the stairs.

"Let me see it, please," George asked. He examined it carefully. "It's simply a dime store music composition book bound in a Gaylord. It seems to be fragments of some material by Wilfred Parton."

"I know of Parton. He was a student of Hindemith. Died a couple of years ago—while I was dating a medievalist who was very big on that sort of thing. What's a Gaylord?"

"This gray cover with the red binding. Libraries stock them in all sizes, already made up. When you get a pamphlet that's not too thick you just glue it into the center of one of these things and it saves the cost of binding it with boards and tapes. I wonder where this would be shelved if it were in its proper place."

George began to walk down the aisle.

"The label simply says Parton Number Twenty-six. Yes, here's a whole case of Parton and Twenty-six would have been here. Well, for what it's worth, it would have been the tallest volume on the shelf, the shelf is chest high, and the piece is close enough to the aisle to be easily seen in poor light."

"What you mean is, if I'd shoved somebody so hard he'd killed himself, and I wanted to make it look like an accident, that is the nearest tall thin gray book I'd come on," said Carson.

"Providing you walked around the elevator and turned right down the center aisle." George laughed. "If you want to push it to the furthest limit, you can say he-she-or-it was probably right-handed."

"How so, Holmes?" Carson responded in kind.

"Because every good librarian knows you put the

books you're trying to push on the left side. Right-handed people always start browsing down the left side of the aisle."

"My God," said Carson. "I'm sorry I asked! I . . ."

He stopped to look toward the elevator. The doors had closed and it descended. They could hear the doors open with a muffled sound beneath them, and then the car rose past, humming steadily until it apparently had reached the top floor.

"Someone must have been underneath us all the time we were talking," said George. "That was mildly stupid of me. Let's see what's down there." He turned back to the stairs and started down.

The floor below appeared to be the bottom of the stacks and thus must be three or four levels into the ground, George thought. The hollow thud of steel flooring was replaced with the sound of a basement floor, although it too was covered with the ever-present gray linoleum. There was no shelving on this deck at all. In its place were row upon row of gray, steel filing cabinets, broken at irregular intervals into aisles so they looked like a giant rat maze stretching off into the dark in all directions. George snapped on a switch by the elevator, and the room leaped into view. It was revealed to be as large as the decks above it, but with a dead, cryptlike feel. At the extreme end, the monotonous rows of cabinets were interrupted to make room for a large cage constructed of heavy wire mesh. The two men walked toward it.

"What is it?" Carson asked.

"It seems to be a bookbinder's room. Those big roller things are a Kleizmesch machine. It's used to seal manuscripts in plastic for preservation. They call it laminating the material. The other stuff is just book-binding presses and cutters and things."

By walking alongside the cage they were able to

come abreast of a worktable. On it were dozens of low wooden boxes, each holding a single book. Some of these were split out of their bindings, some were in chunks and pieces, others appeared to be newly repaired and refinished. Most of the books were leatherbound, although a few were huge, wood-covered codexes. The area smelled of linseed oil, acetone, and scorched glue. A long roll of papyrus ran half the length of the table, held from recurling by a strange collection of glass jars, an enormous paper cutter lacking its knife, a broken yardstick under two pots of library paste, and scissors with its points broken off. At the extreme end of the table, closest to the mesh where Carson was standing, was an unusually high stack of volumes, apparently pushed back to make room for the papyrus.

"That's pretty rich stuff they've got in there. If those old books are as expensive as they are ancient, it's no wonder they keep 'em locked in."

"Age has little to do with book values, I'm sorry to say," George said. "I once knew a rare book dealer who kept a whole case of antique volumes behind his head. When someone would be outraged at the price he'd offered them for the family Bible, he'd say, 'Every book on these shelves was printed before 1690. You can have any one you want for a dollar.' You really could, too. Back in the seventeenth century they made so many collections of dull sermons they're next to worthless."

"Here's some recent stuff, three of these boxes have duplicates in 'em. Hey! Here's two copies of the *Emigrant's Guide to California*. Jesus! That's as scarce as hen's teeth. The nearest copy I could find to Madison was at the Newberry. I finally had our library buy a microfilm of it. Here's two of 'em in one place! Why would they be down here?"

"I can't imagine. If they were common things, they might just be putting them in boards, but you don't case rare books. This is odd. Here are four copies of *Uncle Tom's Cabin* in some cheap edition, and a pair of decayed paperbacks." He squinted through the mesh. "*Twenty-four Years a Cowboy and Ranchman in Southern Texas and Old Mexico*. From the cover style, that could be around the First World War. The three titles seem to be the only modern items in the cage. A strange assortment."

The elevator began to hum again. It stopped at one of the floors above, and shortly afterward they heard someone calling, "Mr. Carson? Mr. Carson?" They walked back toward the stairs and met Speidel coming down still calling, "Mr. Carson?"

"Yoh! Here we are. Just exploring."

"Good Lord, not here! *'The aspiring Guise dares meddle with such dangerous things!'* Quickly, let's get in the elevator before the caitiff sees you. Young man, snap off those lights, please. I'll get the car down." He pushed the button. By the time the door opened, Carson had returned the deck to darkness and they stepped in, headed for the top floor.

"Let me introduce myself, I'm Edward George. I think I'm due to have the pleasure of interviewing you for a book I'm writing."

"Yes, indeed," Speidel said, extending his hand and ducking his head like something out of Dickens. "I've heard you were coming. Delighted to meet you, sir."

"What do you mean we shouldn't be seen down there?" George asked.

"Oh, my dear sir. That floor is the sole property of our resident prima donna, Monsieur Schwartz. He fancies himself the last of the great craftsmen of Europe—though we got him via Vietnam!—and he goes into great rages if he thinks anyone is watching him.

He's threatened to quit at regular intervals for the past decade. He really is so good we humor him, and I haven't been on that deck myself in six or eight months. Frankly, he is an unlovely individual—'*gross and like the massy earth...harsh, contemptible, and vile,*' as Marlowe put it. If you meet him, I would suggest you make no reference to having been in his fiefdom. Incidentally, why were you there?"

They had reached the top and Carson busied himself with getting out of the car, giving George a chance to field the question if he wished.

He did. "I asked Mr. Carson to show me the scene of last night's tragedy."

"'*...illusions, fruits of lunacy...*'" Speidel quoted. "There are certain aspects of what you see, sir, which may not precisely mirror reality. I have it in my mind that we each have some facts which the other could use. Would it be possible for me to give you... possibly trade with you... some information about last night's events?" He turned toward Carson and said in a loud whisper: "Mr. George is spying for Dr. Brooks, you know. He doesn't think we know, so we're all playing along." He laughed artificially.

George was startled and felt his anger rising. It was difficult to know whether Speidel really knew why he was there or was simply baiting him to see what he could learn. "You have the advantage of me, I'm afraid. What is it I'm supposed to be doing?"

"Nothing! Nothing! Writing a book, was it? Whatever you say."

"Hmmm. Is there something that Brooks should be hiring a spy for?"

Speidel laughed and began to move down the hall. "I suspect we hate each other as venomously as any academic community. Rose wasn't speaking to DeVeer. Brewer isn't speaking to anyone Rose isn't. Welles doesn't care and they're all beneath DeVeer's dignity."

"And you, sir?" George asked.

"It amuses me to keep them stirred up." He smiled to show this was just a joke among friends. "Let's say my role is to keep communication flowing in all directions. Can you stop in my office? I think I can be helpful."

George replied somewhat coolly, "I look forward to talking with you. At the moment, however, I have an overdue appointment with your public relations staff. Will you be available later on?"

"I will. Any time before five-thirty. I think I have what you're looking for, so I would urge you to get back to me as quickly as possible."

"Do you indeed? I will be as interested in learning what it is I'm looking for, as I am in learning something about it. In the meantime, Steve, let us see how our ingénue is surviving. Shall we go?" the older man said.

# 5

They passed into the medieval hush of the reading room. The stained glass was casting greens and blues with the light of a perpetual twelfth-century afternoon, and the sense of another time washed over them—to be abruptly dissipated by Miss Brewer. The librarian was perched behind the issue desk, somehow projecting the image of a crane watching a rat hole.

"Ah, Mr. Carson! You ... ah ... will you be needing the diary this morning?" It seemed a verbal lunge based on the nearest trivia at hand.

"Bless you, ma'am. I'm afraid I'm all mixed up in that business downstairs. You won't have to send Olaf back to the shelves will you?"

"Not if you're coming back."

They started forward and Miss Brewer lunged again. "Wait! I mean, what are you ... is there anything I can do to help?"

Carson looked at George with a faintly cocked eyebrow, and the older man grinned and nodded. Carson leapt in.

"Well, yes there is. You could sure sort out some things about last night. I was moving so fast . . . did you get in on any of the excitement?"

"Oh, no. No, no! Dr. Rose and I left early, you remember. You must have seen us go out together. We saw you in the hall. We left together and then went downstairs. We weren't around when it happened at all."

"What do you mean downstairs?" Carson asked innocently.

"Down in the Main Hall. We didn't go into the stacks . . . then we left together—Dr. Rose, I mean. He left me off and then he went on home himself."

George's grin became even more apparent and a thought struck him. While the boy was pumping the poor woman, he might as well improve the shining moment himself. He turned to the left and walked toward the door on the opposite side of the reading room, pulling the panel back and passing through.

The top deck of the Rare Books side was a mirror image of what they had just left on the Manuscripts side. The usual frosted glass carrels stretched down to an elevator and he turned into what would have been the equivalent of DeVeer's office. Here he found Rose with a magnifying glass in his left hand peering down at an enormous codex, his nose barely six inches above the page. His other hand was moving slowly across the vellum, making the sheets pop and crackle as he read.

"Ah, Dr. Rose! May I interrupt for just one question?"

No answer.

"Dr. Rose, I'm Edward George. May I bother you for a moment?"

At this Rose looked up, focused slowly and then suddenly said, "Oh, yes. Yes! They told me you were coming. Come in. I didn't see you. Won't you sit down?" He waved the lens at the only other chair in the room—which was piled high with books. "Oh, I'm sorry. Uh, what can I do for you?" Rose had half risen from his desk, but had not lifted his finger from its place on the page.

"Don't get up. I'll be back to talk with you later. I have just one question now. Can you tell me where I can find that bookbinder who works downstairs? We looked into his cage—room, but he wasn't there."

Rose frowned. "Really, sir, you shouldn't have been down there. Emil Schwartz is a very strange man. He really only works for Mr. Welles, my assistant—and Miss Brewer. I have no idea when he comes in or when he leaves. I send him work by the deck attendants and it comes back the same way. I have no idea where he is. He should be at his desk. DeVeer was always trying to get me to fire him and Welles was always saying how he worked from early morning till late at night and we'll never get another one like him. I've taken a good deal of criticism in his behalf. To hear Welles tell it, the man is always there. There's nowhere else he could be. I have no idea where you could find him—though I'd be surprised if it would do you any good if you did. You can barely understand what he says when he does speak."

George looked down at the book between them and his natural love for a bound volume distracted him.

"That is a magnificent piece. Is it anything special?"

Rose sank back in his chair. "Oh, yes!—that is, no, the book itself isn't special. It's simply a psalter from the Carissi Abbey in Italy—hand-lettered, of course —about 1420 or '30, probably. But the script style may have been the pattern for the type font of the DaVecci *Book of Hours*. What I mean is, if it were, it's just possible that the earliest type font we've ever found in Southern Italy could have been copied from this particular monk's hand. This would be like tying the Gutenberg font to the Great Bible of Mainz!—if you see what I mean?"

"I'm afraid you're way beyond me, but I wish you all success! Please forgive the interruption."

Rose's magnifying glass was up and his nose down before George had reached the door.

As he approached Carson, he found Miss Brewer leaning halfway across the desk speaking earnestly, ". . . and Dr. Speidel is a very impertinent man. You simply cannot believe everything he says. He delights in discussing people, but much of what he says is just what he thinks is happening. I mean, for example, he has always thought there was a feud between Dr. Rose and Dr. DeVeer, and this was quite untrue. Each one was the head of his side of the room, you know, and while they had occasional professional differences, they had the highest regard for each other. Each man . . ." She suddenly noticed George, hesitated a moment as if to withdraw, and then seemed to resolve on a different tactic. She raised her voice to draw him in—and got the attention of half of the readers in the room at the same time.

"I was just saying what a tragedy Dr. DeVeer's loss is. Dr. Rose was telling me only yesterday what a privilege it was to work with a man of Dr. DeVeer's reputation."

George suppressed a smile and said, "Really? Somewhere I got the impression he was a rather difficult associate. Dr. Rose liked him, did he?"

"Well, it's true that no one was really close to Dr. DeVeer, but they had great respect for each other."

"Dr. DeVeer was your boss, wasn't he?"

"Oh, yes. He came to the Library about ten years ago. Of course, I'd worked here before that."

"Did you ever work for Dr. Rose?"

Her rhythm was lost. She looked down at the charging desk and drew back slightly from the edge between them. "No, no. Dr. Rose and I have worked *together* for many years, but I—I've never—I only—I do hope you have a chance to know him well, Dr.— George—he is a very great man. His manner is so gentle, however, that he has never received the recognition that—other people have. His leadership—his staff simply worships him—the people who work for him."

"Is he married?"

"Oh, no!" She had replied too quickly and realized it. "Why do you ask?"

George smiled. "It is just he has a sort of fatherly— no, avuncular—feel about him. Charming. Let's see, does one have to be married to be an uncle? No, of course not. Ah, well. We've taken much too much of your time, Miss Brewer. Thank you for your patience. Steve, can I tear you away?"

They made their exit and George asked, "Learn anything?"

"Nothing except she kept answering questions I hadn't asked. The general theme was that Dr. Rose is the most wonderful man since Adam. It wasn't said quite so clearly, but in vast detail. What happened to you?"

"I spoke with the learned Dr. Rose, who would have us believe he knows no more about the missing Schwartz than we do. He is also nearsighted and reads large books one letter at a time."

When they reached Crighton's basement room they found her, hair mussed and hands slightly smudged, fussing with a duplicating machine but with a light of triumph in her eyes.

"Come in! Come in! You look at Liberated Woman! I

think I'm going to make it. If it doesn't get any thicker than it has to date, there's just a fighting chance I can bring it off. This is more fun than orals!"

George smiled benevolently and Carson said, "By Allah, you are frisky, woman! Far be it from me to comment on such joy over an obituary, but whatever turns you on!"

"This hasn't anything to do with poor DeVeer. It's one of those deep inner things of person over panic and I'm winning. If I can get these releases into the mail, I'll have done right by the professional journals and I'm on top of it. Can you type?"

"Of course, I'm a contemporary scholar."

"Then start addressing these envelopes and I'll stuff. Mr. George, if you'll cover the phone for half a minute, I can finish this up and we'll be even again."

"It will be my pleasure."

Carson looked at the instrument and asked casually, "Get any embarrassing questions?"

"About what?"

"Oh, say, how a man can kill himself falling downstairs?"

"Hardly. Why should they? Hey! What have you two been up to? Where've you been?"

The two men looked at each other.

"Do you want to convince an interested third party?" George asked.

"No, sir. I'd rather hear how you'd present the case."

"Fair enough. Miss Jones, come sit down in your own chair and I will bring you up to date on our morning's tour."

"You stay right there. I'll just stuff and listen. But get on with it, please!"

"Very well. Steve there would have us believe that the story you have been spreading this morning is quite true, but lacks a certain dramatic element which, in a macabre manner, makes it a good deal more interesting than the way you've been telling it.

"He reasons that while it is possible, it is unlikely that Dr. DeVeer was walking down the stairs, stumbled, and struck his head dead center on a steel support, ending on his knees on the floor. He maintains that in order to do this he would either have had to run full speed down the stairs and nearly dive—or he had to be pushed rather violently from behind. Now the first suggests some high emotional state. The latter implies anger, revenge—or hatred. Unfortunately, Steve's idea then leaves us with more difficulties than we started with. If Dr. DeVeer was running in fear or running to help someone, we'd like to know who was with him and why, but our interest would be only curious—and possibly humane! But if he was pushed, we need to know by whom because this would be murder or maybe manslaughter. My knowledge of the law is limited to television, I'm afraid. In either event, we would be expected to do something—either for moral or legal reasons. 'Something,' I guess, means 'tell the authorities' as the cliché would have it."

He turned toward Carson and said, "And Steve, this brings me to an added difficulty which barely an hour ago I was instructed not to mention to anyone! I am taking it on myself to breach a confidence, but I plead with you to honor mine! The reason I'm in this library is that I was asked to assist the Director with a problem. Someone has been telling the press that this library is mismanaged, that its holdings are worthless, and there is evidence of fraud in its operations. I'm supposed to find out who's been generating these unsigned letters and so prevent the kind of publicity which could destroy a substantial part of the Library's funding. You'll note this adds a certain dilemma to your theory. If there's nothing to it but I report it to the police, it will almost certainly reach the papers and I will have revealed the internal frictions in the Library myself. This negates my purpose, and my obligations to Dr. Brooks. If it's real, however, and I fail to report it, I will have withheld information which I'm required to pass on. There is also a bit of justice to be considered here, too. So you see, Steve, you have complicated things."

There was a long silence. George cocked a questioning eyebrow at his audience, and Crighton responded with a worried look. Carson appeared rueful.

"I see when I said I ought to 'tell somebody,' I picked a poor place to start! For what it's worth, I can apply Burkhardt's principle to your dilemma and give you a working solution."

"Really? Burkhardt the historian?"

"The same. He would take your problem and give it the classic test: Is it true? And if so, so what?—to paraphrase. And the first thing he'd say is you don't have enough data to make a decision from! As of this moment, none of us knows anything more than the police do except for two things. We know there were those freak letters you just mentioned floating around, and we know that the thought that 'there's more to this than meets the eye' doesn't seem to surprise anyone we've talked to. If you want to temporize, you can say what we've got to do is to spread out and get as much information as we can as quickly as we can to see if we know what we're talking about."

"It's a wise man who can say he knows what he's talking about in these times," said a new voice from the doorway.

Everyone in the room jumped as if they'd been caught with their hands in the till. They looked hastily behind them to find a well-dressed man with an appealing twinkle in his eye watching them with manifest amusement.

"Excuse me, I didn't mean to break up a conference, I just wanted to check in and offer my services for whatever they're worth. Miss Jones and I know each other—good morning, young lady, you've obviously had a wild morning and it is a tribute to your natural beauty that you look more charming falling apart than most women do after hours of careful decoration. You, sir, must be Mr. George. I have been a long-time admirer of yours. I heard you give your inaugural address, something about 'Let Them Make Their Own Mistakes,' wasn't it? At the time, it struck me as the finest statement on librarianship I'd ever heard. I'm Alan Welles, supposedly assistant chief of the Rare Book Room under Dr. Rose."

"Well, good morning," said George. "I'm delighted to meet you. My first thought was that we'd already spoken, but I realize I'm thinking of your radio voice! I was listening to your interview last night in New Haven. These folks were occupied with more tragic matters."

"Yes, Crighton, I understand you had a harrowing evening. I managed to miss the excitement by the merest fluke. Rosenthal had an early appointment this morning, so as soon as we finished the interview I drove him straight to the airport and then went home. The first I heard of the troubles was when I came to work this morning."

"Had you known Dr. DeVeer long?" George asked.

"Yes, we both came here at about the same time—I guess it's nearly ten years now. He'd been curator of modern manuscripts in Boston, and I'd been at Le-Broun and Grey in New York. To be brutally frank, I found him the most unpleasant 'colleague' I'd ever had to suffer, but his knowledge of his field—and his ability to drag in the donations—were simply unparalleled. Institutionally he is probably irreplaceable. Personally, he won't be missed."

"Ah. That's a harsh thing to say about one so recently gone. I presume your feeling is pretty generally shared?"

"You're quite right—in being disturbed with my lack of taste in talking about it. I find I almost shock myself. Ordinarily I believe in live and let live. My own attitude is that life is really pretty lousy and if we can find a way of getting through it without causing too much pain to anyone else, we should be left to our own way of existence. But that was DeVeer's trouble. He had managed to pick a set of rules for himself that inflicted pain wherever he touched! He could probe the weakest part of a man's armor, and make him look like a fool—not only before his peers, but even more, to himself. In candor, he treated me quite fairly, but I writhed over the way he'd use me for an audience to embarrass someone else. Poor man, and the odd thing was that I don't believe he did it to make himself look better. It simply gave him pleasure and he seized on it for amusement."

"Incidentally," Crighton said, "I hope you didn't think we were ignoring you last night, but we didn't know till this morning that you wanted those manuscripts."

"What manuscripts were those?"

"The ones you asked Dr. DeVeer to bring you. It was some woman's letters, wasn't it? That's what they told me to put in the story."

"I'm afraid you've lost me. I'm supposed to have asked for some letters? Last night?"

"Sure. Didn't you ask Dr. DeVeer to bring you some kind of manuscripts or something for your interview with Rosenthal?"

"Lord, no. I never said another word to DeVeer after you and I saw him yesterday morning."

Carson stood up suddenly and burst out, "You did know that the reason DeVeer went down into the stacks was to get something for you, didn't you?"

Welles looked at Carson with complete lack of comprehension and then a look of horror rose in his eyes. "No, no! I had nothing to do with DeVeer at all!"

George spoke very deliberately. "As we understood it, you called the guard—Wright—in the reading room and asked him to find Dr. DeVeer in the lounge. He was then to ask him to go into the stacks to bring you some material which you had described. Wright came into the lounge, told DeVeer this, and DeVeer followed him out of the room. Speidel apparently began to wonder what was keeping him and went to look for him. He went into the stacks and found Dr. DeVeer had fallen down the stairs and killed himself."

"No! This is appalling!" Welles had complete control of himself, but was looking from George to Carson and back as if to be certain they were genuinely serious. "I had no idea I was involved in this in any way. Why has no one said anything?"

"Apparently everyone thought it would be embarrassing to you. You really knew nothing about this?"

"Great heavens, no! After Rosenthal and I arrived at the Library, we went directly to the sound booth, and blocked out the general outline of what we were going to talk about, and then we fell to it. He was so short of time, I didn't even take him up to see the Director— that's customary in these things. In point of fact, neither of us mentioned manuscript material in any way—and I wouldn't have called DeVeer out of the lounge for anything! There must have been some terrible confusion. I've got to talk to Pop to see what he thought he'd heard. This is fantastic!"

Welles's casual air had evaporated completely. He seemed to be talking to himself, having forgotten there was anyone else in the room. George and Carson were staring at each other, and Crighton sat tensely, her fingers to her lips.

There was an awkward silence, finally broken by Welles, who seemed to have collected his thoughts.

"Frankly, I can't imagine what Pop got confused. He's become harder of hearing just lately, but as a rule he's very good about keeping at you. I mean, if he doesn't understand something, he keeps making you repeat it till he's got it. I've never known him to guess or get it wrong. I must talk with him."

He paused with everyone watching him.

"It occurs to me," he said coldly, "that someone is taking advantage of a genuine tragedy to embarrass me personally. I will not tolerate this."

He paused again, staring absently into the window well. Suddenly his manner changed completely, and his original note of gaiety returned.

"Great heavens! What a mess! What I came down for, Miss Jones, was to suggest that you must be having a wild day and would welcome a chance to get out of this hole. I was going to recommend a dash to Haines's for a late lunch. Can I still talk you into it?"

Crighton hesitated a moment and said, "I don't dare leave the phone. I'll just get a sandwich..."

George broke in. "Go ahead, Crighton. It'll do you good. Steve and I will cover."

"Thank you, sir. I promise to have her back within an hour. Can I prevail on your good nature?" He turned to Carson. "My name's Welles."

Carson accepted his handshake somewhat ungraciously, and said, "Why not?"

"Thanks, all of you. I'll be back by one. I've got to

see Pop Wright to see if I can find out what happened last night."

He rushed out of the room, leaving dead silence behind him. Everyone stared at the empty door. Carson was the first to speak.

"Now you've really got a problem on your hands. Burkhardt would say you have enough evidence to brood on. You're just one breath away from the so-what part."

"Yes," said George. "I can no longer be casual about this. I think I must hear what Speidel has to say—and quickly. Then I had best go to the police."

"Shouldn't you tell Dr. Brooks?" Crighton asked diffidently.

George replied almost to himself. "There are some things about this that distress me. I am just not sure what Nelson's role may have been. If I assume the responsibility for destroying the serenity of this institution, I want to be a free agent. This situation is not good. Not good at all."

"Mr. George," Carson said earnestly. "I'd like to try something. In spite of the fact that this whole mess is sort of my idea, I have to admit that all we really know is: There's something damn strange going on here. What I mean to say is: Apparently you're about to get the pitch from Speidel. Old Brewer would have us believe he's a congenital liar. We need somebody we can trust and as much as I resent this bird Welles," his eyes darted to Crighton, "at least he seems clean himself. We were listening to him when the thing happened. If The Jones here could get him to answer a few questions we might get some background to test whatever Speidel's going to lay on you with. Burkhardt was big on comparing sources! I can hold the fort here while you two wheel and deal."

"Hmmm." George reflected a moment. "What you

say makes sense. I'll go straight to Speidel, and Crighton, if you'll go along with this idea, you can see what there is to be learned from Welles. We can meet at two o'clock and trade information and I'll decide what to do then."

"Will you do it, lady?" Carson asked.

"Sure. I'll try."

"Very well, then," said George. "I guess I'm first on the list, so I'm off."

He gave them a wry smile and started down the hall. Behind him he could hear Carson detailing the information he thought Welles might have and which they obviously needed. Once at the elevators, he hesitated for a moment, pausing uncertainly. He was making a mistake, he felt, but he could not decide whether it was one of judgment or simply an error of timing. There seemed nothing to do but stumble through it. He pressed the button to go up.

# 6

Speidel shifted the chair by his desk a fraction of an inch and indicated its availability with a sweep of his hand.

"My humble cell is honored with your presence."

George looked at him sharply, wondering whether the implied servility was a deliberate insult or merely the result of too much Elizabethan literature. Speidel was, as usual, dressed in black, his Prussian haircut contrasting oddly with his waxen, arthritic appearance. The two men seated themselves and Speidel leaned across his desk toward George.

"Ah, you've come to me at last," he said. "'*Knowledge*,' right? '*The wing wherewith we fly to heaven.*' You'd have saved yourself a good deal of effort if you'd started here, Mr. George. I believe we have some information to trade, have we not?" His eyes sparkled and he seemed to be on the verge of laughing.

"I have no information to trade for anything," George snapped. "I'm afraid I'm unusually irritable this morning, and my sense of humor is fairly thin right now. The casual way everyone around here is taking Dr. DeVeer's death is beginning to tell on my nerves. Business as usual, I gather?"

Speidel rocked back in his chair and chuckled, hooking his hands over a knee which he braced against his desk.

"Why, Mr. George, such an attitude! You should be particularly grateful for the development. His elimination has solved your problem for you. All in one day. How can you complain?"

"What problem?"

"The letters, of course! Or aren't we supposed to know? Surely you realized it was DeVeer who was writing them? The poor man would have been doubly disappointed if you hadn't guessed. He was as eager to be martyred as he was to stir up trouble. I wonder how long it would have taken you to figure it out?"

George found himself trembling with anger. The man's condescension was infuriating. His eyes began to water as they always did when he lost his temper, and he fought to get control of himself.

"Would you like to tell me about it, or am I to ask questions so we can make it a game?" he asked in a strained voice.

"No, no. Relax, relax. The whole thing is most amusing and it would be a pity if you didn't recognize it as such. He makes us '*jesting pageants for their trulls.*' Marlowe, of course. Let me explain.

"It all hangs on the fact that Murchison DeVeer—in spite of being somewhat trying to work with—was incredibly effective at his job! He was in charge of American manuscripts, you know, and he was an absolute genius at bringing the things in. In the last ten years, he's worked his way through half the creative elite of this country. I mean, if you're a scholar and you think anything of significance has happened since McKinley, the odds are high you're going to have to use our collections. I prefer Elizabethan England myself, but even I was awed with the space scientists and the playwrights and the political figures. He brought in their most personal and private papers and what few he didn't bring home with him, he's got on the way! He's got us in their wills!

"So the material's down there," he said, pointing to the decks beneath them, "but there it sits. He could never get the money he needed to process it! As you well know, sir, the material is useless unless it's organized and made available to the researchers. We need collators and catalogers and indexers—and DeVeer couldn't get anyone to listen to him! The more stuff he got, the more help he demanded, but Brooks kept putting him off. Here he was bringing it in practically with his bare hands, and then just when he thought he was going to get some support, the Director would come up with some vastly expensive incunabula and DeVeer would simply come apart at the seams."

Speidel leaned back and laughed in a high-pitched giggle.

"You want me to believe," George said drily, "that DeVeer would threaten thousands of dollars' worth of grants to attract further attention to his own projects? Really!"

"Of course. Come, sir, you're a librarian. You know the answer to that. DeVeer was dedicated. In our profession that's the only possible motivation—besides flight. The only thing that keeps an archivist going is the thought that what he's doing today will be appreciated a hundred years from now when somebody who can really make a difference to society uses the materials. But DeVeer had it carefully analyzed! His cryptic letters would paralyze everything for a while. The press would come thrashing in, the grantsmen would follow the press, and the Trustees would be right behind wondering what was going on. Once the Board began asking pointed questions they'd soon find out how the working money was being wasted on all that sterile trash."

"What sterile trash?"

"Why, those useless first editions and special printings and association copies—all the stuff that Rose can find to waste money on. It's material that belongs in museums, not a working library! No, DeVeer's tempest would kill off a quarter of a million dollars for Rose's rare book nonsense, but in the course of the argument, DeVeer was sure he'd have a chance to make his own case, and when the dust would finally settle, they'd realize he was right. I mean really, sir, if you have five thousand dollars to invest in one autographed copy of *Alice in Wonderland* or making ten thousand papers of the Truckers' Union available to scholars, how would *you* spend it? DeVeer thought he had a way to get his case before the Trustees and bring down Brooks at the same time! It was a fool's move, but I must say, I enjoyed watching."

"He told you all this?"

"No, no. I found the drafts for the first two letters in the wastebasket."

"What! How on earth did that happen?"

"I go through all the wastebaskets every night. It's marvelously informative."

"My God! You're not serious?"

"Of course I am. Years ago I learned that the man who knows what's going on has some control over his destiny. Information is the secret. You wouldn't believe what you can learn from wastebaskets. You can tell about the efficiency of your clerical staff, the decisions of your superiors, and the intentions of your enemies."

"What a marvelous way to be cordially hated."

"I long since quit trying to be liked."

"Have you ever gotten caught at this ... unusual hobby?"

"Yes, that's how I learned about it from DeVeer. He happened to see the two drafts in a folder which I mistakenly opened in front of him. Eh, eh. I believe that was the first time I ever had his respect."

"I would have fired you on the spot if I'd been in his place."

"Not at all," Speidel replied equably. "I, I believe the phrase is, 'knew too much.' He had to keep my loyalty, or what would have been a high-minded strategy for the press and the Trustees would have become a sordid tactic exposed by Brooks, and Brooks would have won the whole round. Anyway, I think DeVeer rather enjoyed telling me about the damage he was going to do."

George ran his hand over his brow.

"This is incredible. With your set of ethics, why didn't you go to Brooks and get the glory of disclosing it all? Why, if you'd played it right, you could have gotten DeVeer's job! This must have been quite a temptation for you."

"No, no." Speidel rocked back in his chair, manifestly enjoying himself. "I toyed with that thought for only a moment. It was obvious that I was going to win this one either way. If DeVeer's scheme worked, we would get the staff and resources we need, and the division would be the finest in the world. Later, De-Veer's role in the matter might well come out, and I was the logical successor. If it failed, I was the immediate heir! *Quod erat demonstrandum*. Q.E.D."

George shook his head.

"I suppose I'm revealing my naïveté, but what is to prevent your being fired by Dr. Brooks should he hear of your failure to report all this disloyalty?"

"You mean when you tell him? Hah! You will find that friend Brooks is not eager for any of this matter to be made public. You will find that DeVeer's... accident... has suddenly made Brooks very cautious. I am a better man than DeVeer for his job. You will see. I am the logical successor."

George started to pursue the insinuations about the Director and then thought better of it. He recalled his own doubts independently raised.

He said instead, "It would seem you have greatly benefited from DeVeer's passing."

To his surprise, Speidel responded very quietly, the mocking note suddenly gone.

"You will find many people have. Suddenly old Rose is a man again. Suddenly Brooks has no letters to worry about. Suddenly fifty members of the staff will no longer dread his walking through their doors. But suddenly Miss Brewer is very worried. It is all most interesting."

The two men looked at each other in silence. Finally George asked, "And how did you live with DeVeer?"

There was no reply for a moment, and then Speidel said softly: "He thought I was a fool. He considered me an intellectual Uriah Heep. But I was useful to him. He shot about the country collecting the praise of the scholarly world, strangely confident that I was caring for his little world back here. I suppose he thought me so weak that I had no place else to go. But I was willing to work for him. Actually, in the area of what I believe to matter, he was a great man."

He stood up suddenly. "Let me show you what he has done. Do you have a minute?"

George started to demur and then thought better of it. The man seemed to be opening doors all around him.

George followed him down the aisle to the top deck where the sounds of typewriters and muffled voices implied processing going on in the carrels at the side. He led him behind the elevators and they walked down a flight to the deck below. Here Speidel turned to the right and began walking slowly, naming with evident pride the collections shelved down each bay they passed. It did indeed sound like the creative elite of the nation. The first deck appeared about evenly divided among colonial figures, Civil War and Reconstruction personalities, and European collections since the Enlightenment. George was astonished at the range of sources. Speidel would step in and pull out a box filled with handwritten letters by Voltaire, and two feet away would be the unpublished poems of a minor Concord poet. The next bay would contain a thousand identical boxes of the papers of an antebellum Secretary of State, while the following shelves carried fifty bound ledgers, the "minutes of the board meeting" from a now-forgotten railway company along the Erie Canal.

"This is incredible!" George exclaimed. "How long has this been building?"

"The material along here came from the original Bok collection which the old immigrant assembled in the 1890s. As we go on, you will see the impact of individual librarians. Langdon got us into the music field and along on Deck Nine you'll see the acquisitions of his period. Barrett, in the thirties, went after the scientists and he got all the papers which make our holdings second only to the Library of Congress in original records of experimentation."

George was genuinely astonished. "I had no idea the Werner-Bok had such breadth. This is very impressive."

Ten minutes later, when the tour had reached the

unpleasantly familiar reaches of Deck Two, George was suddenly reminded of the forbidden cage below.

"Incidentally, considering the tension that seems to lie between your two departments, why is the rare books binder housed in the manuscripts stack? What's his name, Schwartz?"

"Ah, I fear that that has nothing to do with the material he handles. We just had more empty space on our side. Schwartz does an occasional lamination for us, but he's the vassal of the Rare Books people, as you say. Welles brought him here himself, you know."

"Oh? We were surprised to see a number of duplicate volumes in his cage—modern stuff—mixed in with the antique material. Why would he have four copies of *Uncle Tom's Cabin* or some kind of a cowboy book down there?"

Speidel stopped, snapped off a bay light, leaving them in the gloom of the deck, and looked curiously at George.

"A cowboy book? How odd. Was he reading it or repairing it?"

"There was a pair of them in a single tray like the other pieces."

Speidel seemed to think a moment and then turned toward the stairs.

"Come. Will you show them to me? This may be very important."

Now what? George thought. He followed Speidel down the steps, the archivist almost running ahead of him. When they reached the bottom deck, George was surprised to find that all its lights were burning brilliantly. Speidel did not seem to notice this, nor did he hesitate, striding back and forth among the filing cabinets toward the cage. George struggled to keep up with him, wondering as he went what all the talk of 'not having been down here for months' had been about.

As they approached the cage, Speidel seemed to hesitate and look curiously toward the steel mesh. A man was seated in front of the table, hunched over, with his head down. George came abreast of Speidel, who had stopped and was staring intently at the seated figure. What is this?... Oh, surely not, George thought, and passed the archivist.

"Hello, may we bother you a moment?" George called.

There was no response. The door to the cage was standing open and George walked resolutely in. Except for the blood across the open book and table, it was grimly as he expected. The right hand held a gun, the left hand had held the book. The book, George noticed automatically, was a sixteenth-century quarto. George leaned forward. Emil Schwartz lay dead across a first edition of *Tamburlaine the Great* by Christopher Marlowe.

# 7

"Well, actually it was a whorehouse, is what it was."

Welles spun the sports car out of the Mall and headed for Pennsylvania Avenue. A police car with siren screaming shot through the intersection in front of them.

"Haines is in a splendid old Federal house that one of the officer corps built back in the 1830s when they rigged warships at the Navy Yard. If you can believe the prints we've got, the bay was clogged with masts and bowsprits and whatever, and you could look down and see the ships and the sail lofts and the whole bit."

He pulled in beside a curbside mailbox and, while Crighton slid envelopes in by the handfuls, he watched an ambulance roar across the avenue and disappear behind the Archives Building.

"Then along about Grant's time some entrepreneur turned it into a restaurant, and that lasted till the twenties when it had its stretch as a . . . house of ill fame? . . . which got shut down with Prohibition."

They crossed the Mall at the foot of the Capitol and headed for the Anacostia.

"And in sum this rose like the Phoenix in Eisenhower's time as a respectable nineteenth-century seafood spot. Nowadays it looks like late Sturbridge and has a travel sign on the door, so I'm afraid it's wholly reformed. But in spring you must try their shad roe and look at the Virginia headlands in dogwood time."

Crighton laughed. "You do make it sound romantic!"

"It's a little hard to do at high noon, but I try," he said sadly.

A few minutes later he turned the sports car into a well-filled parking lot and opened the door for her. "Miss Jones, that's the first time that seat's been filled with anything like the pictures in the brochure. Brünnhilde and I are both delighted."

"I'm a little awed! I've never been in a Mercedes before."

"Bless you for acting impressed. I was hoping you would be. She's my pride and joy, symbolizing quiet elegance with youthful outlook—the image I try to project."

He led her up the brick steps and she was soon sitting in front of a wide, multipaned window, overlooking the Anacostia as he had promised.

"It *is* lovely," she said. "No wonder you wanted to come here. The room is as beautiful as the view."

"Yes. The Federal period isn't sufficiently appreciated yet, but it will be. I'm very partial to New England architecture myself, and I get a little fed up with Virginia colonial. Everything around Washington—Maryland's just as bad—is neoclassic, Georgian. It's foreign. Federal is much more appropriate for Americans. It fits our way of life. You had to have a plantation full of slaves to keep up the other stuff. But a good nineteenth-century family—with a half dozen immigrant servants, of course—could maintain the Salem homes or something on the Connecticut. They were light and functional. So's this, you see."

"I thought you were a librarian. How come you know so much about architecture?"

"I don't really, of course. It's just like somebody who knows a little something about glass or wing chairs. After you learn the styles, you can drop all the right names and nobody knows the difference. No, that's not quite true. I love New England. I grew up in a clapboard, 1925 house in Asbury Park, New Jersey, so I have no heritage whatever. But I managed to get a good education at Rutgers and then, very fortuitously, I was drafted.

"This got me to Vietnam where I was assigned, of all things, to the Antiquities Corps for no other reason than that I'd had a fine arts minor. I arrived in Danang just when they were setting up those Culture Target Teams—do you know about those?"

"I don't even know what you're talking about!"

"Really? They were far out! Somebody noticed that as we worked our way up the coast the first thing the howitzers took out was the local temple. It wasn't a doctrinal difference, it was simply that the roof was the easiest thing to see across a valley, and when the tower toppled or the dome caved in, you knew you had the range. 'Fire for effect,' they used to call it. You will try the shad roe, won't you?" he asked when the waiter had come.

"I've never had that either, so I'm completely in your hands."

"Two shad roe, please, and a bottle of light Moselle . . . Berncastler '74 will do, if you have it. Well, even the Army got a little embarrassed about destroying the leading monument in every village, so they attached teams of art experts to the bombing commands and the artillery headquarters to identify the really irreplaceable spots in each town. Once we got going, we saved a great deal. I got tied to a fine bunch and enjoyed myself immensely."

"How did you know what was where?"

"The French had been there so long they'd had time to catalog every shrine, so all we had to do was plot them on the military maps and we were in business. We all became overnight experts in Early Khmer, Binh Dinh, and Cam style."

"How did you get from buildings to books?"

"Oh, we didn't specialize in architecture. Any fine art was fair game. I remember being with the 21st Infantry right after the Tet disaster. A beautiful old aristocrat came to us and said that our troops had liberated a solid gold necklace from her house which she believed was sixteenth-century Cambodian scrollwork. She was so afraid it might be lost that she begged us to try to find it and give it to a museum. She said she wouldn't even ask for it back if she could be sure somebody wouldn't just take it home as junk.

"So I cooked up a tragic story about a girl who'd lost a treasured present from her grandmother, and that it had no intrinsic value but if the soldier would drop it into a box outside of headquarters, no questions would be asked. We posted this tear-jerker with a detailed description of the piece on all the regimental bulletin boards. Are you ready for the punch line? It is an actual fact that when we opened the box there were thirty-five solid gold Cambodian necklaces, all seventeenth century or earlier! I am sorry to say the lady's was not among them. So far as I know, it's never turned up and is probably in somebody's attic in Indianapolis. It's enough to bring tears to your eyes."

The wine came, Welles tasted it, and nodded his approval. It was poured.

"You can try a little now, if you want, but you'll find it's just what's needed for the shad. Well, the necklace affair opened my eyes to a great truth—a mission! What Elgin did for the marbles and Napoleon for the Louvre, I was going to do for Oriental art. I went into the black market and made money hand over fist. You may recall that in the sixties the flow of Oriental antiques was all loused up. It was against our law to bring Chinese stuff in, and against the Viet and Cambodian law to take their stuff out. All it accomplished was to deny our museums and collectors one of the loveliest of all art forms, so I did what I could to save us from ourselves—at a fairly generous return for my efforts, I must admit.

"Ultimately, the Provost Marshal began to take a narrow-minded approach to my labors, so I gave the whole thing up and came back to the States. One of the men in my team worked for the New York auction house of LeBroun and Grey, so when my hitch was up I got him to introduce me to the bosses, and one thing led to another and I was a buyer for them through the rest of the sixties. Once Vietnam got to be a dirty word, Asian art lost some of its fashion, so they moved me to the rare book department and that led me to the Werner-Bok, and here I am. Incidentally, I haven't touched Eastern art in over a decade. I'm completely European-American now!"

"That's fascinating. It really is. How many people can make a living out of handling beautiful things? I envy you," Crighton said sincerely.

"I can't deny it," Welles answered. "Heaven knows it beats working. All it takes is a photographic memory and a trustworthy face, and you're a success. In fact, you can go a long way just on the trustworthy face!"

"You're putting me on. You must have to know who wrote what and when and how it looked—that's what makes you an expert, isn't it?"

"I shouldn't admit it, but that's the awful thing about my kind of business. The people with the money really don't know anything. The whole thing is built on a kind of childlike trust, and it is incredibly easy to get away with the crassest fraud.

"You know, the fine arts business is one part appreciation of beauty, and one part avarice. See that Queen Anne chair by the door there? If that is a Roanoake copy, it's worth a hundred dollars; if it's an original Queen Anne, it's worth a thousand! And neither you nor I can tell the difference. Who can? An antique furniture expert, but he doesn't own the chair. You or I do—all on his say-so. And then strictly on the strength of his word, we pay nine hundred dollars more than if he'd said, oh, it's just a reproduction. Why? If we like Queen Anne chairs—the way they look or the way they sit—what difference does it make? Ah, but that's not the point. We want to know that we have one of the really *few* Queen Anne chairs. There aren't many people who have a Queen Anne chair. We do. And we're so glad to have that feeling that we will pay the price of a trip to Europe or two years' clothes or whatever just to know we're one up. Of course, if it gives us a thousand dollars' worth of pleasure, who's to say we're wrong? But it is pretty silly to put ourselves in the hands of a glorified furniture salesman to tell the difference!"

"Is that what you do with rare books?"

"Essentially, yes. I make some small effort to ferret things out, and I'm very big on points (the memory again), but my chief usefulness to the Library—just like it was to LeBroun and Grey—is to say, this is genuine . . . this is a fraud . . . this is in good condition and therefore worth . . . and so forth."

"What do you mean, 'points'?"

"That's the way you tell rare books from used books. Most books since 1700 came out in various printings and only the first edition is worth anything. Since even today they rarely say 'first edition' right in 'em, and they use the same publication date through twenty printings, you learn how to tell which is the first and which isn't. It can be a broken letter or a typo somewhere that gets corrected as the printings progress. Sometimes there are actual changes in the text made by the author—Whitman and Twain were always 'improving' their stuff. These little gimmicks are called 'points' and if you can memorize enough of them, you sound learned as hell!"

"You do private appraisals, too, haven't I heard?"

"Yes, indeed. And that drives our fellow workers at the Library right up the wall—and I can't blame them. Poor Brewer knows the colonial period so well that if you mention the most obscure provincial governor, she can reel off every set of papers that have his name buried in them anywhere—and she makes barely forty dollars a day. I can go to an auction, spend thirty minutes riffling pages and carry back a check for two hundred bucks. The real irony is that I charge a percentage of the sale, and since I set the prices, I can pad my own fee! Oh, lady, I have to shave by memory some mornings. I can't look myself in the eye!"

"I wish I knew if you're putting me on. The way you tell it, it sounds scandalous, and I can't believe you'd actually do anything questionable."

"Oh, no. *I* never do anything questionable. Hardly. I'm only telling you how easy it would be to do it. Do you know anyone who sells things like stamps... or coins?"

"My father collects coins. He's always yelling about Barber quarters and standing liberty somethings—

and Mother's always yelling because he's wasting money."

"He probably isn't. It's ridiculous how everything like that keeps going up in price, but the reason I asked is, I wondered if you'd ever seen the catalogs he buys from? They always say across the top: The Authenticity of Every Item Is Guaranteed. Sounds impressive, doesn't it? All it means is that if *you* find out the stuff is counterfeit later on, they'll refund the money you paid for it. That's the difference between a respectable art dealer and a fraud. If one sells you a Picasso and it turns out to be a copy, the honest one will buy it back. The shyster will say, '*Caveat emptor;* that's why you got it so cheap.' But neither one certifies it to be an original!"

"I don't understand. How do we know that all Queen Anne chairs aren't copies, then, if no one can tell?"

"Two ways. If you really care, you can tear a Queen Anne chair apart at the seams, check the glue, the saw marks, put the wood under a microscope and see its weathering, and things like that. You can X-ray a picture. You can check the specific gravity of a coin, examine it under certain kinds of lenses—almost all of which efforts are more costly than the piece you're working on. *Or* you can buy it through an expert who either knows the entire history of the piece—who bought it from whom when—or whose reputation would suffer so he doesn't dare take any chances."

"But either way, you're just taking the word of the expert."

"You've got the picture, lady! As intelligent as she is lovely. Here comes the food. I will shut up."

The shad roe arrived surrounded with a collection of vegetables, salads, and hot breads which was quite overwhelming. Crighton began at the satellite dishes and worked her way to the center. Everything was delicious—until she reached the point of the feast, and this tasted like the way her uncle's bass boat smelled and was quite appalling. She struggled with it bravely, and with the help of considerable wine, managed to get the majority of it down. Once on to a fruit dessert she was on safe ground and finished the meal somewhat breathless, but triumphant.

"Wow! That was something! Do you do this often?"

"Once a year. Too much would take the edge off; not enough leaves me something to look forward to the next year. I am convinced that's the only way to get through life."

"If someone just listened to you, Mr. Welles, she'd think you lived for the day. If you had your 'druthers,' where would you be twenty years from now?"

"Please, please call me Alan. 'Mr. Welles' is almost as bad as being called 'sir.' I have no idea where—or what—I want to be twenty years from now. I do indeed just try to keep each day from being any more distressing than is absolutely necessary. I don't try to look beyond that."

"Have you ever made a mistake? Is there anything you'd have done differently?"

"Yes. I made a mistake. I married a very beautiful woman with a great deal of money. She gave me a wonderful entree into a world I'd never met in Asbury Park, and I decorated her apartment on the East River with knowing talk about the finest of arts. I became a burden to her, and she kept me from living my own life at all. So we were divorced a few years ago. It was a mistake—the marriage, that is. But I have never been sorry I did it. If I had not had those six years with her, I would not be comfortable in a Mercedes 280 SL, nor could I order wine without feeling self-conscious. She is now married to a real estate man, almost as wealthy as she, but everyone including herself knows that she was once married to a very intellectual art connoisseur. She was slightly vindictive about the matter, and the alimony nearly bankrupted me until she remarried, but except for this sordid detail, it was an even trade."

"You're just a bit frightening to someone still not too far away from Denver."

"No. I was the same person in Asbury Park as I am now, but I was convinced that the jock in the garage and I saw the same scene, looked at the same pictures on the wall, and drove through the same streets. He saw next to nothing. I simply wanted to be certain that I saw everything and felt everything and never let a moment get past me without getting my money's worth.

"Crighton, I don't know if you realize it, but you are much like this yourself. I've been watching you since you came to the Library and you have a frightening—almost compelling—honesty about you. You obviously are fascinated with what you see and hear. You are looking and listening constantly, yet you never try to act like you knew it all along, nor do you do the 'oh, please tell me more' routine. You really want to know!

"I wonder if you realize how attractive this is? Heaven knows I'm not reticent, but you've had me talking more in thirty minutes than I usually do in a morning! But what pleasure it's given me! Would you let me show you some of the world around you? I'm sure I could make the colors richer for you."

"I don't know what to say."

"Wait a minute! I didn't intend to sound like something in an opera cloak! What I mean is, I love to verbalize and it would be fascinating to watch you in a theatre. If I promise only to talk in the intermission, could I take you to The Square this weekend? One

drink on the way home and then to your door. I promise to be the soul of propriety."

"I'd like that. It sounds like fun. Yes, you may."

"Splendid. Come on. Our hour's nearly up. We've
got to run."

He paid the bill and they started home, Welles
keeping up a rolling monologue about how Washington had changed, what this portion and that of the city
had looked like in the past. As they approached the
Mall, Crighton was struck with the sickening recollec-
tion that she had failed to pursue a single subject
Steve Carson had sent her after. Her mind was testing
different openings when Welles interrupted himself by
saying, "By the way, I understand that Mr. George was
in the Manuscripts stacks this morning. Poor Brewer
was about to reproduce. What's the old gentleman up
to?"

Crighton's mind spun for a moment and she started
to panic. But this was the lead she needed, she realized, and said as casually as possible, "I'm not sure. I
couldn't tell whether he was just looking at the scene
of the . . . accident, or he was after something special.
Do you think there was something funny about it?"

"Well, frankly, the idea never crossed my mind until
one of you told me my name had been used. I talked
to Pop Wright and he swears up and down it was me.
Unless I'm losing my mind, it doesn't seem likely. My
first reaction was to think someone was trying to frame
me in some kind of nonsense and I began to run my
mind through everyone who has reason to hate me!
Except for understandable jealousy over my looks and
charm, I honestly can't think of a soul who might have
it in for me! It strikes me that that is a real indictment
of my personality. If, after all this time, a man hasn't
enough character to make at least one enemy . . . But
that's another matter. Having gotten this out of my

system, it finally came to me that if someone were trying to do something a bit close to the bone, mine was the one safe name to use. I was obviously occupied and there was no chance of my walking into a room where someone was supposed to be talking to me. This seems to remove the problem of any animus against me personally—I was just a safe name to use —but leaves me to wonder who placed the call? And what were they trying to bring off? Did poor De Veer's stepping on that pamphlet keep them from accomplishing whatever they called him for, or had they done whatever they intended to, and as a result, he ran off and killed himself? It's intriguing."

Crighton was intently running through everything she had been coached to pursue.

"Suppose someone were mad at DeVeer or something funny was going on in his section, what kind of thing would it be?"

"Well, the most obvious would be theft, of course. It's the first thing you think of in the rare book and manuscripts game. We've got millions of dollars' worth of stuff on those shelves, and it's reasonably easy to steal if you put your mind to it, but it's next to impossible to cash in on. If a book is worth enough to take the chance to steal, it's usually rare enough that its appearance would cause attention. By the same token, if you lifted it from the shelves, the hole you'd leave would be bound to be noticed. Not the physical hole, the absence of the title in your collection. We check every rare book every three years—there's a constant shelf reading going on, it takes three years to come around to the point where you began—and anything missing would show up at the count. Manuscripts are only checked when they're used. Somebody takes out the Franklin papers, and then every box is checked when he returns it and before it goes back on the shelf. If a box isn't used, it could go years without being noticed, but manuscripts worth enough to take the trouble to steal are murder to unload without somebody noticing. They really *are* one of a kind and would be spotted at once. No, I don't see the idea of something 'funny.'"

By now they had reached the Mall area and were slowly working their way through tourist traffic, searching for a place to park.

"If I weren't so vain about Brünnhilde, I'd take the bus," he said absently. "No, this must be tied to some sort of personality clash. Everybody hated DeVeer, but hardly anyone dared cross him. Speidel is nasty and totally without scruples, but he needed DeVeer as a front. I can't imagine him creating a crisis. Brewer is so protective of Rose that if she thought DeVeer was trying to injure the old man, she might do anything—but I can't imagine what the 'injury' might be. Rose could be driven to protect himself if DeVeer were really bearing down on him, but I don't know how DeVeer could get his hooks into him.

"Actually, I suppose Brooks had more reason to work him over than anyone. He was always stirring up 'The Institution,' and Brooks thinks more of The Institution than he does of his wife. Brooks had the power to do him dirt, too, but I can't think of anything DeVeer could have done that would irritate Brooks any more than he always has."

Crighton wondered if Welles knew about the letters and decided to play it safe and not mention them.

Welles looked directly at her for a moment, and asked: "Do you have any idea what might be going on? Does Mr. George say anything?"

"No, Mr. George doesn't talk much to me, obviously, and so far as I know nobody's really speculating," she lied.

He turned the car toward the building, now half a mile away. As they approached it, Crighton exclaimed: "Look, there are police cars all over the place! Oh, dear Lord! What now?"

Welles raised his eyes but made no comment. Finally he said quietly, "This doesn't look good at all. It's no use trying to get closer with them blocking the street. I'll put her in a pay lot. Do you mind walking from here? I'm afraid we both should get back as fast as we can."

"You're right. I'll hop out. I'm terribly sorry you're having all this trouble. Thanks so much for lunch. It was marvelous."

"Don't forget Friday. See you soon . . ."

She stepped out on the grass and hurried toward the Werner-Bok. The rain had stopped, but the skies were low with a cold, damp wind blowing the length of the Mall. The Monument was rain-soaked and black, and the Werner-Bok had strange streaks as water oozed off cornices, down balustrades, and around classic heads staring vacantly out of clam-shelled alcoves. Crighton stared, overtaken with a growing sense of dread. It had once seemed like a refuge of safety, sanctuary. The image of a damp, brooding mausoleum seemed to rise in its place and her apprehension grew as she ran.

# 8

Crighton fled up the steps and into the entrance, now framed by the bronze doors folded back against the walls. It took a moment for her eyes to adjust to the darker interior and as she recovered her sight she discovered the uniformed policemen standing quietly around the entryway.

She elbowed her way through a knot of alien uniforms to the more familiar sight of a Library guard sitting at his desk by the inner doors.

"Excuse me," she said. "I'm Crighton Jones. I'm on the staff. May I use the inside phone, please?"

He hesitated for a moment and then shoved the instrument toward her. She dialled her own number and rejoiced when a familiar voice answered. "Yeah, hello."

"Steve, is that you?"

"Yes, indeed! Where you at?"

"The front door. There are police everywhere up here. What's going on? Should I come down or go to the Director's office?"

"Neither. Just take it easy. Have you heard what's happened?"

"No. Is it about . . . your theory?"

"Could be. They tell me that somewhere around the time you left, Mr. George and somebody—Speidel, I guess—found the bookbinder very dead in that cage of his."

Crighton covered her mouth with her hand. The guard was watching her closely.

"They called the cops and an ambulance," Carson continued, "and from what I can learn from passing staff, they've been trying to cope with it ever since. The Director sent a guard for you and I told him you were at lunch. The guard came back after a while saying the Director wanted you in the Employees' Lounge as soon as you got back. Nobody's taken any notice of me, and I haven't heard a word from George since we all parted. He's hung up in the stacks, apparently."

"How did he die?" Crighton asked quietly.

"All I can find out is what somebody heard from somebody, but apparently he shot himself."

"Oh, no."

"Yeah. It looks like there was something very wrong with the DeVeer thing. Both of these can't be accidents."

The guard reached for the phone meaningfully. Crighton nodded.

"I've got to go. Are you going to wait there or what?"

"Do you want me to?"

"Well, I don't know why you should. . . ."

"That wasn't my question."

"Yes, I'd be very grateful."

"It will give me great pleasure. I'll be here till you release me. Now split. Go up and find out what the party line's going to be this time."

She handed the phone back to the frowning guard and headed for the elevators.

The Great Hall was strangely silent. It was not the hollow hush of an empty room, but a muffled, deadened stillness. She realized that she had grown accustomed to a busy sound from across the mosaic. There should have been a blur of low voices and heels on the polished stone, distracted librarians, shuffling tourists. Today the people were standing in twos and threes, clustered back under arches and in corners, almost furtive.

She walked quietly and alone across the hall and into the elevator. As she came out above, she found the knots of people—here mostly staff members—waiting outside the Lounge. Instead of seeking details of the tragedy, she avoided her fellow workers and was grateful when everyone turned and she discovered that Brooks and George had appeared around the elevator column. They were accompanied by a short, heavyset man she had not seen before.

Brooks walked directly toward her.

"Miss Jones, I should have told you to come downstairs instead of waiting here. I thought we'd be up sooner."

Crighton could see nothing to be gained from admitting she'd just arrived and kept silent.

"I want you to stay with us for a while. Lieutenant Conrad, the Lounge is there ahead of you. I think either this or my own office will be the best for your purpose."

The third man spoke as George gave her a half-wink behind the stranger's back. Conrad was a gray, unhealthy-looking man. He had a thick neck, gray eyes, straight gray hair, and thin lips that looked as though they had been slashed across his face by a master thumbnail. He spoke in a low, somewhat asthmatic voice barely above a whisper—but which somehow demanded attention.

"Yeah. This is better. You go on with your business in your own office and I'll do mine here. First, though, I just want the two of you—and the girl if you want her."

"Miss Jones is the Library's public relations officer," George explained. "Crighton, this is Lieutenant Conrad. He's from the police department. You know about our latest tragedy, I presume."

Crighton nodded and accepted Conrad's cold, rather fleshy hand.

Brooks addressed the groups of waiting staff. "You can go back to work now, and we'll call you if we need you."

They withdrew reluctantly, leaving Crighton and the three men alone in the room. Conrad closed the door very deliberately and stood staring at the floor, making no move to sit or speak. Brooks was clearly irritated, eager to get the thing over and done with. George found himself tired but quietly amused. He had to admit in spite of himself, he was finding the whole affair strangely intriguing. He felt he ought at least to be embarrassed, but he couldn't force himself to make the effort. He looked at Brooks. There was an "administrator" in the classic sense of the word. He wondered how much did his friend know about what was happening in his own library? Was it less than he should, or was it too much?

Conrad raised his head and also stared at Brooks, who frowned irritably and leaned against the arm of a couch.

Conrad asked slowly, "You said something about the man's—Schwartz's—suicide, a minute ago. Why do you think it was suicide?"

"Well, he had a gun in his hand and he'd obviously shot himself," Brooks snapped. "What would you call it?"

Conrad watched him for a moment, and then said casually, "I'd say I saw a man who was dead with a gun in his hand."

Brooks flushed and said quickly, "Believe me, Lieutenant, if it wasn't suicide, I presume it would have to be murder. We don't go around murdering people in libraries, these days. I assume they sent you over when they heard someone had been shot. I suppose you're a detective, then. Just because you're used to looking for crimes, shouldn't require you to find one everywhere. Emil Schwartz not only was not murdered, you will find that there are barely six people in the Library who even knew who he was, and they scarcely had a word to speak with him. Clearly there is some personal tragedy here and I would suggest you discover what it is before you get everyone in the Library excited about 'somebody shot Emil Schwartz!'" Brooks illustrated rumor and panic with waving arms.

"You do get a good number of suicides, hunh?" Conrad asked.

"What do you mean?"

"Well, you said that it wasn't murder because people don't do things like that in a library."

Brooks opened his mouth to reply, hesitated, and closed it, irritation rapidly being replaced by anger.

Conrad looked at the collection of couches, overstuffed chairs, and general furniture around the room and selected a straight-backed, medieval-looking piece which he tilted toward him and dragged back to the others. His audience seated themselves on whatever was closest to where they were standing, while Conrad eased himself into his throne and slid his feet out before him. He looked toward George and said in a tone of mildly bored disinterest, "For some strange reason, nearly every suicide I ever handled left a note. There must be some hook-up between brainy people and suicides. I guess the smart ones get to thinking about their troubles and are bright enough to say 'the hell with it'—but they're also bright enough to want to drop the shoe, if y'know what I mean. They always want to neat things up with a good-bye or an apology or some kind of explanation to get everybody's sympathy. This one: no note.

"The scientists'll be in to measure the angle of fire and all that stuff, but from what I see the gun was held so it could've been done by the body—or somebody else could've shot him and stuck it in his hand. 'Thout the note, I lean toward somebody knocking him off. It makes for wonder, hunh, why would somebody want to do that?"

He looked back at Brooks.

"Who was this Schwartz? What'd he do down there?"

Brooks replied: "He was a bookbinder. Most of our new binding is done under contract with two firms in Baltimore, but any work on rare materials is done on-site—within the department. For security, obviously. He repaired the rare books and did some preservation of manuscript material. He also cared for the leather bindings in the rare book collection."

"What kind of repairs do you need? Things wear out, hunh?"

"No. None of the rare material gets that much use. By and large it is very old when we get it and we immediately do what we can to arrest the deterioration."

"The stuff pretty valuable?"

"Yes, most of it is worth a great deal of money."

"What if this guy had been stealing the things and was about to get caught?"

"Stealing would be very difficult. The material would be hard to sell outside the respectable channels, the room is heavily guarded as is the Library itself, and we are checking the collections constantly."

"You just missed a good chance to sell me on suicide."

"I don't need to..." Brooks flared and then interrupted himself. He sat rigidly, trying to keep himself under control.

"What's this 'caring for the leather' thing?" Conrad continued without changing expression.

"All leather books dry out. Sheepskin turns to dust and flakes off. Pigskin, morocco, ostrich crack and split. You have to rub them with a mixture of oils every year or so. He did this."

"So the man would have to go all over the building picking these books out, hunh?"

"No. He didn't deal with anything except in the two divisions—Rare Books and Manuscripts—and he refused to leave his cage during working hours. He said he was paid as a skilled craftsman, not as a porter. Rose, the head of Rare Books Division, worked up a schedule and the leather-bound books were taken off the shelves and moved down to the cage by the deck attendants methodically every two weeks—year in and year out."

"The repair stuff was brought to him, too?"

"Yes. He rarely left his cage except to go to lunch and home."

"He didn't like people or they didn't like him?"

"No one saw enough of him to know. There was some rumor about his being a collaborator in World War II who'd fled to Indochina. He was French, you know, in spite of his name—came to us via Vietnam.

His English was very bad and I presume it embarrassed him to have to speak."

"Sounds pretty clumsy. Why did you put up with it?"

"Because he was irreplaceable. Master binders are very hard to come by these days. There are very few shortcuts in the job and no innovations since casein glue. You anchor one page at a time. You tool one letter at a time. Like stone masons—it's a dying trade."

"Pay pretty good?"

"Reasonably. We paid him as a professional."

Conrad put his hands behind his head and began to massage his neck, staring at the ceiling. No one spoke.

After a few minutes had passed, there was a respectful knock on the door, and Conrad raised his voice to a near-normal tone to say, "Yeah?"

"Jesse, here."

"Come in."

A young, blonde policeman entered, cap in hand. He had a strange mixture of crisp efficiency and subservience about him that made George think of the "young Nazi" who always appeared behind the Kommandant in the TV shows. George found himself watching the man with unusual curiosity, trying to decide if there was really the unimaginative brutality there, or if the poor soul just happened to look like a television SS man.

"Jesse, run the routine. Check the man's finances. Schwartz's. Find out exactly how much he made and then see if his accounts match. No, sit down, you can do it later. Just sit there and make notes of anything that sounds interesting."

Jesse seated himself and the group lapsed into silence again. Brooks refused to relax, sitting nervously upright; George continued to watch with the same amused interest.

Suddenly Conrad asked, "If I wanted to steal some of that stuff, what'd I have to do?"

The detective continued to stare at the ceiling, and Brooks waited to answer as if there were someone else who could make the reply. He finally shifted his position on the couch, and said grudgingly, "You'd have to go into a room watched by a uniformed guard, pass in front of a staff librarian, go into a deck area where a half dozen people worked, know where the book you wanted was, find it, steal it, and walk back past everybody and out the front door, also covered by a uniformed guard."

"How many doors are there to the area?"

"Just one into the rare materials area, and just two in and out of the Library—the front door, and a basement loading dock which only the staff knows about. It has a guard on it, too."

"I assume there are fire exits which could be propped open from the inside."

"No, there are not. There is only one entrance into the rare materials area and two into the Library. Period."

"Does the fire marshal know about this?"

"He does. Libraries have a special dispensation just like banks. And for the same reason."

There was another wait until Conrad pulled himself upright in the chair and looked at the Director.

"You're convinced there's no funny business about your books. So how do you explain what happened down there?"

Brooks flashed back immediately: "I've told you, it is clearly some personal matter. Find out what's happened to his family. Why did he leave France—or Vietnam, if that's where he really came from? Look for a woman. What kind of trouble had he gotten into? He was really outside the life of this Library. He had no contact with his fellow workers. He had no part of our purpose. He was a little man working in his basement. Get out and see what had happened in his miserable life to make it worth ending!"

"All right," Conrad said quietly. "We'll do that. Jesse, talk to his wife. Has his family been notified? I presume they have."

Brooks replied somewhat hesitantly: "Well . . . I meant his parents. I don't think he has anyone in this country. Not married. He lived in an apartment somewhere."

"Then talk to his landlord and his neighbors."

"Now, Lieutenant?" Jesse asked.

"No. Not yet. I'll tell you."

Conrad turned toward George and said: "When I first got here, you said you'd found him . . . that would be a little after noon, wouldn't it? What were you doing down there?"

George leaned forward and said, "I had been talking to Dr. Speidel up on the top deck and he wanted to show me some of the collection in the Manuscripts Division. We started walking back and forth on the various decks and ultimately worked ourselves down to the bottom level and found him as you did."

"How long were you on the decks?"

"I'm not sure. Possibly as much as half an hour."

"Did you hear the shot?"

"No."

Conrad looked at the policeman.

"Must have had a silencer. A shot would make a colossal racket in a library. Silencers are hard to come by. This might make things go quicker. Wait a minute. What the hell am I saying? The gun in his hand had been fired, hadn't it? That's queer. I wonder why you didn't hear it? Did you take the elevator down?"

"No, we walked from one deck to the other."

"Did you hear anyone else taking the elevator either way?"

George tried to throw his memory back, now nearly two hours past. "I'm afraid I really wouldn't have the slightest idea. If I had heard it, I would have assumed that it was someone getting books."

"Jesse, check out everybody in that room to see who went in and out."

"Now, Lieutenant?"

"Hell yes, now. Go on and get started. Why were you looking at the books again, uh . . . Mr. George?"

George thought, well, here it comes. How much are you going to tell him? Where is your loyalty in this? Candor with authority? Support of Brooks, as an old friend? Maybe a general passivity until you can see which way the land lies? He had waited too long to speak; Conrad was looking at him.

"What do you do here? How come you were down there?"

Brooks shot him a meaningful look, and George replied: "I'm a retired librarian myself. I'm not a member of the staff at all. I was merely discussing some . . . aspects . . . of librarianship with Dr. Speidel and he offered to show me around."

"Did you know this Schwartz?"

"No. So far as I know, I never saw him in my life."

"Were you with Speidel all the time?"

George laughed. "Yes. I think he can provide an alibi for me and, at least from about twelve-fifteen on, I can vouch for him."

"And will anyone vouch for the two of you together?"

George looked at Conrad to see if he was being ironic or was the threat genuine? He could not tell. George chose to assume the question was rhetorical.

"Neither one of you seems particularly distressed at the death of a fellow worker. How am I to think of this?"

Brooks jumped in: "It's simply that I scarcely knew him at all—he was simply a name on the payroll to me. I rarely saw him and hadn't spoken to him for weeks. Ed here had never even seen him."

Conrad looked at George as if to ask, "And what have you to say?"

George hesitated and then said: "I think that we are a bit numb with violence already. I presume you know that we had had another death in the same area barely twelve hours before."

Conrad frowned and Brooks looked furiously at George. "What the hell, Ed! Whose side are you on, anyway?"

"Whose side should he be on, Brooks? No, I did not know you had had an earlier death. What was that all about?"

"The head of the Manuscripts Division—that's the side of the room you were in with the cage—fell down a flight of stairs and apparently fractured his skull. He died before the doctor arrived. His name was DeVeer and he was both well known and deeply involved with the staff. This Schwartz man was scarcely known at all, and if you seem to notice a callousness from the people you talk to, it more likely implies a lesser involvement than the earlier tragedy—not greater insensitivity."

"Dammit, Ed, there's no need to get the staff involved in this. Lieutenant, I really see no reason for your 'talking to people' at all beyond establishing the basic facts of the matter and there's no reason we can't provide those to you directly. We have a highly professional organization here, highly productive, and nationally known. I would just as soon you held off disrupting their morale until you've checked out the possibility of some personal motive—er—explanation."

"I'm afraid we don't understand each other, Brooks." Conrad's voice was low and cold. "I gather you run this Library. I find out about dead people. You look after your books or whatever it is you do here. I'll look after the dead people—my way. Was the coroner here about the other man?"

"Yes," George replied. "I understand he was satisfied it was an accident."

"Did anyone say it wasn't?"

"No."

"Then why did you mention it?"

George hesitated and frowned. "I could say because we were talking about why no one is as distressed about Schwartz as you would expect. But that is not the reason. I must admit it crossed my mind that the precise manner of the accident was unusual."

"When did you get this idea?"

"I'm not sure. Possibly with the additional tragedy. With all respect to my friend, Dr. Brooks here, I must in candor suggest that if there has indeed been deliberate violence—and please recall, we don't know that either of the deaths was other than an accident and suicide—I am inclined to think that the thread will not be either theft or personal matters, but professional relationships."

"Jesus Christ!" Brooks exploded. "Are you out of your mind?"

"Yeah. I'm inclined to agree with him for a change," Conrad said casually. "The idea of a bunch of librarians getting that worked up over their jobs is a little hard to swallow. Believe me, I've been in this business too long already, but the number of these that can't be explained by money, booze, or sex you can put in your eye."

George continued somewhat tensely. "I beg you not to take this so cavalierly. The stereotypes of the librarian are mousy, frightened men or neurotic old maids who hide in the Library, too paralyzed with their own inadequacies to hurt anyone. It is questionable whether this was ever true, but it is certainly not true today. The people who work here are leading experts in their fields. They are both jealous of their reputations and ambitious for their futures. Further, many of them have an almost religious fervor about the importance of what they're doing. Believe me, by the time you're finished, I think you will find warped professionalism in some way at the bottom of this."

Conrad smiled condescendingly. "We'll check it out, but my guess is it's not going to be suicide and it's not going to be any fancy psychological hangup. This is going to be a plain case of cause and effect as soon as we know what's involved.

"Dr. Brooks. I'll have to talk to everybody who works in those two rooms there. Have 'em sent in here one at a time. I don't care what order they come in. And then I think both of you can go on with whatever you've got to do. I'll call you if I need you."

This high-handed dismissal in his own Library brought Brooks to the last edge of fury and only George's firm hand leading him toward the door prevented a major explosion.

Crighton followed them into the hall, and asked, "Dr. Brooks, shall I prepare a press release on Mr. Schwartz or wait . . . for something?"

"Hell, I don't know! I don't know what's going on anywhere. Yes, go ahead, write something, but bring it to me before you show it to anybody. Play it down if it's possible. Hah! That's a laugh. From what I can see, it's too late to salvage anything now. Ed, I cannot imagine what in heaven's name you thought you were doing in there. Fortunately the man is such a fool that he ignored the flag you were waving at him, but I must say that showed the poorest judgment I've ever seen you exhibit. Excuse me, I'm going to arrange Conrad's interviews and get to my office before I say something I'll be sorry for."

George smiled at Crighton. "I don't think Nelson agreed with me, somehow." Crighton grinned, and George said, "I wish I were sure I knew what I was doing myself. Ah, well! You go on. I want to pick up something, and I'll meet you in your office in a couple of minutes. I think we are due for a council of war."

They parted and George turned to the left and followed the hall around to the door opening into the eastern wing: Division of History and Literature. He entered and looked around the room for the first time. It was a large, high-vaulted reading room like any of a thousand others in the country's public and university libraries. He searched for the ubiquitous card catalog, found it, sought a title in its trays, and filled out the traditional call slip. He handed it in at the desk and waited at a nearby table. He was tired. He found he was too tired even to reason, so he stared in front of him musing on all the other rooms like this he'd sat in in the past fifty years. He had enjoyed it himself, he knew, but what impact did all the effort, the getting and the organizing and the keeping have? His mind slipped to a picture of Karl Marx writing, writing, writing in the British Museum and he smiled in spite of himself. Librarians had been using that one to prove they were never quite sure what for years.

His thoughts were interrupted with the appearance of an attendant who handed him his volume without speaking. George thanked him and rose slowly and stiffly. He walked back into the hall and took the elevator to the basement, walking slowly down the corridors to Crighton's room.

"Mr. George," Carson said. "Come in and sit down. The lady is trying to bring me up to date. What a mess! Does it look as bad to you as it does to me?"

George seated himself at her desk without apology, placing the book in front of him. He shook his head.

"It's not good at all. The whole thing may be quite explainable by accident and tragedy, but your fears seem more and more justified."

"This second one...was it suicide? Could he have been the one who pushed DeVeer and then cut out from remorse or fear?"

"The lieutenant has a charming rule of thumb by which he works in these matters. If there's a note, it's suicide. No note, forgive me, it's murder."

"And there wasn't anything at all?"

George sighed. "They found nothing, but I am very much afraid... Schwartz apparently was reading a book when he died, or we are supposed to believe he was. He fell lying across, of all things, Christopher Marlowe's *Tamburlaine*."

"What!" Carson shouted.

"Yes, you're thinking of Speidel's specialty, of course."

"No. I'm thinking that that name is suddenly haunting me. I hadn't heard of the Scourge of God since I was a freshman, when The Jones and I got caught by a fanatic yesterday who gave us an unsolicited lecture on Poe's *Tamerlane*. I mean, twice in two days is a little heavy."

George looked concerned. "I don't understand that at all. No," he continued, "my first thought was that either Schwartz was trying to tell us something about Speidel by killing himself on a Marlowe, or someone was trying to frame Speidel with this rather obvious prop. Then the more I thought about it, I wondered if Speidel were himself involved, putting the thing there to throw us off the track. But wait . . ." George held up his hand, interrupting a question.

"I was sitting there watching that lieutenant look for the obvious, with the growing conviction that this is going to be far more complicated than he has any idea, when it struck me. Wait a minute . . . I could still be very wrong."

He pulled the book toward him, and began to leaf through it, scanning the top of each page.

"The blood had covered everything except the head notes. . . . The page was open to Part II, yes, then Section IV. Here that is. Now, wait a minute. Yes. Oh my, yes . . . I was afraid it would be something like this. Conrad will think he has his note after all. Children, poor Schwartz was lying across this. . . ."

He held his finger on the page, and they crowded around to read:

> I know, sir, what it is to kill a man;
> It works remorse of conscience in me.

"Jesus!" Carson cried. "Isn't that a bit baroque?"

"Yes, Steve, it is. But I suspect your period is wrong. I think we have a Renaissance mind working against us to whom the whole thing is a game of ironies—or we have a Gothic literalist who is getting cold revenge for we don't know what. Either way, I'm afraid we're racing against time before he pulls his next joke—or evens another score. Either way . . . either way," he said reflectively, "I wonder if it may not be me?"

# 9

"What do you mean?" Crighton asked. "What are you saying?"

"Oh, dear. I'm sorry. I didn't mean to sound so dramatic. It merely crossed my mind that I must be a bit of a puzzle to whoever's behind all this. He sees me snooping around the library. He doesn't quite know what I've seen or what I'm after—or what I knew before I got here. It occurred to me that he might think it good insurance to shorten my memory just to be on the safe side." He threw the thought off casually as if he didn't much care one way or the other. "In any event, time is running against me. I've got to get this thing resolved and quickly. Miss Jones, I leave you to your public. You're getting to be an old hand at this, I'm afraid—and Steve, you'd better get back to the research. I am deeply grateful for your..."

"Hold it!" said Carson. "If you think you're brushing me off that easily... What I mean is, sir, this isn't just a casual incident to me. This is the chance of a lifetime. I'm trying to be an historian. I hope to make a living reconstructing things out of the past—usually from words that somehow got left behind. But here's a real live reconstruction! I'm crazy to see if the historical method will work. Think of it! We know some things and we know we know 'em. We probably know some more but we don't know we do. And then we've got some we've guessed at . . . it's exactly what I'm trying to do with that frontier thing. Tests for significance and validity! It's tremendous. Don't let's blow another minute talking about it. Where do we start?"

George hesitated. "You realize that we don't know what we're dealing with here? Whoever's behind all this could either be raving mad or completely without respect for human life." He cocked an eyebrow at Carson and pulled at his lip for a moment. "Ah, well, I guess you're over twenty-one. And I must admit, I'm finding it rather intriguing myself. All right, you've convinced me. Let's go. I think we should get back to that cage as quickly as possible."

Carson slid to his feet and the two men headed for the corridor.

"Dammit! Where are you going!" shouted an outraged Crighton. "Here you two go sailing out without even a write-if-you-get-work! I'm in on this thing whether you like it or not. It so happens I can be useful. I have some access around here you just might need. If you think that chivalry requires you to protect me from danger or something, you can forget it—but what fries me is you didn't think at all! It never occurred to either one of you that I'd be interested in what was going on—much less that I could do you any good."

Both men started hasty explanations which she cut short with a gesture.

"Forget it! You haven't time to lie yourselves out of this one—we'll take it up later. I just want it understood that when you finish whatever you're up to, we reassemble right here. I will not be ignored."

Carson was contrite, and George smilingly embarrassed. "The fact is, Crighton, I am very eager to get a report on your lunch with Welles, and I owe both of you an account of an incredible conversation I had with Speidel. We will return posthaste."

"I'll accept that. Now split. Both of you." Crighton swept them into the hall with her hands.

"Oops!" said Carson. "Nearly blew that."

George laughed. "A charming girl. It's a pleasure to watch her mind work."

Carson let the understatement pass.

They retraced their steps to the elevator, rose, and came out on the top floor. George nodded toward the Rare Books and Manuscripts Reading Room and led the way.

He found the events of the past hours had sharpened his awareness of detail. The high, arched doors were the same as ever. Black, solid, medieval. But this time he noticed the heavy wooden bar slid back on the right one, and recalled that Brooks had insisted this was the only door to the room. He glanced at it casually and was surprised to see a very efficient, wrought iron hasp imbedded in the black wood. Bright wear in the link showed that it could be locked in place and, he assumed, apparently was at closing time.

The men entered and again the curious feeling of drifting back in time swept over them. Again the dark tables, the twelfth-century sunlight filtering through the stained glass. It took only the faintest effort to transform the seated figures into monks poring over Carolingian manuscripts. The two men received Pop Wright's approval and they walked quietly down the slate aisle. So far as George could see, the same scholars were in the same places in the same cataleptic positions he had found them in yesterday.

They turned toward the stacks at right and were suddenly jerked into the present. A large, florid policeman was blocking the door. He made an obeisance toward lowering his voice, but its rumble startled everyone.

"You can't go in there."

"What's the problem, officer?" George asked.

"Nobody can go in there that doesn't work there."

"Ah, I see. Very wise." This could be time-consuming, George thought to himself. He fixed Carson with an intent look and sketched a flanking movement with his eyes.

"Lieutenant Conrad sent us down to get something from my office. Won't take a moment."

Heads throughout the room rose and "shsssses" began to form.

"We're disturbing everyone. Here, let's talk on the deck," George said.

The officer frowned back at the critics and George took advantage of his distraction to pull the door open and slip quickly onto the deck. Carson followed him by inches. The door shut behind them, bringing the policeman with it.

"Wait a minute. You can't come in here. What do you want?"

"I'll show you." George strode quickly toward a darkened carrel. He got inside, snapped on the light, and sat down at the desk before the officer could catch up with him. George discovered to his delight that it was a cataloger's desk, its drawers filled with cards divided into different-sized bundles and held by rubber bands. He seized one and started through it ostentatiously.

"Come on! Get out of here. Is this your office? I didn't see you come out of it. Come on now."

George's earlier alacrity slowed to the deliberate movements of an old man who had finally found what he wanted, read it carefully, drew the materials together again, and carefully replaced them in the drawer. By the time he had permitted himself to be herded back to the reading room, Carson was nowhere to be seen.

"Where's the other guy?"

"He went back to the reading room. Didn't you see him?"

The officer looked uncertainly behind him toward the deck and then assumed a they-shall-not-pass posture barring the door.

"Come on, now. Move along."

George smiled to himself as he started down the aisle. Not bad for the spur of the moment, he thought. He passed through the corridor and took up a comfortable position against a banister overlooking the Great Hall, now cleared of chairs and stage and returned to its ornamental function. Steve should be out in five or ten minutes, he thought.

In fact, it was closer to fifteen, and George had begun to worry that the officer had exceeded the tongue-lashing he anticipated when one of the heavy doors was shoved back and Carson staggered through it, the policeman propelling him with a large hand on the shoulder. Once out of the reading room, Carson could raise his voice.

"Take your greasy hands off me, you Fascist! You touch me again and I'll have you before the board!"

The tone was convincing, but the twinkle in his eyes almost defeated the performance. The policeman started to pursue the discussion and then abruptly changed his mind.

"The hell with it. Shut your lip, Buster, and stay

outa my sight." He stamped back into the room and disappeared.

"Very nice," George said with approval. "What was your theme?"

"Outraged innocence, what else? I merely went into the stacks to get the book I was after. I had no idea he wanted me to wait."

"Ah, but you don't seem to have a book with you."

"It wasn't there."

"Too bad."

Carson's look suddenly became serious. "Actually, it *was* too bad. Listen. We've got problems." He looked around to be certain they were alone.

"I scuttled down the stairs as I assumed you wanted me to, and then slipped out onto the bottom floor. Nobody was there, but all the lights were on and the body had been taken away. If it was lying on a book, that's gone too. And so are the ones we were after."

"Really? Had they removed everything?"

"No. That's just the bit. Listen. Everything was exactly as it was when we looked in yesterday. All those little flat boxes . . . trays . . . are right in the same place with all the fancy books in them. The papyrus is still spread down the length of the table. But get this: the three trays where we saw those books are empty—the only empty ones on the table."

George started to comment but Carson held up his hand.

"Wait a minute. Here's the thing that's got me bugged. Can you see that papyrus in your mind?"

George thought a moment and said, "Yes, I think I can."

"What's holding it down . . . keeping it from rolling back up?"

George stared into space and said slowly, "A bunch

of weights and a ruler and a pair of scissors with broken points."

"More. What's the biggest thing on the table?"

"Ah. A large paper cutter without a blade."

"Right! It's still in the same place—but it's got a blade now!"

George looked at him and frowned slightly. "I'm afraid I don't see what you're driving at."

"You would if you'd seen the thing itself. That blade is sharp as a knife on the cutting side, but the top is nice and flat and smooth and shiny—and just the width of a steel support holding those stacks up!"

George looked at him sharply.

"You think you have figured out how he died."

"I think it's a helluva lot easier to cope with than his kneeling neatly impaled on a T-beam."

George spoke slowly. "Yes, I daresay that's true. There was no blood on the blade, of course?"

"No. Just the opposite. The blade is all shiny black —while the cutting board or whatever you call it is sort of grimy and lying-around looking."

"Ummm. Well, I presume that can be checked pretty easily. I'm afraid we'd better tell Conrad about this."

"Yeah. I'd feel better myself. If I'm right, this is an ugly way to do it. There's a nice, neat handle on one end, and a bolt and spring on the other which would have given it a sickening heft. Anybody who handled that either had to be mighty mad or mighty cold-blooded. This is one for the pros, though."

"I agree. Come along. You'd better tell him yourself."

They headed for the policeman guarding the entrance to the Lounge. The door was firmly shut.

"Officer, I need to talk to Lieutenant Conrad at once. Is he still in there?"

"Yeah, he's run outa librarians. Go on in."

They entered and the door closed behind them. Conrad was still slumped in the black chair, and Jesse was seated at a side table, silently reading his shorthand notes. Conrad turned his head slightly and looked at them.

"So? What's up?" he asked without expression.

"Lieutenant, this is Steve Carson. He was down on the stack deck last night when DeVeer was found."

"What?" Conrad asked quickly. "Did you find the body?"

"No, no. The body was discovered by Speidel, who came back upstairs to get help. Steve and Miss Jones went down to see what they could do, but it was too late. The point is," George continued somewhat irritably, "Steve was just down in the decks and he's come up with something you should know about."

"Down in what decks?"

"Where the bookbinder's cage is."

"What the cold hell was he doing down there?" Conrad sat up abruptly.

"I was talking to the officer and Steve here simply walked past him, not realizing that he wasn't supposed to go in."

"What officer? A big guy with a red face?"

"Yes, I think that would describe him, but what you . . ."

"Come off it. Nobody just walks past Whelan, dammit. What were you up to?"

"Never mind the details," George replied firmly. "Steve, go ahead."

"What we think you should know is this," Steve said quickly to forestall further interruption. "I was passing the cage down there and naturally I looked in to see if the body was still there. I happened to look on the table and was surprised to see that something that was not there early this morning had appeared in the meantime."

"What were you doing there 'early this morning'?" Conrad broke in angrily.

"He was looking around the stacks with me," George said. "What he's trying to tell you is that this morning we saw a large paper cutter on the table, without a knife—you know, the big blade on the side. Now the knife is back on the cutter. Presumably Schwartz had reassembled it before he was killed. But what attracted Steve's attention was that the width of the blade, if reversed, would precisely match the piece of steel that fractured DeVeer's head last night."

"Dammittohell, what are you talking about? I thought he broke his neck or something. No, you told me that he'd hit his skull, but I thought it was on the floor. You mean he ran up against something?"

"Yes. A steel stack support."

"Dammittohell! Those clothheads! They weren't even calling for an autopsy. I guess the bird is still out of the ground so we can make some kind of gesture, but they've probably embalmed him by now and half of what we want'll be gone. 'He saw no reason to suspect foul play.' Dammittohell!

"Jesse, go out and get the scientists back in here. Have that cutter checked for prints and latent blood. Then tell 'em to do what they can with the first body. Jesus H. Christ."

He propped his elbows on the chair arms and buried his face in his hands. Eventually he looked up and sighed. "Come on, let's go."

As they left the Lounge, Conrad spoke to the officer guarding the door. "Johnson, go down and get about six men and meet me . . . where was this body? The first one?"

"Deck Two."

"Right. You heard 'im. Get down as quick as you can. Come on, and on the way let's hear exactly what happened last night, shall we?"

They proceeded toward the carved doors and Carson hurried through a summary as they went. He sketched out the events of the previous evening and ended, somewhat absently, with "We all got home about three o'clock."

"Why in hell did West think it was an accident?"

"Well, you can't blame him—I take it West was the coroner? There was a thin, gray pamphlet lying on the bottom step and it looked like DeVeer had stepped on it and been thrown forward. There was no suggestion of any outside blow. The head was against the support. It appeared to be simple cause and effect—as Mr. George says, you don't expect anything untoward in a library."

"Untoward! Cold hell! Untoward—there's a word for you. Was there a lot of blood?"

"Some, but not an unusual amount."

"Was there not indeed? A scalp wound bleeds all over the place. That nitwit knew that. Wasn't there any blood anywhere but under him?"

"No. None."

They had reached the elevator and George pushed the button for Two without waiting for instructions.

"If everything was so logical—what did you say, cause and effect?—how come you see a paper cutter and immediately think of the body?"

George and Carson exchanged fleeting glances. George thought, a telling point that. He shook his head slightly and Carson, taking the cue from the older man, remained silent as well.

They reached the deck they sought and George led the way around the elevator column. The same plastic smell of linoleum hung in the air, and the pale blue-white of the fluorescent lights lit the central aisle. George snapped on the two adjacent stack lights and the space at the foot of the stairs leapt into view.

"He was kneeling there," Carson explained. "You can see the stains on the support. The floor has been cleaned."

Conrad searched the floor between the stairs and the elevator walls and then walked around to the center aisle and looked up and down. The linoleum showed signs of heavy traffic, apparently left from the night's activity. He walked back into the center aisle and began to examine the stacks to the right.

"What's all this stuff?"

"Manuscript material. It is apparently added just as they get it. As you see, some of it is in boxes on the shelves and some of it's in books, and then the modern stuff seems to be kept in filing cabinets set in where they've taken out the shelves."

"Dammittohell," Conrad said and walked slowly along, snapping on lights and peering down bays of shelves and cases.

The elevator door closed and the car rose to return in a moment with five policemen, Johnson leading.

"Yeah," Conrad said to him wearily, "someplace in this mess there's probably something that doesn't belong. Rags. Gloves. Maybe blood. Maybe a wrench. Maybe a blanket or a plastic sheet. Who knows what the hell. All of you go down to the other wall and start looking. Look in the boxes and the drawers and you're goin' to have to pull the books out and look behind 'em. Turn on all the lights you can find and get started."

Conrad spread his legs and locked his hands behind his back as the men went off down the deck and began their work. Carson and George had either been forgotten or were being deliberately ignored. They stared at the scene for a moment and then at each other. Suddenly Carson grinned.

"I can't tell whether we're being put in our place or he forgot he invited us to the party. I don't know about you, but I'm going to get comfortable."

They returned to the stairs and sat down on the second step.

After a while Carson asked, "You don't suppose they went home and left us?"

They looked toward the other end of the room, but the rows of material effectively screened all signs of activity, and indeed seemed to drink up the sound.

"I was wondering, too," George said with a chuckle.

They sat in silence for a while longer and George said casually, "You know, if there really is something to be found out there, I suspect we could tell him the most likely place to start from."

Carson looked at him curiously.

"Like . . . ?"

"Well, let me try your historical method. How does this sound? If DeVeer really was hit by that cutter knife, somebody must have hit him right on the top of the head, because none of you questioned the way he lay against the support."

Their eyes turned automatically toward the elevator shaft.

"The coroner seemed to think it looked all right, and apparently the rest of you did too, at the time. Now if he had been hit on top of the head, it probably wasn't from the front or he'd have protected himself from the blow. It probably wasn't from the back or the blow would've been farther down his head. So the man must've been standing straight over him. Do I make sense?"

"Completely. Where are you headed?"

"Well, to tower that far over DeVeer—who was a

fairly tall man, as I recall—DeVeer must either have been going down the stairs and been a moving target, or he must have been sitting in a chair—and the nearest chairs are up on the top deck or down in the binder's cage. But there is one other possibility. He could have been kneeling, looking into a file drawer, and his enemy could have stood beside him and struck him down with a firm blow. I'd think there'd be just about room for that in one of these bay aisles. In fact, DeVeer's tendency to look down his nose would have set him up perfectly for such a blow. Is my picture valid?"

"I can see it as if I were there. And so?"

"And so, all they need to do is look in knee-high file drawers to find where it happened."

Carson thought a moment. "You know, that is frighteningly possible."

"Unfortunately, I suspect I can get closer than that. Supposedly, he came down here to get some letters by one 'Esther Hazy,' as Pop had it, for Welles to use in his interview. With a Beethoven concert going on upstairs that was probably Esterházy. One word. Eighteenth-century Hungarians. It would have been believable bait for DeVeer. Do you know the story?"

"Sorry. Out of my period, but your scenario certainly holds. Dare you suggest it? If you're right, Conrad could hang you for it."

They sat in silence, each one testing his hypothesis and trying to anticipate its results. At length George pulled his legs under him and stood up.

"If I don't mention it, we're going to miss supper. I'm inclined to believe I'd rather hang than starve."

Carson rose with him and they walked out onto the deck. There was no sign of anyone, but looking down the aisle they could hear muffled sounds of activity at the other end. As they approached it, they found the men methodically shifting and pulling and searching, with Conrad halfway down a bay gingerly moving books back and forth.

"Lieutenant," George called. "We've been talking about your search and we have an idea which might save you a bit of time."

Conrad looked around without enthusiasm or welcome.

"Yeah?"

"DeVeer had been called out of the Lounge to get some papers for Mr. Welles. We gather he was asked to bring up some letters relating to the Esterházy family. My grip on the Enlightenment is a little weak, but I seem to recall they were patrons of Beethoven and Haydn and who knows who else. For what it's worth, might I suggest your men do a quick check of files and boxes looking for something with those names on them—including Esterházy, of course. The letters could have been to or from them, I suppose." He added somewhat sotto voce as a throwaway line, "You might, uh, urge them to give special attention to things . . . near the floor."

Conrad looked at the two with ill-concealed resentment. He sucked his lip for a moment.

"Dammit. This'll take a week like we're doing now. Let's try it."

He raised his voice and shouted: "Stuff a handkerchief or something in where you are and come'ere. Who are those birds again and how do you spell 'em?"

George repeated his advice and Conrad translated the hunch into orders. The men spread out, reminding Carson of a pack of hounds in a British hunt movie. It came quickly.

"Jesus, Lieutenant! Here it is!"

They rushed toward the man who was standing back, staring appalled into an open file drawer. It was knee-high and it was immediately clear why there had been so little blood beneath the body. It lay before them, congealing irreplaceable rarities into a single, dull, damp, brown-black horror.

George looked toward Conrad. He found him staring straight back at him. George wondered casually why he had not said, "Dammittohell." He wondered with more interest how long Conrad had been watching him. He did not wonder at all what the officer was thinking. That was only too clear.

# 10

"Now you might think that Conrad would have been grateful for all this brilliance and the efficient course of action we made available to him," said Carson with as grand a gesture as was possible from a man straddling a chair. "If so, my bright-eyed lady, you would dwell in error's wood."

Carson had gone straight from the file drawer revelation to report to Crighton, and he found her doggedly coping with a rising spiral of interest from the media. She had followed his recitation eagerly, regularly cutting his hyperbole down to size, but impressed with the way the two men had coped with the events.

"Darn it," she said. "You two have all the fun. I'm stuck down in this hole while you rock around and keep everybody stirred up. What'd Conrad do then?"

"He was about as ungracious as he could be without actually charging us with accessorability or whatever you call it. He dismissed me as being beneath his interest, and then drug poor Mr. George off to the

Lounge. I suspect he's really going to put the screws to the brass now he's convinced he has at least one murder and maybe two."

"Which one isn't?"

"Well, we still don't know whether someone knocked off both DeVeer and the Frenchman, or the Frenchman knocked DeVeer off and really did commit suicide."

"You don't believe that, do you—that it was a suicide?"

"Probably not, but I'm trying to be as professional about this as possible."

Crighton propped her knees against her desk and said, "Are you really serious about this history business? How did someone as loose as you get down that road?"

"Madam, you wound me!" he responded broadly and then quickly became serious. "No, it fascinates me. It really does. I used to kid myself that I was studying history to teach its mistakes to the next generation so they wouldn't do the wrong things all over again. 'The past is prologue' bit. But there's no sense kidding either of us. I really don't much care what we do with it. I just want to be sure we honestly understand what happened back there. Can we really put together any single week or summer or decade in time and know what it was like and what was happening? I don't know. Sometimes it beats the hell out of me. And one of the things that really gets under my skin is that we talk with such assurance about the Romans or the Renaissance, but we have so little idea of what's actually causing our troubles right now! Hell, we'd rather not be pressed too much about what really happened under the last Administration!"

"But you guys always say we're too close to it. We need perspective to tell what were the important things and what didn't matter."

"Bless you for knowing the alibi, but on my depressed days, I get uncomfortable that what we're really saying is: Don't ask us about last year; it's too easy to prove us wrong. Give us twenty years until the old hands tell us what we should believe, then once we've got the party line, we can grind out textbooks and analyses till hell won't have it."

"Do you really care about the people you study?"

"Intensely. I've been trying to figure out why the old boys went west. Why should anybody in Worcester, Mass., or Dover, Delaware, who lived in a nice white house with a clean white fence around it and was really somebody at church on Sunday, sell the whole thing off and head for the Indian-infested prairie?"

"Did they?"

"In droves! The West wasn't founded by the misfits and failures like I used to think. It was the eager ones, the bright ones that went. I've been struggling with poor Olaf in there till my throat aches for his trying. Trying to care for a wife, trying to bring up his kids, watching his crops die and his fences fall down. It's agony."

"But neither you nor Mr. George seem much disturbed that two men are dead. You're as cold-blooded as glass over them."

Carson stopped in silence, looking at her to see what she was probing for.

"You're deceptive, small woman. You look so harmless that a man lets his guard down. What are you needling me about? My inhumanity to man?"

"I don't know. I'm just intrigued that Olaf somebody-or-other is realer to you than those two bodies you saw. Am I right?"

He stopped again.

"Yeah. You're right. But the bodies were just like me, living the scene around me. Right now doesn't seem very real to me—or even matter very much. But back then . . . What are you getting at?"

"Nothing, really. It's just that your eyes snap when you're talking about then and you're so casual about now. You know who I think did it?" she asked suddenly.

"You've thought?"

Crighton flushed and sat up straight. "Just because I'm female doesn't mean I'm a complete loss for bright. You are so damned . . ."

"Whoopss! Cool down, kitten, it's simply that you're so ornamental I can't believe there'd be any other reason for you!"

"That is the worst possible response! You don't under . . . Oh, the hell with it. No! I'll tell you who did it and you won't believe me for the same reason you're so supercilious. I'll bet you anything it was Elsie Brewer!"

"Come off it!"

"No. She's the only one of all this bunch that cares enough about what's going on to do something about it. That poor woman's been watching Dr. Rose, aching for him from afar or something, and every night she goes home thinking, 'nobody appreciates him,' 'nothing nice ever happens to him,' 'why doesn't he get a little credit for the work he does for all those other fools?'—and just when she's simply overwhelmed with pity, those bomb letters start coming in."

She jumped up from her chair and stood with her feet apart, rising to her theme.

"Some way she finds out it's DeVeer who's doing it and she really comes unglued. She's hated DeVeer for years and suddenly he's the guy that's going to wreck everything Rose has put together so patiently—he's the one that's going to keep Dr. Rose from getting his incunabula bought and building a world-wide reputation and retiring with glory. The more she thinks about it the madder she gets. Seethe, seethe. She goes to Rose last night and tries to warn him to get him to protect himself. He brushes her off. So she really blows.

"She sees Rose go up to his cubicle, so she goes off in the other direction. She's just seen Pop Wright at his desk and she knows DeVeer is in the Lounge. She goes back to her office, phones Pop, talking real low, and saying she's Alan. Pop gets DeVeer, sends him down to that filing cabinet. She waits for him down there, casually asks what he's doing, they talk, she sidles up to him naturally and gets the wonderful sensation of splitting his head open with the knife she's pried off the paper cutter. She leaves him hanging in the drawer and hides the knife somewhere close. Then she drags him around behind the elevator, wipes up the floor, grabs the first pamphlet she finds and lays it on the steps—and fades into the stacks. Speidel comes gooping down and we all take it from there!"

"Tremendous!" Carson jumped to his feet and burst into furious applause. "You've done it! It takes care of everything!"

"Hell!" Crighton was crestfallen and a rising flush at the throat seized Carson with remorse. "You see, you never take us seriously. You don't think she'd be capable of doing it and you don't think I'm bright enough to figure it out."

She dropped into her chair, frustrated.

"Wait a minute. I didn't say—or think—either of those things," Carson said hurriedly. "I was just carried away with the presentation. What a trial lawyer you'd have made! Seriously, you're right, that makes as good sense as anything else, I guess. I think it's getting the knife and dragging the body that doesn't ring right."

"Look. I could get a bolt off, and I could drag somebody around, and she's twice as big as I am. You never bat an eye when we hoist a thirty-pound surfboard over our heads, but you think we can't wind up a jack under a bumper. What a bunch of nuts you all are."

"You're getting tense again. Cool down. How do you have the French thing figured?"

"That can be accounted for so many ways it's just a matter of finding out what poor Mr. Schwartz did when he came in to work this morning. Maybe he saw something last night and started asking questions and Brewer found out. Maybe he got suspicious over the way his cutter looked. Remember, at that point everybody thought DeVeer had just had an accident. Suppose he was about to tell everybody DeVeer was murdered, so Brewer had to shut him up and spike anybody's suspicions about the DeVeer bit at the same time. I do wish I knew why she planted that Marlowe thing, though. It could've been to incriminate Speidel —or maybe she's just ambitious! If she could knock off DeVeer and eliminate Speidel, she'd be queen of the heap!"

"Ho, ho! Look who's 'knocking off' the innocent now," Carson said in triumph. "Inhuman, that's what you are."

Crighton stopped and blushed, suddenly caught in the same "detachment" she'd accused him of.

"Never mind. As I was going to say, before I was so rudely you-know-what, maybe she just wanted a literary suicide note. She had no way to get the poor man to write his own, so she grabbed this Marlowe quote she'd learned somewhere, walked up to him and said, 'Hey, want to see something funny?' He looked down and she shot him."

"You've figured out how she happened to have a gun so easily available, of course. Possibly in the card catalog under 'Weapons, see Firearms'?"

He realized his error before he'd finished the sentence and threw up his hands.

"Wait a minute, wait a minute! I'm sorry. I mean I am sorry. It simply slipped out from the long habit of never having met a girl of your insight before. You're quite right, it could very well have happened that very way. Now, if you'll just explain why those books have disappeared without anything else being touched, I will quit thinking completely and type your memoirs."

She hesitated for a moment, and then said firmly: "You're simply all excited about nothing. There were three books there for him to work on—okay, eight. Schwartz worked on them this morning. He did whatever he was supposed to do with them—probably sent them back to the shelves—and went on about his routine. The only reason you even noticed them was that they were the only thing on the table in English that you *could* read!"

"How did you know that?"

She laughed. "I was taken down there once to see something he was doing for an exhibit, and there wasn't anything there *I* could read. Remember, I don't claim to be smarter than you guys. Just as."

"Fair enough," he said. "Now hush up for a minute. I want to think through this idea of yours. Ignoring the source—as you suggest—I shall test some of your suppositions."

He subsided into thought, while she watched him, filled about equally with irritation at his condescension and eagerness for his approval.

# II

"Let's get out of here," said George.

"Splendid thought," replied Welles. "You don't mind antagonizing the lieutenant a bit?"

"The poor man's apparently bogged down with his 'scientists.' I think we could take a short stroll and no one would be the wiser."

George had been sent to the Employees' Lounge to await the arrival of Conrad and, he presumed, a detailed grilling over what now appeared to be two murders. Within minutes of his arrival, Welles had joined him, similarly summoned for information about the dead man, Schwartz. The two men had waited quietly, each lost in his own thoughts, until George had decided to clear his mind with some fresh air and a change of scene.

As they passed the officer outside the Lounge door, George instructed him, "If Lieutenant Conrad asks for us, tell him we're taking a walk for a few minutes and we'll be right back."

Having no orders to the contrary, the policeman

nodded, and they headed for the elevator without challenge. Once outside, they were surprised to find the sky had cleared to a late afternoon blue, and the shadow of the Monument could be seen slicing down the Mall like the pointer of a giant sundial. The two men hesitated on the piazza and surveyed the scene.

"Well! I might live to see another spring yet," said George. "Eternal hope. Winters get longer and longer at my age." He looked toward the Capitol and said, "How about the National Gallery? I see they've got the fountains started, and I have a great weakness for the sound of falling water."

"Fine with me," replied Welles.

They crossed Fourth Street and approached the building, stately and serene, surrounded by its closely trimmed hedges. Moving slowly, they examined the formal plantings around the base, until they reached the central steps where the flash and splashing of the fountains brought George to a full stop.

"Can we watch one of these for a moment? I am completely seduced by the things. I've missed half the sights of Rome for staring at their fountains, and I suspect the reason I have such a weakness for world's fairs is they have such splendid plumbing!"

They leaned against the bronze handrail.

Welles laughed. "I think most people feel that way. I remember the first thing we did when we got back into Hue was to get their fountains going again. I think our engineers did it compulsively, they just couldn't stand to see all those dead, dry, pipes!—but it made a terrific impact on the citizens. They figured anybody who'd get their fountains working couldn't be all bad. Probably eased our PR problems a hundred percent."

"How long were you out there?"

"Years, actually. I reenlisted once—before things hotted up—so I had five, nearly six years out of the

States. I acquired poor Schwartz in Saigon, as a matter of fact. He was slowly dying of something he'd picked up in Laos and I took him on, and got some army doctor friends to look after him. It's interesting, in a way. It's as if his time had really run out back there, and my interfering only held off what was intended to have taken place back then."

"Kismet? Fate? That sounds Mideastern. What's your field again?"

Welles smiled. "The Flowering of New England. No, it's true that I am a fatalist, I guess, but I know it only as the Puritan divines described it. All I know about what you mean is what I saw in *Lawrence of Arabia!*"

"How did you come on Schwartz?"

"Well, I got involved in Oriental art while I was with the troops, and the word spread that I was an easy market for objets d'art, so people would bring me things. I'd rented an apartment in Saigon to use on weekends and one night this battered hulk, Schwartz, appeared at my door claiming he was a skilled bookbinder. He was carrying a half dozen volumes he said he'd bound—and they were magnificent. Tooling and gilding like we haven't seen here since the twenties. He offered to sell the books, but even more he was pushing his own services—could I use a repair man?

"I gave him two beaten-up pieces I had with me and asked him to work on them. Two days later he brought 'em back. Beautiful. He'd preserved the original format, retained the integrity of the volumes, but completely rebuilt them into firm, saleable products. I was still suspicious that the work might not have been his, so I gave him a volume and asked him to tell me what was wrong with it—what would have to be done to restore it. He did it right in front of me, in fairly acceptable English.

138

"So I took him on, and when I finally came back myself, I paid his way over. Then when I came to the Library, Brooks very kindly gave him a job here. All along he was quite withdrawn. He wasn't frightened —he was a surly son of a bitch till the day he died— but he wanted to work at home in his apartment. That was out of the question, so we finally installed him on that empty deck, and he's been there ever since... had been, that is."

"Did he have a family?"

"No, I'm sure he wasn't married, but I really have no idea about his personal life. I rarely saw him outside the Werner-Bok."

"He seems so alien to the Library's normal life, I wonder how he became involved with DeVeer? What linked them together?"

"I've been trying to figure that ever since I heard about the suicide. The only thing I can imagine is that DeVeer found out something that Schwartz was trying to hide. There was a rumor running around that he had collaborated with the Germans in France—he was French, you know, in spite of his name. I'd never heard of it myself, but maybe DeVeer got wind of something. DeVeer was always using some mistake or weakness to get one up on somebody. When he'd find a cataloging error, instead of bringing it to the woman who'd made it, he'd report it at the next staff meeting before all the professionals.... Maybe he'd been working Schwartz over without my knowing it, and Schwartz simply decided to do something about it instead of taking it like everyone else did. I really can't imagine."

"Could DeVeer have communicated with him to that extent? I thought I'd heard you were the only one who could talk to him."

"It's true, I did use my French because it was more

precise for instructions, but Schwartz's English was perfectly adequate. He only used his '... ne comprends...' as a device to keep people away. Actually, the only person he allowed into that cage was Elsie Brewer! I think she felt sorry for him and somehow she seemed to have broken through. Come to think of it, I stumbled on the two of them together outside the Library on a couple of occasions—socially. It always amused me. Neither one of them were much for talking English, but they seemed to have endless conversations in Elsie's basic French!"

"Interesting." George pushed himself away from the rail and looked up toward the entrance. "How about doing a couple of rooms? What do you feel like: the Old Masters or Impressionism?"

"Ordinarily, I'd say very early Italian, but with our careful library world falling around us, I think I'd like the order of the Flemish. How about some Hollander interiors?"

"Most appropriate. You lead the way," said George, as they started up the steps.

Once inside, with the rich leather doors silently closed behind them, George was once more overwhelmed with the sublime serenity of the place. The black marble columns framing the Bologna Perseus in the center. The restraint, the unhurried beauty of this fountain compared to the sound and surge of the ones they had watched before. They walked slowly, relishing the flawless relationship of halls and dome, polished wood and marble, pigment and gold in the paintings themselves. They resisted the pull of the Botticellis and the Raphael Madonna, and turned into the well-ordered world of the Dutch.

Ultimately, George spoke. "I wonder if the precise, purposeful society we see here reflects your Puritan interests?"

"It probably works the other way. I like things neat, logical, and utilitarian. Both the Dutch and the New Englanders were sparse, clean, and dry, so I respond to them at times of tension and dissolution. I find I have very little rapport with the florid and the over-stuffed. As you may know, I wrote a history of early American libraries—I guess I've visited a couple of hundred in the past ten years—and scarcely anything has given me such pleasure as browsing through those little town collections up in Maine or the Massachusetts hills. They were so neat, so self-contained and purposeful. I think I've always preferred art in the miniature to those monumental, Rubens-like things that fill up the museums. Give me a Vermeer or a Holbein anytime."

"Doesn't that tend to be a bit cold, though? Without a little drama and embellishment, it seems to me both things and people get sterile."

"I find that warmth is almost always demanding. I resent feeling I 'ought' to respond. With a thing, I prefer to hold it and examine it for what it is without its demanding anything from me. I'll give it what appreciation I wish, not what it 'deserves.' I feel the same way about people. I do not require their affection or praise, and I resent their insisting I give it. I'm a great believer in 'do unto others as you would they do unto you.' Since I wish they'd let me live my life to the fullest—so long as I do not impinge on theirs—it seems only fair that I return them the favor and leave them alone to do as they wish."

"I presume you feel that if everybody lived by your rules, we wouldn't have had those tragedies back at the Library?"

"Precisely. DeVeer was a classic example of living at the expense of everyone around him. Schwartz—I'll admit I can't quite account for, but I'll bet you dollars to doughnuts if we knew what he was trying to do to someone else, or what someone was trying to do to him, we'd know what brought on the disasters."

"Yes," said George, "and you may have pointed the way to the answer we're seeking. We have tended to assume that DeVeer was the major disaster, and Schwartz was an aftermath. It just may be that Schwartz was the heart of the problem, and DeVeer got swept in accidentally."

"Possibly," said Welles, "but I would correct one thing in your thought. What *you're* seeking, not we. So long as my own life is not endangered, and I cannot see how it is, I am not involving myself in this. It's somebody else's worry, not mine. I think you'd be well advised to detach yourself, too, or you'll find that you've lost your own independence of purpose!"

He smiled warmly, and George replied: "I'm afraid you're only too right. Ah, well, now that we've got ourselves thinking about it anyway, let's go back and face the authority of the law. I presume you think Lieutenant Conrad is the proper person to do the seeking?"

"I do. I have enough troubles of my own, and I suspect you do, too." Welles laughed, and they headed back to Conrad's growing wrath.

# 12

---

"I believe Dr. Rose is on Deck Seven in the Houdini collection," said Miss Brewer. "Is there anything I can do?"

"Brother!" Crighton replied. "Not unless you know more about poor Mr. Schwartz than Personnel does. I've got three sentences so far. Do you?"

"Well, hardly anything you could use as news. We used to go out together occasionally."

"You did! You dated him?" Crighton realized she had overreacted. "I mean, I had no idea anyone could help me at all. I'll be grateful for any crumb you can throw. Did he have any professional ties? Did he belong to anything—any organization? Whatever?"

"Oh, no. No, Mr. Schwartz was terribly misunderstood and it distressed me that no one seemed to make any effort to bridge the gap to him...although it is true he made very little effort to meet anyone from his side either. He was convinced that he was disliked and then went out of his way to prove it. He'd talk to me about his experiences in the Second World War and then in Vietnam. Apparently he was a lonely person even then."

"When you . . . when you went out with him, what sort of things did you do . . . I mean, where did you go? What did he like to do?"

"Well, it was difficult. He didn't like music or the theatre. And I don't enjoy motion pictures or television. Mostly he would just come to my apartment and talk."

Dear God, Crighton thought. How do I put some edges on this? I can hardly ask her if she made out. What do I need to know? No, what do I *want* to know? Who did he hate? Where were the two of 'em, when? How well did they know each other? She tried another gambit.

"Why do you suppose he bottled himself up in that cage like he did? Was he ashamed of something? Or afraid? Or . . . ?"

"No, he thought people didn't like him, and he . . . knew he didn't like them."

"Was he mad at anyone in particular?"

"No. Everyone equally, I suppose."

"Was he . . . ?" The hell with it, Crighton thought. I give up. "Thanks, Miss Brewer," she said. "Maybe Dr. Rose can give me something, too."

"Yes, he's on Seven. He's checking a list for New York Public. Mr. Welles ought to be doing it, but I don't know where he went. A policeman came and got him an hour ago."

"Thank you. I'll see if I can find him."

Crighton veered off to her left, irritated and frustrated, and pushed her way out onto the deck. The door to Rose's office was open, but although the light was on, it was empty. She continued to the elevator, conscious that typewriters in each of the three catalogers' carrels had stopped. Either the catalogers' traditional curiosity was showing, or they were feeling the growing unease that she carried herself. She looked ahead and saw the long rows of shelves on either side—suddenly remote, dark, and threatening. Odd, they had always looked so appealing before. All those books to be read...

By the time she stepped out of the elevator onto Deck Seven she had generated a firm case of jitters. The deck was dark in both directions except for the single line of fluorescent tubes running down the center aisle. She listened to see if she could tell where Rose was working. Damp, muffled silence. She started to call his name and then realized you didn't shout in libraries. On second thought, why not? These stacks weren't connected to anything.

"Dr. Rose?" she called. Her voice sounded small and smothered. The ranges of books clearly worked like baffles and drank up the sound as efficiently as the walls of a broadcasting studio.

"Dr. Rose?" she tried again, louder.

She was aware, more from the vibrations in the floor than anything else, of someone walking down a bay of books in the distance. A familiar head appeared in the center aisle.

"Yes? Oh, yes, Miss...ah...Jones."

"Right. Can I bother you a minute?"

"Why, of course. Uh...here?...where? Should we...do you want to go to my office?"

"No, it won't take that long."

She had reached him and could see several piles of books stacked on the floor in the bay behind him.

"With poor Mr. Schwartz's death coming so close after Dr. DeVeer's, the papers are getting interested in who the men were, I'm sorry to say. I got out a short note on the 'apparent suicide,' like they're telling me to call it, but I can barely find anything about Mr. Schwartz himself. Here's all I could get from Personnel. Can you help me pad it a bit?"

Rose very deliberately pushed his glasses back against his eyebrows and read the page. Without looking up, he began to shake his head.

"No, young lady. Not only do I not know more than this, this is the first time I'd heard where he came from in France—and that he had had so much formal education. Some way I'd always assumed he was merely a craftsman. He really had a degree in the classics? I could have used him to check my Greek. I take some pride in my Latin, but my Greek is as clumsy as a woman's. Oh, excuse me."

"Think nothing of it, everyone's doing it these days. I don't know whether the stuff's true or not. All I know is that that's what the personnel folder says. Didn't he belong to any kind of a union or guild? Wasn't he a bat watcher or rubbed headstones or something? We look pretty silly having a man here for ten years and can only tell three lines about him. Did he ever do anything special for the Library?"

"No. I'm sorry. Most of what he did was pretty routine. He did it very well, and his preservation techniques were as fine as those of anyone we ever had, but we don't do much creative work, and not too much repair either. Our specimens are usually fairly sound or we wouldn't take them in the first place. We rarely purchase anything less than Fine or Mint. Except for a very few items which are unique, if a book is much worn it just goes into the public collection out in the reading rooms."

"You wouldn't put first editions out there, would you?"

"My dear, almost every book a library owns is a first

edition. Libraries buy books when they first come out and they're all first editions. Even a bookmobile is loaded with first editions. No, they come to us only when they get valuable. Occasionally when something goes sky-high—like a Thoreau or an early Melville, we might withdraw it, but there's not much point. By the time a library has 'processed' a book—punched it and stamped it and circulated it a few times, it's next to worthless for bibliophilia. The books you see around you here are both rare and fine. In many ways we're like an art museum. Museums don't buy a painting just because it's a Rembrandt. They buy fine Rembrandts. There are literally hundreds of Utrillos owned by private individuals. But his masterpieces belong to the institutions. Our books are masterpieces."

Crighton looked around her. "Do you keep the expensive things in a special place?"

Rose looked baffled for a moment.

"What? Oh, no. Anyway, it's so hard to know what's expensive!"

He laughed at this as if it were a traditional joke.

"Of course most of our vellum material—hand-lettered, you know, from the medieval period—is all pretty valuable. Very valuable, I guess you'd say. But then, we have many linear feet of fourteenth- and fifteenth-century legal records that are not excessively costly. Let me show them to you."

He suddenly shuffled off in the opposite direction and led her down the deck and into a separate area where the shelves were very wide and the material lay on its side, stacked three and four high. All of the volumes were leather-bound, most with huge straps around them, and occasionally the top one would appear to have stones set in its face like the Codex she had held the day before.

"Are those real jewels?"

"Yes, we keep them to show the various styles of bookmanship—as well as for their contents. Here's a good one."

He pulled a huge volume off the shelf in a matter-of-fact manner, and flipped its heavy pages until he came to a brilliant illumination painted in reds and purples and surrounded with gold leaf.

"That's tremendous. It must be terribly valuable!"

"Let me think. Yes, I suppose it is. It was part of the McCullough bequest, and as I recall, altogether it was worth two or three million dollars. There were several hundred pieces, of course. But look at the craftsmanship! Do you see? The letters are as beautiful as the painting. No wonder Gutenberg could start so well. Look what he had to copy!"

"Wow!" said Crighton, as he slid the book back on the shelf. "Aren't you terrified about fire or anything? Think of the responsibility we have for these things! Here people have taken care of them for hundreds of years and what if *we* lost them?"

"You're quite right. It would be inexcusable. However, we hope we've thought of everything we need to."

He began to walk down the aisles, pointing to devices overhead.

"These things here are some kind of gadget with little plugs in them that melt if they get hot. The plug drops out and that interrupts the wire or something and lights go on all over the building—in the guard office and in the reading room upstairs, I guess even in the fire department, maybe. It's pretty old, but I trust it still works. I hope somebody's checking it.

"Then, every so often you see these strange-looking things? They're smoke . . . wait a minute, I thought the word was so appropriate . . . sensors! No doubt from the Latin *sens*, participial stem of *sentire*, to feel. In any event, they're supposed to be able to smell smoke! The main thing, of course, is not to let a fire get started. This part of the building is completely sealed off from the rest of the Library. The walls are nearly three feet thick—actually, this whole part of the building is like a vault. About the only thing that could cause trouble is electricity, and we turn it off when there's no one around. You see the lights all have timers, so no one can leave them on accidentally."

"Really? You mean there's something ticking in there?"

"Well, I don't know whether it's ticking or not, but it will stay on for only half an hour. Then just the . . ."

He stopped, frozen with horror. Crighton covered her ears with her hands and suddenly burst into an hysterical scream. From inside the wall behind them, high over their heads, a feminine shriek, tiny and distant like a knife point scraped across a slate, had risen to a piercing scream and then fallen past them into the reaches below, almost fading from earshot. A fraction of silence was followed by a rumbling shock that rose up the steel decks from floor to shelf to floor until the whole vault shuddered and groaned.

"Oh, no!" Crighton cried. "What was that? What was it?"

Rose was absolutely paralyzed with shock, his eyes wide, his hands hanging helplessly by his side.

"I don't know. I cannot . . . I don't know."

Suddenly he stumbled sideways against the shelving and threw his head back as if to stare through the steel ceiling above.

"Elsie! Was it Elsie? What have we done?"

Suddenly the stacks filled with the rumble of steps pounding down the stairs. Crighton ran back toward the elevator to see Speidel shoot out from behind, wild-eyed and hysterical.

"My God! My God! I could have been killed! I could have..." He huddled against a support as Alan Welles pounded into view, running down from above. Others could be heard thumping behind him.

"Crighton! What in the name of heaven is going on here? Did you hear that? Dr. Brooks! What the hell was it?"

"I'll be damned if I know."

The Director, arriving barely twenty steps after the others, was panting and looking up and down the deck as if he expected the whole place to crumple beneath them. Except for the rumble of more feet on the stairs, there was no further evidence of the terror that had seized them all, but the scream still seemed to hang in the air and each one of the group could hear it throbbing in his memory.

"I could have been killed, I tell you. Do you hear me? I was almost killed!" Speidel whirled on the group demanding its attention.

"Shut up, man, and pull yourself together," Welles snapped at him without sympathy. "What do you mean, you could've been killed? By what?"

Before he could speak, Miss Brewer hobbled from behind the elevator, and Rose suddenly cried from halfway down the deck: "Elsie? Is that you? I...I..." He suddenly realized everyone was staring at him and he stammered, "Ah, Miss Brewer, we heard a woman and..."

"That was no woman, you fools!" Speidel shouted in a high-pitched voice. "It was the book lift. It fell. It must have tons in it. It fell from up there somewhere, straight down. The rope broke or was..."

"What book lift? Goddamn it, what the hell is he talking about?" Brooks looked from one to the other.

Welles shrugged, indicating ignorance; Crighton shook her head automatically. Rose seemed to pull himself together, thought about it for a moment, and then began to nod.

"Yes. It must have been the lift."

He turned toward the Director. "Back when the building was first built, they put a hand lift—a dumb-waiter sort of thing—in the wall. It runs all the way from the top to the bottom of the stacks."

Speidel shouted again. "I was looking down it, do you hear! I was halfway in it looking down and it fell from above. If it hadn't made that noise, I'd have been cut in half! Do you hear what I'm saying?"

Brooks said, "What the hell were you looking down it for?"

Almost simultaneously Welles asked, "Is it still used?"

"My, no," Rose replied. "I don't think it's been touched since I've been here. I didn't even know it would work."

Welles looked up with a half-suppressed smile and asked, "Yes, Sydney, why were you looking down it?"

"Well, I happened to be down at the end there..."

"Where?"

"A couple of decks above... and I happened to see it, and I... well, wondered what it was. I'd never seen it before, and I opened the little door... and looked in." He ended the sentence as if he were surprised to hear it himself.

"Wait a minute," Welles said suddenly. "Crighton, where were you in all this?"

"Dr. Rose and I were talking back there and all of a sudden this scream seemed to go right past our heads."

"Yes," Rose interjected, "I realize now we must have been standing just a few feet away. The thing is..."

"Goddamn it, Speidel! You were eavesdropping!" Welles fairly shouted it and then burst into uproarious laughter. His delight and relish for the situation washed over the group and smiles broke from all the participants except Speidel, who looked more waxen and discomfited by the second. He opened his mouth as if to try another alibi and then seemed to think better of it.

"I'll not dignify your insults with a reply. If you don't see what this all means you're such fools you don't deserve it explained."

With this attempt at an exit, he strode through them to mount the stairs. His withdrawal was marred with the very evident trembling of his hands and his unsteady walk. He appeared to have been genuinely frightened to the verge of hysteria.

"Well, let's see what damage it did below," Brooks said with a broad smile. "From where I was standing, it sounded as though the whole deck frame had been torn loose."

Welles had his handkerchief out, wiping his eyes and breaking into chuckles at irregular intervals.

"Where were you when the sky fell, sir?" he asked.

"I don't know, up there on Ten or Eleven, I guess. Where were you?"

"I'd just come down to Eleven and I didn't see you, so you must've been on Ten," Welles explained as they all started down the steps to the lower levels.

"Yes," volunteered Miss Brewer in a weak voice. "I had come in to look for Dr. Rose and it sounded to me as though it started somewhere below me, but I could hear it come out of the wall clear at the end of the deck."

They dropped lower and lower until they finally reached the First and final level, immediately apparent from the solid feel to the floor. They streamed toward the end, Brooks in the lead, snapping on lights as he went. When they reached the wall, he doubled to the right and found the waist-high door, the shelf in front of it grimy with dust and grit.

He lifted it and looked in. The others crowded around. Beneath them was a splintered wreck of yellow library oak and iron, shattered into a thousand pieces. The two guide rails on either side showed the streaks where the runners had protested against the rust as they fell.

Crighton looked into the darkness, wondering if she could see what must have been left of the rope, wondering if it would prove to be frayed or cut. Rose stood beside Miss Brewer, who appeared to be afraid to look. Brooks shook his head.

"Dammit, what a mess!" he said.

"My God! He was eavesdropping!" Welles suddenly shouted, and returned to deep, satisfied laughter.

# 13

"Children," said George, "I think I know *what* was happening and *why* it was happening. I am not yet certain who was making it happen. I think something Welles said to me had greater truth than he knew. I think Schwartz is the reality in this. DeVeer was just an accident."

They were creeping home in a shared taxi, each of them both physically and emotionally exhausted from a day which was so far outside their normal, orderly patterns. They had met finally, when George had been released from his session with Lieutenant Conrad. Once together, Crighton had reported in great detail the demise of the book lift, and George had generalized the various avenues down which the detective had tried to lead him. Looking back on it, George said, he had learned only two things that might be useful to the amateurs. It appeared, oddly enough, that the one man who could easily have been involved in both murders and Speidel's near miss was Nelson Brooks, the Director. He had been seen by someone in each of the three appropriate areas, each time perfectly reasonably, but nevertheless at a most unfortunate moment. The lieutenant had asked if there were any reason why Brooks might have desired DeVeer out of the way, and George had said that he did not know of any. He had emphasized the *know* hard enough that his own conscience was mollified; he was not so sure of The Eternal Record Book.

The other item which had been revealed was money. Conrad, in steady pursuit of money, booze, and sex, had excavated more about their financial condition than George had thought possible, and three members of the staff appeared to be living on a scale considerably above where the detective thought a librarian ought to be: Brooks, Welles, and Schwartz. George had wondered how much was attributable to outside income, and how much to questionable activities. He also wondered if this did not make these three the most satisfied with their lot and the presumably starving Rose, Brewer, and Speidel the more likely to lash out at the system or somebody. Carson had reported an hysterical day trying to cover for Crighton, having to admit that even his glib improvisations had been inadequate to hold the press at bay.

He pursued George's thought. "Do you mean DeVeer's death was only an accident, or it was only an accident that DeVeer had to be killed?"

The taxi stopped for its fifteenth time as they crept around the rear of the White House.

"The latter," said George. "Strangely enough, your *Tamerlane* and those three books on the table may well be the wedge that splits this thing apart. I do believe they represent an unforeseen aberration which will give us the key.

"Steve, if we all survive the night—I meant that figuratively—if we're all functioning tomorrow, I want you to ask your friend Miss Brewer for that *Tamerlane* again, and the Stowe and the emigrant thing. Can you remember what that third volume was? I've lost it. Anyway, I want to see what she does when you ask for them, and I want you to look at the three and see if there is anything about them that strikes you as being unusual. I don't want to say more for fear of leading your conclusion."

He turned to the girl who sat quietly beside them, drawn with fatigue but following the conversation closely.

"Crighton, you poor child, go float yourself in a hot bath and just lie there for an hour or so! It's been a long day for all of us. But I can't help but say: I told you so! I seem to recall way back this morning much fear of failure. And I think I remember a very grand-fatherly lecture on how it's impossible to anticipate trouble—all you can hope to do is cope with what comes. I must admit I had no idea it would be quite as dramatic as it turned out, but I think you'll have to agree, I was righter than I knew!"

"Mr. George, beat as I am, I feel wonderful. I did do it, and if I could survive today, I can survive anything!"

"Precisely." He looked at her with pride and affection.

"Children, I am going to leave you. We seem to've crept our way to the Corcoran, and I think I'll walk from here. Drop me off at the next light, please," he said to the driver.

Carson groaned. "You look in one helluva better shape than we do! We should be in your condition. What do you do? Take vitamins?"

George looked sideways at the young people.

"You are too kind. All I can say is, I will not admit how old I am, but given the choice of two sins, I now take the one that will get me home the earlier. To-night, I don't even have the sins to choose from. I am going to make two phone calls and retire. Here's the money for my fare. I will see you in the morning."

The older man got out carefully, examined the various threads of traffic and worked his way to the curb. As the cab inched ahead, they could see him walking with all deliberate speed toward the World Bank Building.

Carson was suddenly struck with the realization that he was alone with Crighton for the first time—*alone* alone, he said to himself, not interruptable alone. For some inexplicable reason, he discovered, he was uncomfortable and embarrassed.

He turned to look at her and was amazed to recognize the proprietary feeling she awakened in him. She lay back against the seat, slowly unwinding from the tension of the day, staring at the familiar buildings of official Washington passing slowly in the dusk. Her mind was clearly accepting the scene without registering and Carson was reluctant to force his presence on her.

Reluctant, hell! he realized. Unable! He noted with despair that not only had his glibness evaporated, but suddenly here was a girl he had no wish to be glib with anyway! The act he'd spent so long getting together had become inappropriate. Even he had to accept it. Here was the one he wanted to keep—no open-handed "relationship," just *his*—and the fear that he could not get her attention, much less hold it, was more a source of rage than of challenge. Why just this one, dammit?

Suddenly his long-accepted ends, his scholarly time-table, seemed too superficial and too distant. Tonight he wanted to do something or be somebody—now—so he could shout, look at me! You want something good? I'm it! You'll never do better. Great God Almighty! She was distorting both his values and his timetable.

"I'd have walked, but they don't expect me till the train gets there," he said weakly.

She laughed. "It's hardly blinding speed, but I'm so beat I'm not going to be good for anything anyway. Aren't you going out of your way? Where are you staying?"

"I am. I room on Capitol Hill, but to be at your side I would tread the world!" He sagged even further. He was so used to hyperbole, he couldn't even carry on a casual conversation. He added, sadly, "'Yup, that's the way to Bangor, but it's twenty thousand miles and there's some pretty rough wheeling along the way.' Old New England joke."

"I'm very grateful." She turned to watch out of the window again, and the stillness returned.

The cab finally broke loose from the knotted bypass and accelerated up Connecticut. It can't be much farther, Carson thought, and writhed with frustration. A hundred million women and just this one suddenly makes a difference. What to say? How to tell her? He was still floundering among a dozen verbal gambits when the cab stopped and she looked at him, expecting him to get out so she could cross the seat.

He straightened up, got the door open, and in ten counts she had blithely thanked him and was gone. He threw himself back on the seat and slammed the door.

"Downtown, dammit. I'm going back to Monday and start over," he told the driver.

George had walked along, unhurried but steadily, through much of the seedier part of downtown Washington until he had come out at last onto Massachusetts and dignity. The impressive fronts of the embassies began to appear and ultimately he reached the Minerva Club and "home."

He was amazed that he was not more tired. The walk had been good for him, he thought. Today he had been on the defensive most of the time, and while he had found it challenging, he had also found it wearing to have had to "doublethink" every reply. His respect for Conrad had risen with the probing he'd undergone, but he felt brain-weary.

George checked at the desk to see if there were any messages and, finding none, started for the elevator. Mahogany, leather, marble mantelpieces—an air of peace pervaded the huge rooms. A very restrained clink of ice on glass came from the lounge, and he was tempted to go in and test an old-fashioned, but no, he told himself, get the calls out of the way and then you can reward yourself.

Once in his room and in his shirt-sleeves, he seated himself at the miniature desk and called the operator.

"I would appreciate your getting me John Cotton, the Head Librarian of Hodges Institute at Ann Arbor, Michigan. It's part of the University there."

He glanced at his watch. Six-thirty. John always worked later than his office staff. Let's hope he has today.

The necessary progress through switchboards was made and Cotton picked up his own phone.

"Yes? John Cotton here."

"John! This is Edward George calling from Washington."

"The hell you say! What are you doing in Washington."

"I'm supposed to be on a project for Nelson Brooks at the Werner-Bok but I've gotten sidetracked into a strange situation which I'll write you about if we ever get it sorted out. Did you know Murchison DeVeer?"

"Of course. I know him very well."

"I'm sorry to say he was killed in a bizarre accident yesterday that's involved in the thing. I'll tell you about that later, too. Right now, I need a name. Whom can I talk to that's up on the purchase and repair of rare books? Who'd know all the angles—theft and faking and fraud—the whole thing?"

"Why, I'd call Melville Dana at the Hetherington. Do you know him?"

"Only by name. I always considered him fairly unapproachable. Could I just barge in and get some answers without an introduction?"

"Oh my, yes. Tell him I urged you to call. You'll find him easy to talk to."

"Very well, I shall do so. If we ever get this thing figured out, I think you're going to be shocked—and fascinated. Don't mention it to anyone till I tell you. It may be we'll be able to keep it quiet. If we don't it could cause a good deal of trouble with your own rarities—tell you more later. For now, many thanks."

He said his good-byes and placed a second call to the Hetherington Research Library in Los Angeles. With the time differential, he had less fear of failing to get his party. It was three-thirty on the coast, and the distant librarian was easily reached. Introductions and explanations were exchanged and he said, "Sir, I would like to pose you a few odd questions about the care and handling of rare books. Are you free for about five minutes, or could I call back at a more convenient time?"

"No, indeed, Mr. George. I am completely at your service. Go right ahead."

"Thank you. For the sake of this discussion, please assume that the absolute worst is happening to a very valuable collection. In other words, think in terms not of what usually occurs, but what might occur given the worst possible situation. First, then, what are the possibilities of faking very valuable books?"

"Assuming that they are indeed 'very valuable,' it is possible. If they weren't very valuable, it would scarcely be worth the time. On the other hand if they were, it would have to be done very carefully, because they would be examined in such detail. I assume you mean for them to be sold—to a dealer and then to an institution possibly? Or just the latter?"

"I don't know, but sell them to someone knowledgeable, yes. How would they be checked and examined?"

"Well, the paper would have to be of the appropriate texture and period. It would have to be sufficiently foxed to look its age, but not so much that it reduced the book's value. These are printed books, not vellum or hand script?"

"That's right. Printed—and fairly modern, I suspect. Eighteenth and nineteenth century. Probably no incunabula, although I could be wrong there. What do you mean, 'foxed'?"

"Foxing is the brownish stains that develop in old paper. It used to be thought of as an acid stain; now we think it's a kind of fungus or mold. In many respects it's what makes a book 'look old.' You can fake it by staining with weak tea, if you don't do too much of it."

"What if it works the other way? What if you have a very 'foxed' book—something terribly worn—can it be eliminated?"

"Yes, it can be bleached out a page at a time. You would soak the sheets in a succession of potassium permanganate and metabisulfite, if you're interested in the details."

"Anything may be helpful! What if you started with a terribly mistreated, a really worn-out book, and you wanted to pass it off as one in better condition? Can this be done?"

"Oh yes, you could trim the pages slightly to get rid of some of the wear—this would square the corners a bit, too, if they were rounding—and then you could restain the cut fore-edge. You can fill in any holes with wet pulp and let it dry and rub it down. If you can find some old thread you could catch any signatures that were starting and . . ."

"Signatures are the folded sections, of course. What is 'starting'?"

"Just pulled loose—slipped, so that a portion is not tight and smooth with the adjacent signatures. If the covers are scuffed or rubbed or the hinge is cracked, this can be touched up, and glued from the back. All of these things will improve the condition of a book if done with restraint, but if the book is obviously repaired, it is almost worthless except as a curiosity. Has little bibliophilic value, that is."

"When you buy a book you check for all these things?"

"Oh yes. They make the difference for all the steps between a Fair and a Mint. In a good piece of eighteenth-century work—a Diderot's *Encyclopédie* or a Johnson's *Dictionary*—they could make a difference of many thousands of dollars."

"How about faking a whole book?"

"It's been done, but very rarely. You'd have to get antique paper, antique ink, an antique type font, probably a handpress, the whole thing. It can be done, but it's time-consuming and probably not worth the risk."

"If I could get a fraud past you at the point of purchase and it became a part of your collection, what is the chance of its being found out later?"

There was a long wait from California. Ultimately Dana replied slowly: "I am not sure. If it were one of our gems which is frequently requested for loan to exhibitions or were one that is being reproduced, it would probably be caught very quickly. If it were in the middle range of value and use, it might go some time before being identified."

"Months or years?"

"Months or years, yes."

"I heard a man on the radio talking about the *Bay Psalm Book* supposed to be worth some fabulous sum . . ."

"Yes. Probably a quarter million dollars in today's market."

"Heavens! What if I suddenly turned up with another one?"

"It would be examined with a fine-tooth comb. Every letter on every page would have to match. The paper would have to be precisely right. The paling of the ink. And you'd have to have a pretty convincing story of where it came from, too. I was at the New York Public when they got their *Murders in the Rue Morgue*. Cost some $25,000, as I recall. It was worked over so you'd have thought someone was trying to sell them a second copy of the Declaration of Independence! I am to think in terms of someone wishing to make some easy money, is that right?"

"Exactly. Is there an easier way than *Bay Psalm Books?*"

"Well, that would draw so much attention. Why not fake something like *Leaves of Grass*, it's worth five or six thousand dollars, or an early *Alice in Wonderland?* I think ours cost around five thousand but there must be forty or fifty of them around. How about early Mormon stuff or the westward movement? For some reason that brings in a couple of thousand dollars a volume every time one turns up."

"That reminds me," George broke in, "I've been

trying to recall a cowboy book I saw recently—an old one. Are they valuable?"

"Cowboys? Well, some of the journals of the early drives are pretty rare. Do you remember what part of the country it came from?"

"Was it Texas? I seem to think so."

"How about Will Hale's *Twenty-four Years a Cowboy in Texas and Mexico*?"

"That's it! That's the one! Is it worth anything?"

"Oh yes. It's the sort of thing I was talking about. I once bid five thousand dollars on one and lost it by six or seven hundred. It was printed around 1920, so they don't have to be old to be valuable. Of course, if you're planning to make a living out of this, you'd best find a dealer who'll take a kickback." He laughed to emphasize he was making a joke. "And that's pretty hard to do, too. One mistake and he's out of business forever. And he just couldn't make enough to make it worth the risk."

George sighed. "Every time I think I have a solution for my troubles, someone tries to talk me out of it. But you've been most kind and most helpful."

"It has been my pleasure, Mr. George. While we've never met, I've read your articles in *Library Journal* and A.L.A. things many times. I'm delighted to be of some assistance. I'll look forward to hearing from you."

George said his good-bye and cradled the phone. Rather than appearing disheartened, his eyes flashed with more satisfaction than at any time in the past two days.

I will have that drink now, he thought. "'Something attempted, something done, has earned a night's repose.' Longfellow," he said to himself.

# 14

The following morning, George arrived at the Director's office somewhat later than he had intended. He had slept well. Retiring with the feeling that he was at last on the way to the resolution of his unknowns, he had risen tardily but refreshed, and treated himself to a full breakfast. He had had less trouble getting a cab than he had expected—behind the government workers and before the lobbyists, he thought. Congratulating himself on his timing, he went straight to the Director's outer office.

The middle-aged secretary looked up. "Good morning, Mr. George," she said.

"Hello again. Is Dr. Brooks in? Could I see him?"

"Was he expecting you?"

George smiled ruefully. "I'm not quite sure. I suspect he either wanted to see me much sooner, or very much later. Perhaps that's the reason I'm here—to find out which."

The woman showed neither cordiality nor interest at

this and very deliberately dialled a single number on her intercom.

"Mr. George is here. Is it convenient for you to see him?"

The phone appeared to remain silent, but the secretary said, "All right. You may go in."

George walked to the closed door, opened it, and passed into the office of the Director. Brooks was seated at his desk, proofing letters which lay in two neatly stacked heaps on either side of his blotter. He finished signing a sheet before him, very deliberately slipped it under the flap of its envelope, and lifted it onto the pile at the right. He raised his head and looked at George. The movement was one of great fatigue. His eyes were red and the dark circles around them seemed to fuse into unhealthy patches on his cheeks. George was shocked at the change that had appeared in so short a time.

"Good morning, Nelson," he said quietly.

The Director made some kind of sound in his throat and nodded toward a chair. George seated himself, watching the librarian closely.

"I'm going through the expected motions of administration rather waiting to see what will happen next." Brooks spoke with a voice as tired as his appearance. "I no longer know whom I can trust, nor what is going to happen to the institution, so I am just sitting— waiting—I'm not yet sure for what."

"Really, Nelson, what are you afraid of? What makes you so sure this is going to hurt the Library?"

Brooks looked directly at George, searching his eyes as if trying to find what was in the other's mind.

"Don't be naïve. This is supposed to be a center of scholarship, staffed with people of distinction, in an atmosphere of professionalism and wisdom. We now know that there was such bad blood between two of our divisions that there was backbiting, academic blackmail—and apparently murder. We've got two men dead, and the killer still loose. By the time this is finished, the reputation of this place will be wrecked for a generation. What kind of staff can I recruit after this mess is spread through the trade? 'I can recruit'— there's a laugh! I'm finished myself, and you know it. Do you think the trustees are going to give me anything... *anything* I ask for now? Either I'm going to have to resign, recognizing my usefulness is past, or they'll invite me to quit to try to salvage something of the place. And who'll hire me after letting a mess like this go on?"

"What do you mean the killer is still loose? Don't you think Schwartz killed DeVeer and then took his own life?"

Brooks stared at him. "Do you?"

"It is possible. If you take the facts that we know and arrange them properly they could come out like that."

"You mean you think this may be over?"

"It could be. Unless... what do they think caused that lift to fall yesterday?"

The other man sank back in his chair.

"They don't know—or at least they're not telling me. Conrad says the carrier must have been resting at the top deck all these years, and the rope was bent over the pulley at the same place all the time. It appears to've rotted away and anything could have happened. Someone could have tried to pull the carrier down for some reason and the rope just tore apart. It might have been so rotten just the vibration of lifting the door could have parted it. And, of course, someone could have twisted it apart with their hands—it didn't actually have to be cut. They'd have me believe there's no way of knowing what happened. Still, if it did fall by itself..." He seemed to be trying to convince himself the two deaths were the end.

"Nelson," George asked suddenly, "if you'd known what DeVeer was up to, what would you have done to him?"

George expected a furious reply of outrage. Instead, Brooks looked at him again, searching intently with his reddened, watery eyes. He finally replied in a low voice, "I suppose he would have had to have been disciplined, but I think I would have given him a chance to resign first."

"Wouldn't that simply have set him up for playing the martyr? The more I think about him, the more impressed I am that he'd organized the whole thing very prettily. If you raised a hand against him he could go before the trustees—hell, the whole profession—crying he was a man of principle surrounded by fools and small minds! It seems to me he held all the winning cards. I don't see how you could have defended yourself against him."

Brooks rubbed at his eyes with his hands. "No doubt you're right. He was a worthy adversary."

There was a long pause, and then Brooks said slowly: "I have been thinking about the life of institutions—how very fragile they are. We look at buildings or campuses or 'names' and we assume they will go on forever from a sort of perpetual momentum. They won't. They run down. They become second-class. They can even die.

"Do you know which was the greatest name in humanities at the turn of the century? Which school had graduated more doctorates in history and English and the classics than all the other universities combined? Johns Hopkins! Now it's just 'a good school in Baltimore.' Do you know what was the greatest museum of the nineteenth century—the one they came from all over the world to see and copy? The Agassiz in Boston! Who knows it now? Look at Columbia and Berkeley—crippled. They may never recover. Running one of these things is an awful responsibility. I mean awful as in awe! Your obligation to the institution transcends every other consideration! It must be here, strong and viable. It affects the entire community—not just individuals—whole generations of creative minds. It must not falter! Nothing or nobody had the right to threaten it. It could not—it cannot—be tolerated."

He subsided and stared into space. He appeared to have no more to say. George could not decide whether it was simply because Brooks was lost in thought, or because he no longer thought it was safe to confide in him. When it was clear the conversation was at an end, George rose.

"Nelson, I want to snoop among the records. If anyone asks may I say you've given me permission to examine them?"

The librarian focused and then seemed to reconstruct the question. "Go ahead. Say anything you want." He looked at the other man intently. "You would anyway, wouldn't you? Whose side are you on, Ed?"

George averted his eyes and replied airily: "A mere observer of the passing parade, Nelson. Any significant thinking I leave to the authorities. I'll check with you if I hear anything I think you should know."

He left the room and hurried through the outer office. Time is moving much faster now, he thought. He started down the winding stairs, having forgotten the elevators. Striding purposefully over the endless cascades of marble seemed to fit his mood. He was in control of his thoughts and actions. He was enjoying himself.

———

Crighton swished down the hall, chin up and heels clicking on the basement floor. Either a Renaissance mind looking for laughs, or a Gothic ghoul getting revenge. She'd been thinking about George's choices right up till the moment she'd dropped off to sleep last night, and she'd resolved that the minute she could pry a second loose, she was going to visit Personnel. Jealousy, a questionable past—there must be something which would point to somebody and give them some idea of who—or what—they were after.

After exchanging pleasantries with Mr. Owens, the personnel director, she had secured permission to search the files and she plunged in. She had found the ones she wanted quickly, and read them in detail—ending up more confused than ever. She was sure it was there, she had read it herself, but she just couldn't tell which fact it was that mattered. The whole bunch looked so ordinary, and yet . . .

Speidel had started as an Elizabethan scholar at a fancy prep school, he'd taken an Ivy League Ph.D. in Marlowe, and been hung on their Rare Book Room as a teaching fellow. From there he must've gone into librarianship, and by way of three equally impressive libraries, made the Werner-Bok. Period. That was all there was to it.

Miss Brewer had gone to a ladies' college library school farther back than Crighton thought possible. She'd worked as a cataloger in her hometown library till World War Two, then she'd come to Washington to take a cataloging job at the Werner-Bok. From this she'd edged into her present spot. Though she'd majored in American history as an undergraduate, there was nothing in the folder that quite explained all she seemed to know about colonial history. Still, Crighton thought with a shudder, she'd certainly had long enough to learn it on the job.

Alan Welles's dossier looked precisely as he'd told her at lunch, but Rose's was at least something new. No wonder old Brewer kept calling him "poor Dr. Rose." The man had started by collecting a summa cum laude in classical history from Vanderbilt and must have graduated as the pride of his class. He'd been granted a year's fellowship in Europe from the Berenson Fund, and he'd come directly from abroad to the Werner-Bok as their curator in the classics and medieval period. Thereupon everything had come to a complete stop. He'd blown fifteen years between changes of either salary or title, and any fool could see that the old boys around him had been hired at higher pay with a lot less experience than he had. They finally made him head of his division ten years ago, but even then it had taken four more before he saw anything in the paycheck to cover the added responsibility. It occurred to Crighton that Rose had far greater reason to resent Brooks than DeVeer had had.

Brooks's file was the very model of the successful administrator. With a Master's from Yale and a doctorate from Chicago, he'd started looking great on paper and he'd made the most of it. He'd moved every four or five years, and he'd shot from public libraries to university libraries to the Werner-Bok. Every step had been just right—appropriate and remunerative. He'd collected sheaves of recommendations from board presidents and university chancellors, and Crighton figured he must have had 'em eating out of his hand. She suddenly saw how painful the present situation must be to the man, ending his career discredited and with his reputation clouded. For some strange reason, her mind slipped to lions. How did that thing go? If you meet a lion in the jungle, you're all right as long as he can retreat. Corner him and he'll kill you. With a flash of insight, she wondered if Brooks's professional vulnerability had made DeVeer so sure of his attack, or whether DeVeer might not have miscalculated at this very point.

Schwartz's dossier was just as thin as the last time she'd looked at it, and it was the last one. She stared at the heap of folders and chewed her lip.

"Rats!" she said. "If I was half as bright as I want 'em to think I am, I'd have seen something. I know it's there. I just know it!"

She gathered up the papers and handed them back to Mr. Owens.

"Many, many thanks. They were most helpful," she lied. As she started toward her office she said: "Damn. What do you suppose you missed, Jones? Double damn."

Carson, in the meantime, had plunged directly into Mr. George's assignment. Resisting a desire to see if Crighton was in her office, he had headed straight for his medieval Chapter House and the omnipresent Brewer. On arriving, he saluted Pop Wright and progressed down the aisle toward the chancel, but Brewer was nowhere to be seen. He stared at the empty desk, feeling as if a part of the furniture had been removed without being able to remember how it had looked before they took it away.

As he stared, he realized that Speidel was working quietly at the catalog on the right. Presumably he could provide the same service that Brewer did. The question was, what was George after? He'd implied he wanted Steve's "reaction." Was it to the three books he was supposed to request, or was it to Brewer's reaction to his request for the books? Was it essential that Brewer bring the books to him, or would anyone do? His natural impatience and curiosity won out. He walked to the desk and stood attempting to project scholar-requiring-assistance. Speidel finished his work and as he replaced the catalog drawer he noticed Carson.

"Yes? Do you want something?"

"Yeah, thanks. I need three books. Can you get 'em for me?"

Thus far Speidel had shown no sign of recognition, but as he approached the issue desk, he peered out from under his rather prominent eyebrows and said, "Aren't you the boy . . . of course, you're George's assistant, aren't you?"

"Not exactly. I've been working in your American manuscripts—Miss Brewer's been helping me, but I don't see her now—I could use some books. Do you get things, too, or should I wait for her?"

"No, that's all right. '. . . *when I to watch supplied a servant's place* . . .' I'll get them for you. What do you want?"

"I need the Poe *Tamerlane,* first edition, and first editions of *Uncle Tom's Cabin* and the *Emigrant's Guide to California*. I'm getting hung up on some social history."

There seemed to be no particular change of emotion, but Speidel replied, "Oh, none of those circulate. You can get them in the general history reading room on the west side."

"No," Carson tried to sound casual, "I particularly need a first edition of each one of them. I want the exact version that would have been available at the time of my study."

"That's all right. Their *Emigrant's Guide* is a photocopy of our first edition, so it will match. The *Tamerlane* is very rare, and cannot be handled except in the most exceptional circumstances. I suppose I can bring you the *Stowe,* if you insist on it."

"Thank you, but I'm afraid I insist on the others,

too. That's what they're here for, isn't it? Have they been lost or something?"

Speidel's appearance seemed unchanged, but Carson suddenly became aware of an unblinking stare. He could not tell if he simply had not noticed it before, or his insistence on the volumes had seized the man's attention.

"I assume they have not been lost, but possibly we should see, eh? You are eager to have these three books, are you? Well, we wouldn't want Mr. George to think our service is at fault, would we?"

"Mr. George has nothing to do with this. I am working on the midcentury frontier..."

"Of course not. Of course you are. I'll see if I can find them."

As he watched the familiar pattern of the search in the catalog and then the disappearance into the decks, Carson wondered if he might not have committed an expensive error in judgment. It was impossible to tell whether Speidel had known all about the three volumes from the outset and had attempted to keep them out of Carson's hands, or whether the titles had meant nothing to him in the beginning, but he had sensed some dramatic overtones in the request and was now eager to pursue them.

The search appeared to be running into trouble. Minutes stretched into a longer and longer delay. Carson's imagination began to accelerate. Were the books missing and could not be found? Were they there, but Speidel was getting rid of them? Was he back in there going over them with a glass, probably finding whatever it was that George had expected him to see? Would whatever it was he was supposed to find still be there when Speidel had finished with them? Would ...? He was on his tenth permutation when Speidel appeared, carrying the slipcase and three old volumes.

The librarian held them in his left hand and carried them before him as if they were stacked on an imaginary salver. His expression was one of quizzical watchfulness. I don't believe he's found anything yet, Carson thought.

"I believe these are what you wanted. Each one right where it belonged. I trust Mr. George would have been impressed. I'll sign them out for you."

He handed over the volumes and Carson took them to his table without comment. Once seated within his circle of light, he spread them before him and instinctively looked toward Speidel at the end of the room. He had gone behind the issue desk and seated himself as if waiting for further customers, but his casual glances toward Carson were so regular it was clear he was under close surveillance.

Carson made a show of moving note cards around, pantomimed the selection of two which he laid in front of him, and then picked up the slipcase after rather ostentatiously consulting the nearest card. He let the little drawer slip out as he had seen the professor do only two days before—thinking that it seemed like weeks. Once again the beauty of the slipcase fascinated him and he examined its workmanship. The leather box was so tactile, he had to resist a desire to rub it against his cheek. And once again the brilliance of the leather and gold and silken lining clashed with the tawdry volume it protected. In contrast, the book was so trashy it was distressing to touch. It seemed to present nothing for his imagination to pursue.

He lifted it, aware of Speidel's attention. He turned its pages. Without knowing what he was to look for, he examined the piece in detail, and then placed it back in its tray and closed the slipcase.

He then picked up the *Emigrant's Guide*. It was in almost as bad shape as the *Tamerlane*. It was water-soaked, the corners of the pages were worn, and the paper covers were warped and tended to bend up at the edges. Nevertheless, the volume caught his interest at once. Poor Olaf might well have carried one of these with him in 1859 when he headed west—in fact, he may have read this very one and it could have been the force that moved him from his ordered, Delaware life. Carson recalled that professor's assurance that he would respond to an association copy, and he realized that he did feel a sensual thrill at the thought that this very volume might have been the one that Olaf had in his hand in the wagon.

Carson opened it carefully to see if there were any identification marks to show where this particular volume came from. Nothing. It had no library identification other than a small card with a call number sticking loose out of the pages.

Carson knew Ware well, so he had little interest in its contents other than a casual leafing to see how it looked "in the original."

Having satisfied his curiosity, he started to lay the *Guide* down beside the *Tamerlane* when he remembered he was supposedly looking for something significant. He drew it back and worked it around under the light. Except for its general wear and decay, the two volumes had little in common, and he certainly could find no identifying marks which might indicate a single owner.

Now somewhat bemused, he abandoned the frontier piece and picked up the *Uncle Tom's Cabin*. He was promptly surprised to see that what at first appeared to be two identical copies were in fact volume one and volume two of the same title. His mind ran back to the bookbinder's cage and he realized the "stack of four" was really only two duplicates again. The two volumes were in somewhat better shape than the others he had looked at, but not much. He opened the first to its title page and smiled at the Victorian run-on: "Uncle Tom's Cabin or Life Among the Lowly, Harriet Beecher Stowe."

He pulled the book closer and methodically turned its pages. It looked about the way he had expected it to. The one thing which struck him as being at all newsworthy was its length. The old girl was a lot wordier than he had remembered. The idea of writing six hundred pages with a quill pen made him shudder and his mind slipped away trying to remember when quill pens went out of style. This generated pictures of Ben Franklin sucking on a feather which reminded him of drying wet ink by shaking sand on it, and he was in the midst of thinking what a mess that ought to have made and why didn't it, when he forced his attention back to the book in hand.

These pages were in better shape than the earlier ones he'd looked at and he riffled through them looking for something out of the ordinary but the whole thing appeared routine. He finally abandoned the Stowe as well, and, puzzled, stood up to return the collection. As he started down the aisle, he was again conscious of Speidel apparently staring out through the false, leaded windows. There is a man who has been watching out of the corner of his eye, Carson thought. He wondered again if he had blown it. He returned the volumes to Speidel without words on either side, and returned to his table space, irritated with his search and with himself. Buster, he thought, you loused that one up royally.

Edward George was in high good humor. Unlike Carson, he had gone to Crighton's cubicle, found it lighted but empty, and then proceeded to the medieval gloom of the Rare Book Room. He, too, nodded at Wright, and he had seen Carson deeply engrossed in the examination of his books, but not wishing to interrupt him had passed down the far aisle and on to the rare books deck. He started back toward the shelving, listening for life among the carrels along the way. Rose was in his cubicle hunched over a book and apparently oblivious of all traffic. Welles was also in his room, and George had passed him and gone several steps beyond his carrel before he realized that Welles's door had been folded back in such a way that it formed a mirror to anyone in the corridor and he realized that Welles had been looking straight at him from behind his wall. It gave him a slightly uncomfortable sensation, and he found himself intrigued with the thought that from his detached position Welles was maintaining a close surveillance over the traffic on the deck. George shook his head impatiently as he walked. You're getting jumpy, he told himself. The door happened to have caught his eye for a moment; there is no reason to believe he sits there like a cat all day—in fact, that is much more appropriate for Speidel. The thought brought him up sharp. I wonder if Speidel can do the same thing with his glass? That would be very useful to a man like Speidel. He could use it like a periscope to watch the elevator; he would know who goes where and when. Very useful indeed. Thinking he must check this phenomenon, he reached the last cubicle on the deck before the shelves began. He had been told this was where he would find the cataloger.

"Are you Miss Hester? May I bother you for a moment? I'm Edward George."

"Oh yes, I understand you came here in all innocence and got caught up in these frightful murders. Do sit down, Mr. George." She pointed to the other chair in the room, an uncomfortable-looking folding model. George seated himself and thought it was as painful as it looked.

Miss Hester was a very large woman, neatly groomed and wearing the kind of dark dress supposedly useful in reducing the size of the wearer. She appeared to be efficient and well-organized.

"How can I help you?"

"I want to ask you how you keep track of all this material of yours. I walked through the stacks yesterday and I was shaken by the enormous value of the holdings. A call slip returned 'not on shelf' could mean a thousand dollars missing with the kind of material you're handling!"

Miss Hester laughed cordially.

"Mr. George, it's hard to believe, but we aren't conscious of the value at all, really. The books come in, we catalog them, all the usual cards are made up—my shelf list is in the next room, and the full catalog's out with the readers—we put the call number on a shelving slip and it's just another book for the stacks. They do tell us how much they spent for the things, and we put it on the shelf list card for insurance purposes, but it's simply another notation, so far as we're concerned."

"The shelf list tells all, huh? I suppose you use it to see that nothing's missing?"

"Yes, every summer we hire a group of college kids and they work their way through the collections to see if it's all there."

"How would they know if it wasn't?"

"The shelf list cards are arranged exactly as the books appear on the shelves, so they work as teams, and one of them calls out the author and title, and the other pulls it off the shelf to see if it matches."

"And if one's missing?"

"They tilt the card up. Usually they come on the

book in a few feet and they move the book and drop the card."

"Ever fail to find something?"

"Very rarely. These are closed stacks, you know, and there's no place for a book to go. They all turn up eventually."

"Always?"

"Always in my time. There are stories about someone way back stealing handwritten sheet music and selling it for the composers' autographs, and they lost three of Oscar Wilde's diaries in the thirties, but that's all."

"Were they recovered?"

"No. The consensus seems to have been they contained some salacious material and some enthusiast destroyed them to protect Wilde's reputation—not stolen for money."

"Had he any left?"

"What?"

"Reputation."

"That's a fair question, I think."

"Where is the shelf list kept?"

"Next door. Want to see it?"

"I'd be grateful."

He followed the cataloger into the neighboring carrel where a low, heavy safe sat in the corner. Miss Hester pulled back the thick door revealing card drawers inside. She slid one out and set it on the safe.

"Fireproof?"

"Yes, it's supposed to resist flames for ten or fifteen hours, or something. By then the fire's supposed to be out, and we can pull the trays and sue the insurance company."

"Is the safe locked at night?"

"No, we leave the combination taped to 'open.' The

only purpose for the safe is to protect the records against fire."

George casually examined a few of the cards. They were typical of any library, the ones he was holding proving to be sixteenth-century German herbals, each running from fifty to two or three hundred dollars.

"Are these the prices originally paid, or do you keep track of their increase in value?"

"That's what they were worth when we got them—either what we actually paid or, more frequently, their market value. Most of our materials are donated."

"So I've heard." He looked up at the cataloger. "By the way, do you think this publicity will cut down on donations?"

She replied seriously. "I don't know. There's a lot of talk about that in the Lounge. One of our chief sources of material is vanity. People like to say, 'The Werner-Bok asked for my collection.' It's sort of an intellectual laurel wreath! The trouble is, everybody is competing for material now. If we should go out of favor with the market, the Library of Congress or Texas or a dozen others would be only too happy to pick up the pieces."

"Ummm. You don't want to risk your respectability, huh?"

"That's the problem."

George started to take his leave and stepped back into the corridor. It suddenly struck him that Miss Hester was nearer the wall with the book carrier in it than any other office on the floor.

"Ah, Miss Hester. I suppose you've heard about poor Speidel's near miss yesterday! Do you have any guess what happened?"

Her manner was slightly less cordial, and appreciably less casual.

"If you mean, did I see anybody go toward that dumbwaiter thing, I've been asked that by everybody on the staff and most of the policemen. The fact is, yes, I did see someone who might have tampered with it: the Director, Dr. Speidel, Mr. Welles, Dr. Rose, Miss Jones—and Miss Brewer."

"I don't understand."

"Every one of them walked by this door and two deck attendants besides. That is a fool's question, Mr. George. This is a library and people have to use this corridor to do what they're paid for. That's like asking a filling station man if he noticed his helper at the pump. Of course he did. That's what he's there for."

George was a bit startled at the analogy, but properly repentant. "Sorry. I can see you've been asked that question once too often."

She smiled again, her cordiality returning. "No, about ten times too often. You just happened to start the second decade!"

"That's enough. I've taken too much of your time already. I'll leave you to your casual recording of all these jewels. I do admire your nonchalance with thousand-dollar volumes!"

"I don't know whether it's familiarity breeds . . . or fools rush in, Mr. George—and I'm afraid to think too much about it to find out!"

They parted with a smile.

George strode back toward the Reading Room, the deck vibrating slightly as he walked. Once through the entrance, he could still see Carson at his location, methodically writing on note cards. George decided he would make one more visit to the bookbinder's cage before disturbing him.

He crossed straight in front of the issue desk which was now quite empty, neither Brewer nor Speidel being in sight, and no third person covering. Like Carson, this struck him as being somewhat unusual, but presumably accountable for. He passed into the steel world of the Manuscripts side and proceeded to the elevator. The usual sounds of telephones and typewriters were missing, and he had the feeling that he was alone on the floor. He pressed the button, but nothing happened. After pressing and listening for a moment he concluded that either it had been cut off or a door was propped open below and he decided he might as well start down the stairs. He smiled to himself at the thought of the endless notices he had posted in his time, "Anyone holding open the door of this elevator will be subject to disciplinary action." Deck attendants learn to prop elevator doors before they can hold a book, he thought fondly.

He descended three levels and wondered if the elevator might be visible from this point. The thought of walking down another nine flights struck him as tiring, and he started back toward the center of the deck. As he progressed, he realized that he was hearing a woman sobbing. Whoever it was suddenly cried out, "What kind of lies were you telling him?" He recognized Miss Brewer's voice.

"I was only telling him what I saw and what I knew. It was up to him to decide what to do about it." It was Speidel.

"You knew he'd do the evilest thing possible."

"If Rose had done nothing he had nothing to fear."

"He just isn't that kind of a man," she replied passionately. "He couldn't defend himself and you knew it."

"Then he doesn't deserve to be running a division."

"Well, you've got what you wanted. You've got an opening for yourself."

"Don't be foolish, woman; while I believe in survival of the fittest, I don't expect to advance over dead bodies."

"Don't you care what you do to anyone?"

"Who cares what they do to me? If I can't be on top, I can at least make the high ones jump."

"You're despicable."

"My dear woman, that is scarcely original. You stand around snivelling about everyone and everything. I do not intend to leave the solution of this unpleasantness to the hands of a ham-handed policeman who is liable to hang these crimes around the first neck he finds convenient just to get back to his office. From what I can observe, his boredom is matched only by his frustration and at any moment he is going to do something dramatic. I don't think he has the faintest idea of what is going on, and I think it behooves me to be certain he lines up what he has seen in, shall we say, a legitimate fashion? In any event, I am going to let myself be locked in tomorrow night, and by the time this building is opened Sunday afternoon, I shall have what I need."

"To do what?" There was flickering anxiety in her voice.

"Protect myself, what else?"

At this point, one of the speakers began to walk, with the other apparently following close behind. Not knowing where they were headed, George was relieved to hear the elevator doors closing and the car beginning to descend—presumably with them aboard. It stopped somewhere well below where George was standing.

He now found himself completely frustrated. He could scarcely continue down via either the elevator or the stairs without running the risk of meeting the two, and there was even a possibility that they were themselves at the bookbinder's cage. Irritated by this enforced change in his plans, he retraced his steps to the Reading Room.

"Steve," he said, placing a hand on his shoulder.

The young man jumped violently.

"Forgive me, I didn't mean to startle you."

"Excuse *me*," said Carson. "I didn't mean to come apart, either. I had just figured out a way to prove that Pop Wright did it, when I thought he'd grabbed me!"

A half dozen heads turned toward them projecting silent shushes, and George motioned for Carson to join him outside. He hurriedly gathered his materials into a pile, and followed the older man through the door.

"Have you seen our young lady?" George asked when they reached the hall.

"No, have you?"

"I have not. Let's go find her."

When they reached her room, they discovered her, coated and buttoned, on the verge of turning out the light.

"And where do you think you're going in the middle of the day?" Carson asked sternly.

Crighton colored, and looked past them into the hall.

"Well, I . . ." She thought about her excuse for a second and then said aggressively: "I am going home. I have a heavy date tonight, and I'm going to get ready for it."

"The hell you say!" Carson's reply hung between a laughing retort and a hint of irritation that she might be serious.

"You heard me. I've never done anything like this before—but then I've never had a week like this before, either! I told Personnel I had a sick headache and had to take the rest of the day off." She turned to George as if to beg his approval. "I haven't had a day of sick leave since I came to work, and I'll come in tomorrow to catch up, even if it is Saturday—but, well, things have been in such a mess that I haven't had a chance to do my hair or anything and I want to make an impression tonight. Do you think Melvil Dewey would turn in his grave if I cheated just this once?"

George smiled. "As an old administrator, I couldn't possibly condone it. On the other hand, from the look in your eye, if you don't take off you really will have a sick headache, so it's only a matter of time one way or the other."

Carson frowned. "Who's important enough to get you to pull a stunt like this?"

"I don't think it's any of your business," Crighton snapped back too quickly.

"Forgive me for living!" Carson said. He looked deliberately toward George. "If you want a report on the books, I'm at my usual place. I think I'm trespassing here." He headed for the door, obviously tense about the mouth.

"Wait a minute," Crighton started after him. "I didn't mean . . . oh, the hell with him."

She came back to her room and dropped into the chair behind her desk.

"I don't know what's the matter with me, Mr. George. I'm falling apart. There's no use kidding myself, I am on the defensive . . . I don't know whether I should be doing this—any of this. I've never quit work to have my hair done in my life. And I've never had a date with a divorced man, either! Mr. Welles asked me to The Square tonight, and I've talked myself into wanting to impress him. As if there was anything a beauty parlor could do that would help. Should I go ahead?"

George leaned casually against the desk, not wanting to interrupt her thought.

"You know, it's always easiest for an old man to say, 'You do what you think best, my dear,' because it really is the only thing he should say. Nobody can know what to weigh against what for anybody else— and of course, it's the safest answer, too! This way, you've got no one to blame but yourself! But really, why not? Tell me, what makes this date so special? You must have been dating young men for years."

"Not really. I went to a girls' school where we went in hordes to neighboring campuses and spent a week-end of dances and football and a movie or two together and then we all went back to school in a horde and there was never any occasion to try to get just one man. By the time I got to graduate school, most of the men were married already, and what was left didn't interest me much—and I sure didn't interest them! So I sort of got all the way here without any practice! And now I'm afraid to try.

"Alan says all the right things about my being intel- ligent and curious and sensitive and that's what I want a man to say. So here I am, trying to talk myself into being able to live up to the billing! Tell me honestly, should I try for it or am I way out of my league?"

"I don't know, Crighton. I'm not sure what it is you're looking for, and even worse, I don't know what he wants or why. I find him most interesting, I must admit. Either he is a bit more steely under the surface than I first thought, or he is much more vulnerable, and is trying to protect himself from something. As long as you keep control of the situation—don't wear your heart on your sleeve for a while—I don't see why you shouldn't get to know him better. This business of getting your hair done or whatever is nonsense, of course. The only possible use for it is psychological. If it makes you feel pretty, I suppose it's worth the time, but a good face washing and a short nap are all you really need. You are a most attractive young lady, needing only the amount of messing with that is required to make you look like the going style. You have beautiful hair, stunning eyes, and the kind of complexion half of the women of the world would give a year off their lives to have. Brother Welles will be very flattered to be seen with you tonight, no matter what you manage to do to yourself. Your presence will enhance him, if only to imply that he could interest a girl of your obvious intelligence. Though you devalue it, I suspect it *is* your brains and curiosity that have seized his interest. Beauty parlor jobs must be easy to come by—though I'll admit it's been half a century since I was looking—but brains were hard to find even then!"

Crighton smiled wanly. "You are a real, genuine-type dear. Your line is even better than his." She held up her hand to stop a denial. "I think what you've said, though, is, I'll never know till I've tried. I'm going to do it. When will I see you next? Are you coming in tomorrow?"

"I am. I'll tell you what. Let me drop you off wherever you're going. I'll phone up to Rare Books and leave a message for Steve to meet us here in the morning. I think it's time for a council of war. I want to go home and do some careful thinking and I'll use you as my excuse. May I borrow your sick headache? I don't think you're well enough to take a cab alone."

# 15

The evening had started well. A few minutes to H-hour she had stopped in front of a mirror to make a final check and found it good. The hair had come out nicely, even she had to admit there was a flash to her eye and style to the ensemble, and she felt good. She also felt she was getting too close to the edge of something, but a rising key which would ordinarily have threatened stage fright, tonight came out excitement and she let herself revel in it.

He arrived within minutes of her readiness, and as she slid across the red leather seat of the sports car she thought, he looks just right for the occasion. In fact, she suddenly realized, that was the reason he was slightly different. He was always completely appropriate for the time and the place, completely at ease and quietly relishing each moment.

He made pleasant small talk on the way to the theatre, and as they worked their way through the lobby, properly crowded with the usual well-dressed Washington theatregoers, she was pleased with how many people knew him and wanted his attention, and his very apparent pride in presenting her to them. It was a new experience for her, and she wondered fleetingly if it came about because of a maturing on her part or only that she had never been with his kind of person doing this kind of thing before. They took their seats inside the rather self-consciously dramatic theatre with the squared stage in the center. She reminded herself that she had been here many times, but she realized she had never felt quite like this before. It must be him, she thought, and the way he treats me. I wonder if he treats everyone like this, or could he really have meant it when he said I make things different for him.

The play was Anouilh and they both enjoyed it. Once again it seemed to fit. She usually saw Shaw here and she thought that Shaw's acid teaching would have been inappropriate for him. While you enjoyed Shaw along the way, you always ended up feeling you ought to go out and do something about something. Anouilh didn't care what you did so long as you recognized the irony as you passed it by. As ever, it was the proper thing for Alan Welles to watch.

When it was over, they returned to the car and he said, "That was interesting. I hope you liked it, too."

"I did very much. I think theatre-in-the-round works best for real sharp dialogue. I'm never quite comfortable with it if the play's about something that really matters. I keep seeing people run up and down the aisles and I keep looking at all those people looking back at me and I never do believe what's going on in between! That's wrong, isn't it? Isn't the idea of being up close supposed to make you part of the action or something?"

"I completely agree with you! I don't care what the idea is supposed to be, I can lose myself in a darkened theatre with an old-fashioned proscenium, and no matter where I'm sitting I'm up and across those foot-lights in nothing flat. In-the-round, the people never stop being actors no matter what they're saying. You're absolutely right."

They drove along the waterfront and the bobbing lights on the boats made the night seem velvet black.

"It's odd," Welles continued, "but half the time I find real life about the same as I do theatre-in-the-round. Do you ever have days when you seem to be watching everything from a seat on the side? I get times when I'm even watching myself! Understand, I'm always delighted at how well I'm doing, but there does seem to be a note of unreality about everything. Ultimate irony: the bizarre events of the past few days seem more real than most of the past months! Incidentally, Crighton, you are realer than anything I've noticed for years. I wonder if you have any idea how attractive you are? It is a joy to watch you in a theatre. Your eyes nearly give off sparks when you're caught up in the words! I enjoyed that play more watching you than I could possibly have alone."

They swept through the antiseptic white tile of the Southwest Tunnel and out again beside the Reflecting Pool and the Jefferson Memorial, chalk-white across the water. The cherry trees were lost in the night.

"Thank you," Crighton replied. "That is beautifully said and I promise to believe at least half of it, but the thought of your going to a play 'all alone' is a little hard on the imagination. I find it much easier to see you as a Playboy Bachelor with a different woman every night . . . every one six feet tall with bare shoulders!"

He laughed easily. "I can't deny that I do my damnedest to live up to that image, but you wouldn't believe how hard tall blondes are to come by (they were blondes, weren't they?), and how stalking around regally seems to sap their brains. The taller and handsomer they are, the glazeder they seem to be! But I try. You should see my apartment. It looks so much like a bachelor's movie set it sometimes even embarrasses me!"

He looked at her as if he were genuinely surprised.

"Yes, you *should* see my apartment! I hadn't intended to invite you up for the etchings, but dammit, I think you might enjoy it. Have you ever been in one of the Legate Towers? I have a magnificent view of the Kennedy Center and down the Potomac. I had intended to stop by the Windsor Lounge and then take you home, so you have your choice." He looked at her with a boyish grin.

Crighton hesitated and noticed a slight swirl of panic creep up before she thought to herself: Don't be stupid. All you have to do is say, no. He wouldn't take advantage. Take advantage! Have some Madeira, m'dear.

"I'd love to!" she replied a little too firmly.

He laughed. "I'd give anything to know what went through your mind just then! Hang on, I'll show you how gracefully Brünnhilde corners."

The sports car accelerated toward the Mall and then swept along behind the Lincoln Memorial. Once on the Kennedy Center bypass, he gunned it beside the sheets of marble and black glass and cut to a fast stop in the garage beneath his apartment. As they stepped into the elevator he said, "You're perfectly safe for a minute or two. This elevator is covered by television. See?" He pointed to a pale mirror near the ceiling. The outline of a lens could be detected through its reflection.

"Well! Who's watching?"

"The front desk has a whole battery of monitors under the counter. It's a nice little conceit—implies we're all so valuable we need guarding, and it lets a man indulge himself. You know, think only of pleasure, someone else is watching out for you."

"What's a Sybarite, Daddy?"

He laughed. "You've got the picture."

He unlocked the door to his apartment and followed her in.

"Whoops!" she said. "He wasn't kidding. It's luscious."

It did have an air of comfortable opulence—deep rugs, much leather, soft, unvarnished woods. There were rows of small bronzes, some enameled silver, and even a surprising number of etchings.

"Hey! You do have some, don't you?"

"Of course. How else could I ask beautiful women to come up and still be honest?"

"I'd think they'd be mutually exclusive."

He motioned her toward the balcony which showed through a wall of glass.

"This is what we pay for, though. The view. It may not be Venice, but it comes as close as you can get on a monthly salary."

He rolled back a panel and they stepped out into the cold black night. The lights of Rock Creek Drive snaked beside the river and out of sight. The Potomac itself was shiny black and visible only where the Memorial Bridge marked its width with floodlit arches in the distance.

"Lovely!" she said. "No wonder you want to show it off. It must be the most beautiful view in the whole city."

"I wouldn't be at all surprised," he agreed.

They watched a jet rise from National Airport and scream overhead as it climbed toward Georgetown, silhouetted on the horizon behind them.

"That's enough. You'll get chilled out here."

They returned to the living room and she dropped into the low couch.

"What can I get for you to drink? What would you like?"

"A scene like this must call for wine or brandy. Whatever you think is appropriate."

"Nonsense. Don't ever let a setting influence what you think is desirable. You decide what you want and then put that around yourself. The most damning thing you can do is to do what's expected. What would you like right now?"

"To take my shoes off and have a cup of instant coffee."

"Good girl. You take care of the first and I'll have the second for you in a second."

"Can't I do it?"

"You stay right where you are."

She slipped off her shoes, but disobeyed him by walking slowly round the room examining carvings on tables, tiny, mounted miniatures, and one Florentine helmet standing on a magnificent piètra dura table. Each item was masculine, but precise. There were no rich lithographs, only line drawings. No landscapes, only portraits.

She gingerly lifted a tzarist Easter egg and opened the top to find another of contrasting colors inside. She started to open this in turn, but felt as though she had her hand in the candy jar, and stopped. She set it down carefully and looked around the room. She was suddenly struck with a thought. There was not a book in sight in any direction. She had dropped back on the couch before he arrived with the coffee for both of them.

"How come no books?"

"I live with them by day. I want other things at night."

"Don't you have any at all?"

"Oh, yes. I have a few favorites in the back room."

"What kinds do you collect?"

"Pretty ones. Ones that show somebody's skill or imagination in making them. Stuff that feels good to the hand and interests the eye."

"Don't you read them?"

"No." He sat down across from her. "If I want to read a book, I get it from the library or buy a paperback. I feel foolish reading something in leather—or even a fancy edition. It detracts from what the author is trying to tell you."

"I thought the idea of good book design was to make the contents more appealing."

"That's a myth. A good, workmanlike job of page design is one you never notice—either its goodness or its badness. If it's hard to read, it's bad. If it calls attention to itself because it's pretty, it's just as bad. Really fine editions are splendid to look at—but the margins are self-conscious, the lines are too far apart, the initial letters demand your attention—they're all lousy to read."

"How can you be a rare books librarian if you feel that way about it?"

"Does a stockbroker have to be in love with AT&T? No, I do love beautiful books for themselves. Let somebody else worry about what the words say. The hell with print! Don't you want some music? How about a Beethoven quartet or some Purcell?"

"I'm sorry. If I'm supposed to be honest, I'll have to ask for great swatches of music. I love Brahms or Franck—and Beethoven if there are thousands of instruments. I like to have it wash over me. I suppose that's terribly gauche."

"It is—not because it's unfashionable, but it's clear you've never really tried the other stuff. After I've had you in hand for a year (I'm offering you a contract, do you hear?), you'll feel like a full orchestra is all blurred. You'll want the cleanliness of the ensemble." He smiled at her fondly, without hint of patronage. "You know, the Kreutzer that was playing the night of the late unpleasantness is probably the finest ensemble in the world now. The tapes are still at the studio, but when I get them back, I'll play you the program we all missed. If it was up to their usual standard, it must have been splendid."

He threw himself sideways in the chair and gulped at his coffee.

"That hall of ours is perfection in sound, you know. Those hard walls make every note as clean as a break in a glass. Just splendid."

Crighton frowned. "I wish you hadn't mentioned our 'late unpleasantness.' Tonight has seemed like a thousand years away from it. But you know, I think it's about to be resolved. The lieutenant has stopped coming around as if he's got what he's looking for, and Mr. George has a sort of home-stretch look about him— and poor Dr. Speidel is going to lock himself into the stacks tomorrow night and says by the time he comes out Sunday he'll have the proof to clear himself."

"I fail to get your image of 'poor Dr. Speidel'—he deserves your sympathy like a hungry black widow, but I didn't realize he was under any more suspicion than anyone else."

"I didn't either, but Mr. George says he seems to think so. Is he normally paranoid?"

"I assume you mean usually paranoid. No, he thinks nobody loves him, and he's right. What a pair he and DeVeer made! We should all be grateful they hated each other so. If they'd been in collusion, with their attitude toward life, we'd all be dead!"

"You don't suppose they were, do you?" Crighton

asked with a new thought suddenly forming.

He, too, hesitated as if to explore the idea for a moment. "You know, that would open a number of possibilities. Speidel was certainly the last one to see DeVeer alive, and I understand he was the one that led you and George to the two bodies. We'd all wondered about his unlucky timing. I don't think we'd really pursued what the two of them might have been up to together. Could something have driven one of 'em to eliminate the other? The assumption has always been that DeVeer was the master and Speidel the slave. I wonder if Number One overshot and the worm turned on him—to mix the metaphor. This deserves a bit of thought."

He jumped up. "But I promised you music. You want noise; we've got noise. I'll split the difference with you. How about Ludwig's Pastoral? Four movements and I take you home. I want to leave you wanting more. Soon."

She snuggled down in the cushions and lost herself in cascades of sound. When the last note had been absorbed by the furnishings, he got her coat, and keeping up a casual flow of small talk, replaced her in the car and drove her directly to her apartment. She had wondered how he would end the evening, and as she turned to him, somewhat wide-eyed, to thank him, he took her hands in his and she felt, how appropriate: a Continental farewell for a rather Continental evening. But instead he suddenly dropped her hands and cupped her face in his palms and very gently tilted her mouth up to his. He kissed her then, gracefully and with restraint. When he had gone, she thought about it. It was as if he had lifted a piece of his art, examined it, and found it beautiful. She went to sleep wondering if that was how she wanted to be loved.

# 16

"All right," said George. "I'll tell you what's been going on—or at least the considered conclusion of an ancient mind."

They were back in Crighton's office. Crighton had arrived first, bright-eyed and cheerful. She was feeling one up on the world and giving everyone and everything the benefit of the doubt.

George had come soon after and was making small talk when Carson appeared somewhat diffidently at the door. Rather than the bluster and resentment that George had expected, his role was one of the chastened errant, eager to be returned to the fold.

"May I come into your presence, ma'am?" he asked.

"Nobody threw you out, you removed yourself. Come in and stack out of the way. Never mind the excuse. Mr. George, here's your council. How goes the war?"

He smiled benevolently. "My, you are frisky this morning, young lady. Very well, let's get down to business. I can't recall having expended so much mental energy on a problem in fifty years. I don't know whether it was the contempt of that policeman, or a need to prove to myself . . . in any event . . ."

He sat very straight in the chair beside Crighton's desk, his hands folded in his lap. Crighton perched on the edge, and Carson watched quizzically from the heap into which he had dropped on the floor.

"When one thinks of rare books and something going wrong," said George deliberately, "the first thing that comes to mind is theft. It was the first thing that each of us thought of, and I think that that is precisely what has been going on here. I think that someone has been stealing books from the Library, steadily and methodically over an appreciable number of years.

"I am inclined to think it is this prolonged performance that is remarkable here. I did a superficial research job upstairs, and I find that people have been stealing rare and costly books ever since they invented the scroll. But one piece taken by one person from one place. Not seriatim! But that seems not so here. If my analysis is correct, I'm afraid a great many people are going to be shocked at the number—the really vast quantity of treasure—that has been liberated from this library in recent time."

The older man cleared his throat drily, and continued in a quiet, didactic tone. "I note an odd thing about book thefts—indeed, about theft in general. In every case I read, the incident became known because the volume was discovered missing. Except for the time a questionable student lifted a hundred-thousand-dollar item from the UCLA library—he made the mistake of dropping from a second-story window directly on top of the night watchman!—it was never the act of stealing that attracted the attention. It was the absence of the material that was stolen." George stopped somewhat dramatically, as if attempting some kind of effect.

Carson looked puzzled, and said: "I don't see what you're driving at. Isn't that what gives away any theft?"

George appeared pleased at the question. "No. And that's where this man's—person's—scheme is so different. You notice a bank robbery because the teller is held up or the door's blown off the safe. You find the house burgled by the broken window, the drawers open, and the jewel case upside down. And in a library, the book is missed because it isn't in the glass case, or there's a hole when the summer inventory's run. But our man—or woman—solved that. He stole the books and then put another copy of the same thing right back in its place! No one would ever know they were gone and he could keep on stealing indefinitely!" He stopped in triumph.

There was a moment of silence, and Crighton asked: "But what's the percentage? If he has to get another copy to put back, what's he gained?"

"Condition, that's what. From what I can see from my brief examination of the rare book market, these bibliomaniacs are not so interested in getting a readable copy, as they are of a 'specimen,' an 'exhibit.' There seem to be all kinds of first editions and things which can't even be sold simply because they're too badly worn or damaged to be worth anything. It is my considered conclusion that somebody here is getting junk copies of rarities, cleaning them up to look as respectable as possible, stealing the Library's fine copies, selling these—and putting the trash in their place. As you would say, Steve, help me test my thesis. Did you ask for those titles yesterday?"

Carson pulled himself into an alert position and replied with animation, "Dammit, I did! I sailed into the Book Room up there, looking for old Brewer, and she was missing, but Speidel was there, and after brooding a minute, I asked him to get me the titles. He put up a big delaying action. First, he tried to con me into facsimiles in the public reading rooms. Then he claimed they didn't circulate, and only when I put the blast to him did he produce, under very funny circumstances, it seemed to me. I thought it meant that he knew they were missing or were involved in the murder or something. Are you saying it didn't?"

"No," said George. "I am saying it did not necessarily mean that. It might very well have meant exactly what he said: that the operating rules of that room are such that use of the volumes is always discouraged if there are reprints or facsimiles available elsewhere. I presume you've never had that kind of resistance when you asked for manuscript material?"

"No, because what I want usually exists only in the original. Nobody's ever reprinted it."

"Good. That's what I suspected. They try to protect their rare material even when it is right where it belongs! Thus not only would a reader have no reason to know that the book he was using had been substituted for a better edition, it is most unlikely that a reader will ever get his hands on the book to find out! I think DeVeer was right. The Manuscripts people collect materials for use; the Rare Books people resist use beyond all else. Incidentally, did you examine the three volumes? Was there anything unusual about them?"

"Nothing. The only news I could come up with was that those were first edition Stowes down there. The first edition came in two volumes—over six hundred pages—so we just had a pair of them, like the Ware and that paperback. But if you're right about this substitution thing, I was missing the point of what I was looking for. Wait—but you were right! All three of 'em were in lousy condition. One—no, probably at least two of 'em—even looked like they'd been repaired."

"Good," George replied, but with restrained satisfaction. "We may have learned something. We may only have proved we have not been refuted. If I can prevail on your assistance today, I would be much obliged if you would go up to the Library of Congress, and do exactly the same things: ask for the three books, tell me if they are as difficult to get there as they were here, and when—or if—you do get them, what kind of condition their copies are in."

"I can hardly wait!"

"Well, do. I've got some other things I want you for. But first, let's see where just this much of a . . . hypothesis? . . . gets us.

"First, let's don't lose sight of your first reaction. Maybe there was 'something funny' about the way Speidel responded to your request for those books. Look at all the things that could mean. It could have been DeVeer who was stealing the books either to get the money for himself or to embarrass Rose or Brooks. By blowing the whistle when he chose, DeVeer—and his professional view—would have gained ascendancy. One of them, or both, may have cut him down. Schwartz then may have been an unexpected witness or a silenced partner. Speidel knew so much about what DeVeer was up to, maybe he knew he was selling off the Rare Books collection! Ah, but maybe he knew nothing whatsoever about the scheme. He could just as easily be protecting the books because of routine orders. It still leaves us with all sorts of lovely possibilities!"

"You're enjoying it again," Crighton said. "You both should be ashamed."

George laughed and went on, his enthusiasm undimmed. "Brewer and Rose could be stealing them to get even with Brooks's treatment of the poor man. Or they could simply be after the money. Indeed, as far as that goes, Welles could be doing it to pay for that black sports car of his."

"I like that one best," said Carson quietly.

"The only person I can't see benefiting from such thefts is Brooks. It would seem he's got too much to lose."

"How do you tie the stealing to the murders, though?"

"A fair question. Again, I get so many combinations that either it shows it could be simple, or it suggests the whole thing may be a delusion. Suppose that De-Veer was not doing it himself, but caught someone else at it. This could have been what the implication of fraud was all about in his letters-to-the-editors. Speidel would have us believe the letters were meaningless, but what if they were real and Speidel was just trying to get me to forget them! Then whoever was doing it could easily have killed DeVeer to keep him from telling or turning in evidence against him. You can explain Schwartz's death in any one of three ways. He found out from someone and was killed to keep him quiet. Or, since we found the doubled volumes on his desk, he could either be helping the man who was stealing: as a craftsman, he could be rehabilitating the trash volumes up to a point where they would pass if they weren't examined too closely, or he could be doing the stealing and substituting the trash himself. If it's the former, the real thief could have killed him for knowing too much. If it was the latter, DeVeer could have found out, Schwartz killed him and then actually committed suicide from fear or remorse.

"The highest irony would be that all DeVeer was doing was making noise about 'fraud' in the sense of poor judgment in the use of the Library's money—

that he didn't know the thefts were taking place at all and was simply trying to frustrate Rose's 'useless incunabula' thing—but his letters panicked the thief into killing him for knowing something the poor man had never heard of! As you can see, the scheme explains everything but fails to focus on anybody."

"When you said you knew what but not who, I thought you were being coy," said Carson. "You meant exactly that."

"Yes. Unfortunately, most of them could have been involved in either one or both of the deaths, most of them have the reason, and oddly enough, I've convinced myself that most of them have the personality to have done it, too. Each one of them seemed to be having something he held most sacred either threatened—or suddenly made possible. The thefts and the deaths would benefit nearly every person involved!"

"Where does Speidel fit in here?" Carson asked. "He's the most repellent one around, and all that quotation stuff is enough to drive somebody to knock him off on general principles."

"He seems to think that he has more to fear from the police than from the murderer—which, of course, would follow if he were the one! I still don't know whether that *Tamburlaine* book was a clue or a coverup—and of course it is doubly interesting if my guess is right that the Poe *Tamerlane* is a junk substitute for a fine copy."

"Mr. George, why is Speidel locking himself in tonight? What good will that do him?" Crighton asked.

"I've been wondering about that, too. If he's the one who's doing the stealing, I suppose he simply wants to cover his tracks or to plant some sort of alibi—but if this is so, why would he tell Miss Brewer? This makes it look more logical that he really is innocent, and is trying to find out or prove who really did the thefts or murders or both. Working from this position, I asked myself, what would I do if I had a whole night to work in the stacks? I think I would go to that woman's shelf list and look at the prices on those cards. I would pick out as many expensive volumes as I could find on the probably foolish theory that the highest prices meant not only the rarest pieces, but the finest specimens. I would then spend the rest of the night going to each one. If I was right, I would come up with the largest pile of junk of any rare book department in the country! And if I were Speidel, I suspect I would also go through the desks of my fellow workers with a fine-tooth comb, hoping to come on some proof that would tie somebody to these particular volumes."

There was a long silence. Each of the three seemed to be taking some element of the theory and running off mentally with it, applying and testing it in his own way.

Crighton revealed her own pattern by saying defensively: "It couldn't have been Alan. Not in the murders, at least. He was with that book dealer from the time he picked him up at the airport till he took him back there after the interview. And we were listening to him when DeVeer . . . I don't see how you can say they all have the personality to do it. It doesn't fit him and he would get no benefit from it at all."

"Quite the contrary, as Mr. George says, either the thefts or—" Carson suddenly stopped, thinking this was a fast way to win a battle and lose a war.

"No, Crighton," George replied gently. "I am only trying to be as dispassionate about this thing as possible. You naturally wish to defend Alan Welles, and I assure you I have no reason to suspect him in particular. I am equally reluctant to suspect my friend from many years past, Nelson Brooks. Since he brought me here to look into this whole matter, it seems most unlikely it is he who is creating the mess. However, I am trying to be as objective as is humanly possible. I have forced myself to realize that I could have been brought here to provide an alibi, as some kind of character reference for him, and I will ultimately be asked to cover for him. I may indeed have been used in some way already which I don't yet know about. His whole purpose in life is indeed tied to this library. If DeVeer pushed him to the wall by overplaying his hand, I do not doubt it possible that Nelson could kill him. And therefore, while it is not comfortable for me, it is rational to recognize that the murders, at least, could have been done by Nelson Brooks. The first out of professional self-defense, the second, possibly because Schwartz discovered him doing it, or tied him to the murder of DeVeer."

"That's horrible," Crighton said flatly. There was no feminine delicacy in her remark. It was hard and cold. "I can say just as clearly in Alan's defense, he is sensitive, appreciative, finely tuned to any human relationship. It would be impossible for him to kill anyone."

George replied quietly. "Not so. He is sensitive to his own values. He is appreciative of what he finds beautiful. He is tuned to human relationships as they affect him. If any of these were marred—turned against him—I believe he is quite capable of eliminating the pain to himself. I strongly suspect his philosophy of live and let live is equally real in reverse, if someone refuses to let him live as he wishes, he could see that that someone does not live either. Did you find yourself genuinely in rapport last night? I do not apologize for being personal. You are very valuable to both of us, although Steve has not yet found a way to express it."

Carson looked up with genuine astonishment and then smiled a slow thanks. Crighton appeared not to notice the implications, indeed even respond to the thought. She was staring into space.

"It was a strange evening in many ways. Yes, I found him gentle and responsive. He was interesting—almost fascinating, and there was a sort of unfinished feeling about being with him as if there was so much more to be said about everything he touched on. He lives beautifully. His feel for . . . for . . . culture, I guess you'd call it . . . seems to be very genuine. He surrounds himself with rich, sensual things. He has beautiful furniture and pictures and artistic pieces which seem absolutely to belong. Nothing for effect. Everything because it actually matters to him. We drank coffee and talked and listened to his music. He's determined to sell me on chamber music, he says. He's promised to play the tapes of that concert the other night when he gets them back. He . . ."

Carson's eyes suddenly became preoccupied and then his hand flew up involuntarily as if to seize a word or thought out of the air. He started to speak when he discovered George looking directly at him with a sharp look of annoyance on his face. The annoyance seemed to be with himself, because when he became conscious of Carson's reaction, he hurriedly shook his head and glanced toward Crighton, who was still talking, as if free-associating to an analyst.

". . . No, I was not in rapport with him. If you mean did he turn me on—no, I guess not. But for some reason I felt that I wanted to get next to him—to let him lead my thinking along with his so I could get to feel about things as he does." Her eyes suddenly shifted to George and she said cheerfully: "I've never heard a man who has rationalized his aesthetic reactions so. Not only does he like culture, he's thought about why he likes culture, and why he likes liking culture!" She laughed, completely oblivious to the intense change in the atmosphere of the room.

There was an awkward silence. Crighton had exhausted her thought, Carson seemed eager to press something but felt he had been instructed to stay silent, and George seemed to be thinking furiously to himself.

He spoke: "Yes. There are several things that must be done. Assuming that we're right about the thefts, we must find out who's doing it, and quickly. The books must be being sold somewhere and somehow. Such a flow of rare material must have some kind of impact on the market. I am going to New York and talk to some dealers." He looked at his watch. "Nearly ten o'clock. I can be there by noon on the shuttle. That'll give me the afternoon at least.

"Steve, I want you to get up to the Library of Congress and go through the three books all over again. When you've got the books and looked at them, see if you can find out where they came from, how much they're worth, find out if my idea of condition rings true. Anything you think might be helpful; just don't let them know you have anything to do with the Werner-Bok."

He looked at Crighton. "What are you going to do this evening?"

"Liz Stroup wants me to go with her to a recital at American U. Why?"

"Nothing. Just do it. Don't let anything change your mind. Go and forget all about the Library here. Steve, we start."

They said their good-byes, and it was not until the men were completely out of earshot and climbing the stairs to the street floor that George said: "You're absolutely right, of course. Before you do anything else, find out if that interview was taped and when."

"Shall I call the station or ask around the Library?"

"Try the station first, and if you can't find out there, go to the music people upstairs. Stay as far away from that medieval charnel house as you can, and use any story that comes to your mind. I have great confidence in your ability to improvise. I'll be back by seven or eight tonight. As soon as you know where you'll be after that, leave the number at the Minerva Club and I'll call you."

By one o'clock, George was in the Rosenthal Galleries in New York, Carson was at the Library of Congress signing the entrance book, and Crighton was thus alone when she learned Speidel had left town. It was Elsie Brewer who phoned with the message.

"My dear," she said, "have you any idea where I could find Mr. George? Dr. Speidel asked me to tell him he was going to Philadelphia this afternoon, and he wanted to speak to him first thing tomorrow. I've tried to reach him at his club, but they don't seem to know where he is. Miss Jones, my dear, could you possibly tell me where to find him?"

Crighton was surprised to hear that Speidel was gone, but equally startled to learn she was now "my dear" to the Manuscripts people. Suddenly, she was "in," she thought, and in this crowd this was a consummation devoutly to be questioned.

"I'm sorry, Miss Brewer. He was here this morning, but I don't think he's even in the Library this afternoon. Did you leave a message at the Minerva?"

"No, I only inquired. Perhaps I should call them back and do so."

"Do you know what Dr. Speidel wants to see him about? I could tell him if he comes in later."

"Oh ... no. No ... he just asked me to say he was going to Philadelphia and would appreciate his calling him at his home as early Sunday morning as was con-

venient." She seemed suddenly ill at ease as if she had
dropped the script. "Yes, I think your suggestion is the
very thing to do. I'll call the club right now. Thank you
so much. Good to talk to you. Thank you again . . ."
She was still talking when the dial tone came on.

"Well, damn," said Crighton, returning her phone
to its cradle.

"Double damn!" she elaborated. She frowned at the
top of her desk for a moment, and then instinctively
prepared herself for some hard thinking by slipping off
her shoes and sitting on her stockinged feet. Here's a
pretty mess, she brooded.

Mr. George is in New York to case the book business. Speidel's in Philadelphia—which is just as book-
ish as New York, almost. Has he got it psyched like
Mr. George? Or is he panicked about what Mr.
George is up to, and is off to alert somebody to bury
the evidence? Maybe he's off across the border!
Should I tip off the lieutenant? Darn! When's Steve
coming back? Hell, we never set up the next meeting.
Why would Speidel pick this particular time to . . .
Wait a minute! He was intending to lock himself in the
stacks tonight. This means he won't be here. Has he
done what he was going to do, or does he think they're
closing in on him too fast? Suppose . . .

It took barely five minutes of such circular conversation with herself to come to the conclusion that she
would take advantage of Speidel's absence to get herself locked in instead. She tested the idea from every
side and found it sublime. It satisfied all the requirements—and best of all, it resolved her rolling irritation that whenever anything important happened,
George and Carson sailed off without even saying what
they had in mind, much less asking for her help.

No, if she could get herself locked in, she could do
the very things that George had implied he'd like to

do himself: check the shelf list for the most expensive items, and see if they satisfied his theory of mass, methodical theft. He'd also said he was sure Speidel would go through everybody's desk to see if he could tie the thefts to someone. Wow! She wasn't sure of the ethics of this, but if she could come out of the place with proof of who was doing what . . . There was simply no question about it. It was too good a chance to miss.

She proceeded to think logically. What would it take to bring it off? The Library closed at five on Saturdays. She presumed that someone checked the decks to be sure everybody was out, and then went out those big black doors, locking them behind him. This would mean she would have time to hide somewhere long enough to get everybody out, and then she could start through the records. As she recalled, once the doors were locked they were not reopened until nine the next morning. No, she corrected herself. Tomorrow would be Sunday. They wouldn't be opened until one o'clock. This gave her nearly a whole day to work! Surely she could come up with something by then.

There were details to be considered. She would have to lay in enough food to cover supper and breakfast. She would tell Liz she was going to spend the night with someone and not to count on her for the recital. She'd have to figure out the who and why of this alibi. She straightened up in her chair and slipped her shoes back on. It would be a busy afternoon between making phone calls, collecting provisions, and getting herself hidden in the stacks. She noticed a feeling of elation as she started to work and hastily assured herself it was the hope of a final resolution of the "mess," not the pleasure she was getting out of the disaster.

By four-thirty she had everything accounted for. She packed all her supplies in a typing-paper box, and then slipped this into a stack of manila envelopes, some file folders, and various other papers which together yielded an armful which could pass for something being taken to someone. She arranged her desk carefully, and turned out all the lights, aware of the feeling that she was about to leave on a long trip and wouldn't be back for some time. She scooped up her materials and set off down the hall and into the elevator. A gallant payroll clerk pushed the button for her and she soon found herself struggling with the iron ring on the black, cathedral doors. The wooden bar was very evident, and she felt it represented less a lock to keep her in than a bar to keep intruders out while she accomplished her purpose.

Inside, the usual stained glass gloom lit a half dozen forms at the tables. Pop Wright was talking to a scholar who appeared to be on his way out, and merely waved at Crighton over the visitor's shoulder. She started down the center aisle, and was somewhat chagrined to see Miss Brewer enthroned behind the issue desk, staring directly at her. Crighton exaggerated the weight of her armful, and forestalled any conversation by saying hurriedly, as she approached earshot: "Hi! No sign of Mr. George yet, but I left a note on my desk. Anyone in there?" She nodded toward the Rare Books side of the room.

"Yes, I believe both Dr. Rose and Mr. Welles are in. Two of the girls are in back, too. Whom did you want?"

"Fine. I'll scoot on in and leave these. See you."

Crighton walked busily toward the side door, and slid through it with considerable effort. The iron deck was empty, but four of the carrels had lights on, and the sound of a typewriter was coming from one of those closest to the shelving area. Her armload of papers seemed to have been adequate to get her into the work area without painful explanations, but she was doubtful if it would survive a direct conversation with any of the staff. She therefore almost ran toward the elevator and the shelter of the stairs behind it. Once there she stopped to listen to see if anyone seemed to be reacting to her presence. The typewriter continued in spurts, and there was no sound of movement in the other carrels.

She paused to consider. Where to hide? Which deck would be the safest? At the bottom ones, a searcher would be looking hard; toward the top, he'd be losing interest, but too close to the top, someone might whip down and catch her off guard. She decided on the third deck down and began to descend as quietly as possible.

Her feet on the steel treads seemed to make an uncomfortably obvious rumble, but there was no evidence it had aroused any activity above, so she reached her level and instinctively turned to her left to get as far away from the elevator as possible. It was not until she had reached the far wall that she realized she had headed directly toward the book carrier shaft where she had been so frightened two days before. She retreated a few bays, and slipped down between the bookshelves.

She was now in the gloom, the only light coming from the center aisle, and she felt more comfortable. The stacks were divided into two long ranges by the center aisle and then given further access by aisles against the walls at the outer ends. Crighton assumed that anyone checking to be sure the deck was cleared would go down the center aisle, looking both ways, and presumably turning off any bay lights that were still on. She decided her best bet was to wait at the far end of a bay, and whip around the end of the shelving as he passed. If he happened to walk down one of the outer aisles instead, she would not be exposed by accident, and she hoped she could outrun anyone and dash back to the center aisle before he arrived. The thought of having to move quickly—and quietly—led her to slip out of her shoes again and set them carefully in an open space on the shelf beside her. The steel and linoleum floor was cold under her feet, and she laid down some of her file folders to stand on. The rest of her supplies she distributed into spaces on nearby shelves, with her food at waist level for easy access. Thus fortified she decided she might as well be comfortable, and she removed a large volume from a shelf and laid it on the floor to sit on. It was too dark at this point to read, so she arranged herself to await the Library's closing.

Preoccupied by a mental review of who might be stealing the books and then speculation over whether he was the murderer or had simply tripped the murders accidentally, the time slipped past quickly, and she jumped at the sound of the elevator doors closing overhead and the car descending. It hummed for so long, she was sure it had taken someone to the bottom level, presumably to make the final check. She struggled to her feet, returned the book and the folders so they would not call attention to anyone searching down the aisles, and prepared to slip around the corner at the proper time.

As she waited expectantly, she found that the area was totally silent. Not silent with the absence of sound, but silent as if the vibrations of life had been blotted up by the books—a sponged-up silence, deadening and oppressive. As she waited, she found herself becoming more and more excited. What could he be doing down there? How far down was he, anyway? She began to calculate where she was standing in relation to the complete stack extending below into the basement. With her attention distracted by the problem, she was slow in realizing that she knew he was coming.

It was still perfectly silent, but she could hear his footsteps. It didn't make sense. And then she realized that she was feeling the vibration of someone walking as it was transmitted up the steel columns supporting the bookshelves and across the steel and linoleum floor. The area was vibrating, barely perceptibly, with the rhythm of a man walking deliberately to and fro on each floor beneath her. She found herself involved in trying to guess where he was down there, and how fast he was rising. Again, after it had been occurring for several moments, she realized that she could now hear—not just feel—him as he rose. He was two decks down. Then he was one deck down. Now he was walking up the stairs behind the elevator, and turning toward her end of the deck.

It sounded like a heavy man, older, walking deliberately, apparently giving himself time to look carefully down one side, and then coming back, examining the other. She centered herself at the end of her row of shelving, standing rigidly at attention, and trying to pull herself into the tallest, thinnest silhouette she could achieve. The steps approached, walked past, returned, and searched the far end of her deck. They returned to the stairs and slowly walked up them to the deck above. She held her position but relaxed. She was safely "in."

As she listened to the steps cross and rise overhead, she tried to guess whose they might be. They could easily have belonged to poor Dr. Rose, she thought. They could have been Pop Wright's, too. They did not sound like Alan Welles or Speidel. Not Speidel. He was gone. For the first time she realized that her subconscious had not fully accepted Miss Brewer's story of

Speidel's leaving town. Was it possible that Brewer's story was simply a way of accounting for Speidel's absence and he, too, was somewhere in the stacks, waiting for the building to be closed? She suddenly found herself tensing. She had no special reason to be afraid of Speidel. He had never been particularly threatening to her, but the idea of running into him here in these most peculiar circumstances could be most embarrassing—and the thought of his coming up behind her when she thought she was alone was downright frightening. She was in the process of reassuring herself that he couldn't be here... when the lights went out.

The stacks had resumed their dead silence, and there was no sound when the distant glow from the center aisle simply disappeared. It did not flicker and die. There simply were floor and ceiling and shelves and books, and then there was nothing. Absolutely nothing except black nothing. Total and complete darkness.

She instinctively grabbed for the end of the shelving to steady herself and then feeling vertigo about to seize her, dropped to the floor, still holding the stack support as if it were the only solid thing in the world to keep her from falling into a bottomless void. She knelt, clinging to the support with one hand and feeling the floor with the other and tried to get control of herself.

She suddenly realized that she had never been in total darkness before. She had been in dark rooms, she had hidden in closets, she had worked in photographic labs in journalism school, but they were never totally dark. They sometimes started that way, but little by little her eyes had begun to find the crack under the door, or the window with the night behind it, or the faint safety light over the tray. But never before total darkness. Trying to keep her sanity, she began to examine it. It was not dull black, it was brilliant, shiny black. Streaks of color seemed just to have passed. They were never there when she looked at them, but they had just been there. Purples, and oxblood, and orangy yellows. And the darkness had taken everything with it. The walls and shelves had disappeared, and there was nothing but black nothing, without limit, around and above and below her.

What to do? Just sit and wait until she was sure everyone had left above her, or flip on one of the bay switches that were at the end of each bank of shelving? She decided that the sound of a switch might carry up the steel and attract attention. It was better to wait. Why had the lights gone out? Was it a blown fuse or something? No, she decided, they must be turned off up at the offices so as not to waste electricity with the stacks empty. Probably to cut down the chance of fire, too, with no one in the locked part of the building. No, she had better wait a bit before she turned on even a local light for her own use.

She adjusted her position carefully, always with the feeling that if she moved from the precise spot on which she knelt, she would roll screaming over a ledge. She found the sensation of staring wide-eyed into black nothing almost sickening, and she suddenly covered her eyes with a hand. The pressure of her fingers against her eyes seemed to explain why she could not see and she found this more comfortable. In this position, with one hand clinging to the shelf support, she waited for time to run away. She noticed the smell of linoleum around her, the smell of paint on steel, the odor of books—they *were* musty, a strange word, but appropriate. She counted to a hundred a few times until she lost interest. She counted her pulse, and once she looked between her fingers in hope that a light might be visible somewhere. It wasn't, and as she thought about it, it was just as well. It might indicate there was someone still there and she wanted to be alone and the sooner the better.

She finally decided she had waited long enough. She struggled to her feet, still holding on to the stack support, her only contact with the world as she could remember it, and staggered from lack of circulation in her legs. Once fully erect, she took her hand from her eyes and tried to see where the switch would be. The blackness told her there was nothing there, but she felt down the steel until she found the switch, and with relief, she threw it.

Nothing. The blackness stretched away as endlessly as before.

There was no light there. Panic flooded over her and fear made her gag, her throat closed and she sucked for air. She felt she should scream or cry or call out, but the blackness kept her silent and what rational thought remained told her there was no one to hear her. She struggled to hold her sanity. One of the lights must work. It must be a faulty switch. She held to her support, but groped for the next one down the aisle, found it and its switch, and again nothing. The larger center aisle seemed more like home; this distant one beside the wall was new to her. She suddenly felt that safety must lie back toward the middle of the deck. She began to pass herself down between the books, letting the edge of shelves lead her. Again, the cool, hard steel had reality. The blackness above and beyond was empty and endless. She had almost reached the center aisle and the opposite end of the bookshelf when she realized that her shoes, the food she had brought, her little cache of familiar things were lost somewhere in the void behind her. She rushed on, found the end, found the switch, but again there was no reassuring light. She dropped to her hands and knees in the aisle, leaning hard against the support, as her only point of reference in the velvety blackness.

Rather than swirling out of control, she found herself regaining logic. She decided she had to get up to the offices. Surely, there must be light up there. The switches controlling the book decks must be different from the study rooms and the great medieval hall. The thought of that artificial afternoon coming through the stained glass seemed painfully desirable. She tried to reconstruct the appearance of the deck. The elevator, with the stairs behind it, must be in that direction, and eight or ten bays away. No, probably more, but she would be able to find it.

She rose to her feet, and reached for the next support. It came just at the last possible point before she had to relinquish the one behind her, but in this way she shuffled hand-over-hand toward the staircase.

She found she was beginning to lose her sense of time. She worked her way along—it was much farther than she had supposed, and for a terrifying moment she wondered if she had become confused and was going in the wrong direction—but at last the shelves ceased, there was a frightening gap, and then the cool, flat steel of the elevator walls met her hand. She slid over to it, and found it large, solid, and reassuring. She pressed both her palms against it, and leaned her cheek along its cool surface. She began to edge around behind it, toward the stairs, turned its corner, located the narrow T-beam on which poor Dr. DeVeer had been impaled at *"another time and in another country,"* she thought. How odd, she'd once heard Speidel say that. Marlowe, she supposed. She cautiously dropped to her hands and knees and crept into the void across the floor and gently met the gritty steel of the bottom step. She was on real ground again. She had only to go up two floors to light and sanity. She sat down on the step to reaffirm her bearings.

As she sat there, she heard the footsteps again. Heard? No, she knew it was like the last time. She was feeling them in the steel. The floor was trembling, the supports were carrying the sound, but there was nothing to hear. Someone was walking, not as heavily as before, still deliberately, but not so slowly. It was a walk of someone looking for something, not going from somewhere to somewhere. Her heart began to pound so loudly in her ears that she felt she was too deafened to hear anything.

She half rose, holding on to a support, but poised to run back toward what had been a sanctuary when there had been lights and shapes and edges to things. She stopped herself. Why was she frightened? It could simply be someone working late. If she wanted light so desperately, why not just call to him and ask for help? Some unreasoning feeling held her back. If this was all perfectly simple, she would have sacrificed her chance to resolve things. If there was something wrong, she did not want him to know she was there. And who was he? And what was he doing here? She listened and felt and tried to match the stride with the people she knew. Then he began to walk down the stairs above her and she could both feel and hear him.

He was now on the first deck below the offices, she decided, and he was walking deliberately down the center aisle to the far wall. He was searching just like whoever it was who had come before. She listened as he turned and walked the full length of the deck to the opposite wall, where he turned and stopped. There was a long silence, and then he came back toward the staircase above her.

Crighton crouched trembling and looking up, and as

the footsteps began to descend the stairs, she saw the thin beam of a flashlight reflected off of steel planes. He was in darkness, too, and he was searching the deck above her. She froze until the steps had gone around the elevator overhead and started down the aisle as before. She waited, forcing herself to stand when everything within her cried for her to run wildly away. Her arms and legs ached from holding until the steps were at the far end above her, and then she felt her way behind the stairs and slid down the railing and over the treads to the level below. She had put another deck between them, but she dared not descend farther. The steps were returning. She felt as if she wished to run blindly away from the open point of access and hide among the books, but the thought of being boxed in, surrounded with walls of volumes, steel, and blackness, was even more terrifying than trying to drop down before him. There was the same pause at the end of the aisle, the long walk, and then a very clear chuckle of amusement.

It was chilling. This was madness, she thought. No sane man was up there. Who was he seeking? Did he know she was in there—or was it someone who thought Speidel was coming back? Who could know it was she? Anyone who had seen her run down the aisle by the offices and not come out, of course. Who knew that Speidel was planning to come back? Mr. George had told Dr. Brooks. She had told Alan; had he told anyone? Was the man stalking someone special or anybody who was there to find his secret—whatever it was? She dared not take a chance. She shrank back from the stairwell until he had walked away above her in the same measured, inexorable cadence and proceeded down on the deck overhead. Now ready, she slipped down the stairs again and pivoted in the blackness, hoping to put yet another floor between them before he returned.

Holding to a support with one hand, she began to double back when she was struck in the stomach with something hard and flat. She stumbled and tried to protect herself, crouched with her arm raised defensively. She could hear something in the darkness in front of her, and she realized she had fallen against a book truck which was rolling away from the impact. She stood frozen, waiting for it to come to rest, praying for silence. It was denied her. The truck rolled against the wall of the elevator, striking with a ghostly rumble in the darkness, shortly followed by the drum of books falling on the steel floor beside it.

She pawed her way from support to railing, around the back of the staircase. Lurching and falling she tumbled down one flight after another. As she dropped into the darkness, she heard the pound of his feet overhead, a beam of light flashed, and a deafening explosion made the darkness throb around her. Fighting for her sanity, she realized it was a gun firing toward where the truck had crashed in the darkness. A high-pitched ringing in the blackness held the sound of ricocheting metal as the bullet sheared off the steel wall. Far enough below that the light had again disappeared, Crighton stood frozen in absolute silence again. Whoever he was above her waited. Finally, he moved, almost tentatively, down the flight of stairs, apparently paused to examine the source of the sound that had attracted him, and after hesitating for a moment, began to search the deck she had been on. Apparently he did not know whether she was hiding among its bays, or had fled farther below him.

The resumption of the pattern gave her a moment of confidence and she began to think ahead. How many decks were there below her? How long could she run before him before there were no more floors and he would be in the same room with her? Could she hide from him as she had from the first searcher, possibly huddled behind something and then trying to run past him toward the offices and lights and phones above? The darkness which had been the enemy was now protection so long as she could avoid that single beam of light. But there was no end to it. It would be hours before help could come. She feared that she would go mad or crumple in hysteria unless this could be ended. There must be some way of attracting attention.

The deliberate rhythm of the search gave her control over her movements. Now she waited for the halt at the end of the deck, and then slipped quietly down. She thought she must have three, maybe four decks between them now. As she stood, seeking desperately for some resolution of her troubles, she suddenly remembered: the fire warnings. How did they work? Sensors . . . sensing heat, was it? Could she break one? What would happen?

Working desperately in the blackness, with the sound of footsteps pacing evenly overhead, she searched the low ceiling of the deck. Books, supports, brackets, fluorescent lighting fixtures, everything but what she sought. Then she found it. A round thing, covered with wire mesh, with wires on either side. It must be it. She tore at it, pitching back and forth in the darkness, fearing to steady herself for fear of pushing something off and revealing her presence, but clawing at its impersonal shell. Nothing. In her fury, she seized the wire leading to it and tore it loose. She nearly fell with it, cutting her hand—but no sound, no light, nothing. For the first time, blind terror and despair seized her and she fell on her hands and knees, listening without thinking for the sounds above, and fleeing before them.

Animal-like, her hands gritty from the floor, hot tears on her cheeks, running and cringing, she barely realized that time was slowly disappearing and she was dropping down and down toward the point where he would be beside her, with only the darkness and the impersonal walls of books to protect her. Time and space and sanity smeared together and she lost bearings and reality.

And the lights came on.

Fluorescent, they flickered, one here and one there, gradually lighting the center aisle, and revealing the stairs and railings and supports she had been clutching level after level. Her eyes, totally adjusted to darkness, caught the meaning of the very first glow. With intelligence slipping back, she ducked under the staircase, scuttled to the far end of the nearest bay of books and huddled behind it, every muscle tense and prepared to twist and flee when he appeared.

The space was there again, gray at the extremities, light at the center, in total silence. The perpetual footsteps overhead had evaporated as completely as the darkness. She put a grimy hand to a damp forehead and pushed back matted hair. Had it all been hysteria? Was it simply hallucinations of the black void? Then way overhead, the pounding of many feet, shouts, and a rumble of steel running again through floor and walls. Now he was running immediately overhead, vaulting down the stairs, pivoting, and running lightly into the decks below her.

She could make out the shouting over the rumble of feet.

"Crighton! Crighton! Where are you?" Carson was bellowing from above.

She tried to answer and found her voice cracked and dry. She tried again.

"Here! Down here!"

As if unable to believe the reality, she huddled in her darkened aisle, waiting to see if the sound above her was real.

Carson burst down the stairs, all too evidently solid and very present. Three Library guards were behind him, all crazily jumping two and three steps at a time as they plunged down.

Crighton stumbled out to meet them, rushing into the arms of Carson, who seized her as if he had been holding her like this for a lifetime.

"Oh, how wonderful you look," she said. She seized him violently. "I was terrified!"

Everyone stood momentarily without purpose, beaming as if there was nothing more to be done. Carson began gently to disengage her, and said, "My love, you look beautiful to me, too—though I must say, you are the most God-awful mess of any woman I've ever been in love with!"

She looked down. Her pantyhose were twisted and drooping, her skirt was streaked with dirt, and an air of total dissolution prevailed. She put a hand to a grimy, tear-stained face, about to dissolve again.

"Look," said Carson. "What happened here? Are you really all right?"

His questions returned her to reality.

"It was awful! I hid in here to spend the night like Mr. George said—Speidel isn't coming. He's in Philadelphia. When everyone left, they turned out all the lights, and before I could get upstairs someone tried to kill me. No, I mean it! There's someone down there with a gun. He was looking for me and actually shot where he thought I was."

The four men exchanged looks and instinctively

drew back from the staircase where Crighton had pointed.

Carson thought quickly and said, "We'd better get out of here. She ought to be upstairs, and there's no sense in us playing heroes either. Call the elevator before whoever's down there does. Come on, let's get back from here."

The group retreated, still watching the staircase, until the elevator had arrived, been gingerly peered into, and finally boarded. They slipped hastily in and rode with it to the top. Crighton noticed with a shudder there were only two buttons below the one for the deck they were on.

As the car rose, Carson said, "When we get to the top, kill the elevator to keep him from using it. I'll take her down to the guard office and call Conrad. Why don't you all cover the door to the deck from the Reading Room? It's steel-covered, and you can prop it with a chair or something to keep him in there till we can get the cops. Princess, do you have any idea who it is?"

"Just that it's a man. I kept trying to match his walk with everybody we know, but it never made sense to me."

"Don't let it bug you. We'll give it to the professionals."

Leaving the guards to cover the door, they headed for the guard office through the empty, half-lit library, and soon were swept up in a confusion of assignments, explanations, calls, and speculations. Before the last were finished, the results of the first materialized. Conrad and George arrived together, at the head of a dozen uniformed and armed men. Conrad was looking even more irritable than usual, but treating George with a new respect. Carson thought, the Old Boy must've found what he's looking for.

"Mr. George," he said, "do you know who's down there? Is he really dangerous?"

"I think I do, Steve, and if I'm right, he may well be. It's hard to know. Very hard."

Conrad broke in sharply. "We're going now. You stay here with the girl. How are those decks laid out? Can he get out anywhere except the stairs?"

George said firmly, "I am going with you, Lieutenant. I think it is possible I can convince him to give himself up. We know he's armed, and he has absolutely nothing to lose. If you try to bull him out, somebody's liable to get killed. I think I can talk to him."

"Yeah, I'm going too," Carson said belligerently. "I began this mess with DeVeer and I expect to be in on the end. Anyway, I can tell you how the decks work and where the approaches are."

"All right. Come on, both of you, but stay back. Way back." Conrad either agreed with them or felt it wasn't worth the time to argue.

The group went forward silently. At the door to the stacks, they discussed the layout of the area, and Conrad described how he wished to pursue the search. Carson, listening from the margin of the group, was reminded of street fighting in basic training—rush the open spaces and drop to cover fast—and they began the operation.

With the stairs the only point of access to each deck, the quarry knew precisely where to lie in wait for his pursuers, and with no way to flank the area of search, each floor was a test of nerves. Conrad worked slowly, minimizing the chances of danger as much as possible, and searching each deck with total thoroughness, every square foot being examined before the next floor was rushed.

Nearly two hours had passed before they reached the final floor. Following their established pattern, six of the men surrounded the stairwell with guns pointed, and three more plunged down the steps to run to the nearest cover. They found a deck without shelving or books, brilliantly lit, and filled with the same dark filing cases that had surrounded the binders' cage in the opposite stacks. Two-thirds of the way toward the end was Alan Welles, poised, smiling, a long-barreled target pistol in his hand. He was leaning comfortably against a row of cabinets.

"Good evening, gentlemen," he said.

# 17

---

"So you finally made it! I was tempted to call to you, but it seemed a shame to spoil your fun."

The group spilled onto the floor until they were all watching him down the long deck. They spread out across the rows of files, waiting for an order from Conrad on how to proceed. My God, Carson thought, we're back in the trenches.

"Where's Speidel?" Welles asked. "I thought I had the son of a bitch about the third level down. Did I wing him?"

"That was Crighton Jones, Alan," George answered calmly. "Do you see where your plan has taken you?"

A look of genuine horror crossed his face. "My God, no! You're not being candid, sir. Why would Crighton have been there?"

"Without my knowledge, she came back to verify a theory of mine." With his hands hidden by the filing cabinets, he pantomimed two end runs. Conrad understood and drifted toward the end of an aisle, looking pointedly at the farthest policeman. George continued in the same even tone. "I had it in mind there might be a certain deterioration in the quality of the collection upstairs. Crighton was testing my assumption."

Welles laughed. "Good for you, sir! And did she verify it? She is all right?" His concern appeared real.

"She's all right, no thanks to you. No, she had no chance to pursue my thought. I spent an interesting afternoon with David Rosenthal, however. Tell me, was he the only one you were selling through?"

Welles began to laugh again, easily, pleasantly, apparently genuinely enjoying the situation. The policeman at the extreme end of the row shifted his billfold from one pocket to another, dropped it, stooped to pick it up, and failed to reappear.

"I'll bet you left poor David in a state. I'm sure nothing like this ever happened to him before. As you must know, he had no idea of what I was doing to him. If the news didn't carry him off on the spot, it should strengthen his character. How did you leave him?"

"As you say, shocked, but still in good health, I think. Did he have them all?"

Welles smiled again. "Now that is something I think I'll leave for you to work on. Let's see. David must have handled seventy or eighty of them, I suppose. The question is, how many more were there, and how can you find out? Well... no. No, I don't think I'll answer that. Brooks can look in the remaining hundred thousand volumes and try to guess which ones were mine. It will be my legacy to him." He smiled pleasantly.

"Where did you get the substitutes, Alan?" George continued. A policeman at the other extremity leaned over to tie his shoe and disappeared from sight.

"Mostly from my research in those New England libraries. They were absolute gold mines! Little collections which were town libraries back in the Flowering of New England had first edition Emersons and Hawthornes and de Tocquevilles. I found a complete set of the Federalist Papers just sitting on the shelves in Woodstock which were the actual honest-to-God essays bound together! Nobody in the place had the slightest idea of their value. That was the beauty of the thing! The little libraries never really missed the books because they were so old and faded they needed new copies anyway, and the substitutions here put the mint copies back in the hands of collectors where they belonged. It's inexcusable to bury really rare volumes in institutions. I was liberating the prisoners and returning them to hands which would love them." He nodded gracefully.

"I'm glad to hear there was some high purpose to your folly," George said.

"Don't you believe it," Welles replied. "I was after the money. And it made a right good living, too. My beloved wife set me on the path. She was well-heeled herself, but recognizing my affection for luxury, she insisted on alimony to twist it where it hurt. Among the objets d'art I'd bought with her checking account was a really fine collection of rare books so she let me sell them off to help meet the payments. She was right. It was agony to part with the things, but I'd present them to David and he'd turn 'em into cash and she'd get it every month. The books brought about half of what she had coming, so the rest of it came out of my hide. When it began to affect my standard of living, I was driven to some creative thinking."

"When was that?" George asked casually.

Welles smiled. "Let's say 'several years ago.' Anyway, I began to add a few of the Werner-Bok's better volumes to the monthly sale, and poor David never knew the difference. My wife's books ran out a good long time ago, and the alimony ceased when she re-married, so it's been clear profit ever since. You can't imagine how much I've appreciated the skill of the W-B's selection officers. They built a splendid hoard to choose from."

"Alan," said George, "had DeVeer really found out what you were doing?"

"Well taken, sir!" He nodded the long pistol in George's direction as a pedagogue would flourish a pencil at a class. "You know, I don't know to this day! Those letters of his were so ambiguous you couldn't tell whether he really had something or was just trying to drive Brooks into the asylum! The trouble was, I couldn't afford to take a chance."

George checked the far sides of the room out of the corners of his eyes. The men must be well started by now. "Did you think it fair to kill a man just to be . . . on the safe side?"

"DeVeer? He should have been dispatched years ago! He had so many souls on his conscience, someone should have removed him long since! No, I haven't the slightest regrets over him. I do feel badly about poor Schwartz, though. He'd been doing the repairs, of course, so as soon as I released DeVeer from his mortal coil, Schwartz guessed it must've been me, and promptly sank his teeth in my neck! I'd been giving him twenty-five percent and I couldn't blame him for trying to enlarge his portion. We all try to get as much as we can for as little as we dare, but I could see there was going to be no end to it. I had no intention of working for *him!* He was so unreasonable—all it would have taken was a little moderation. Whatever happened to the Golden Mean?"

"I'm afraid it never was. What was all that *Tamburlaine* nonsense?"

"Oh, I'd hoped your friend Conrad would take care

of Speidel for me—I was only trying to eliminate the world's second greatest blister! But I finally had to try it myself. There was too big a chance he'd heard about the books from DeVeer—if DeVeer knew—but it'd have been very little loss in any event. Where is he, by the way?"

"In Philadelphia, I understand."

"Great heavens! How disappointing!"

Welles straightened up from his casual position until he was standing firmly behind his case. He gently placed the pistol against his temple.

"Mr. George, sir, your two uniformed friends must be about down here by now, and I have no intention of suffering restraint. I've got my money's worth. If I had it to do over again, I wouldn't change a thing. It's been good and I intend to quit while I'm ahead. Do give my deepest apology to Crighton Jones, will you? I never intended to harm the innocent. Now, to spare you any unpleasantness, I bid you all good evening."

He must have bent his knees, because he sank slowly out of sight behind the cases, still perfectly erect.

"Rush him, dammit!" Conrad bellowed.

There was a rather dull, very localized explosion and the sound of his falling.

"The poor man," said George. He turned to Carson who was staring aghast at the spot where they had last seen him. "As you would say, baroque to the last."

They leaned against a wide banister where the stairs spilled into the Great Hall, George, Carson, and Crighton, watching the flow of police, ambulance men, the coroner again, all duplicating the actions of the earlier tragedy, but this time on a far grander scale. The half-lit hall and the echo of footsteps from shadowy vaults gave a ghostlike, slightly unreal air to the scene.

"How under the sun did you manage to turn up when you were so badly needed?" George asked.

Carson, who was standing by a considerably repaired Crighton, replied, "I can ask you the same thing! I went off to the Library of Congress, had a very profitable afternoon—they have three first-edition Stowes, one *Guide*, and no *Tamarlane* at all—and then came back down just before closing time. I went down to see The Crighton here, and found her light off but her coat still hanging on the hook. I concluded she must be around somewhere, so I sat down to wait her out. When five o'clock came, there was still no sign of her, and the guards turned up and threw me out. I figured there must be some logical explanation, so I took off home, but the more I thought about it, the less I liked it.

"I finally looked her up in the phone book, got her roommate instead of her, and she gave me this bit about your staying with friends." He looked at her fondly. "That didn't make much sense after Mr. George's warning, so I kept calling this Stroup person you were supposed to be visiting, and she finally got home on the third try. She'd never heard about the nonsense, of course, so I really did get spooked. I tried you, sir, at the Minerva, ground around a while, and finally decided to go back to the Library.

"I beat on the door till they let me in, and then I got involved in a great rhubarb and after they went down and searched your room and were trying to throw me out again, I was arguing and raising hell when that bell went off like a ring from Heaven!"

"What bell?" George asked.

"One of those on the wall there in the guards' room where they keep track of all those fire signals. They've got a gadget that shows the condition of each deck, and one of the deck bulbs lit up saying 'tilt' or something. Apparently it signalled 'system inoperative,' not fire, but it got their attention and that was all I needed. I yelled that was it—something was wrong up there, and we all roared up. Where did you come from?"

"I'd had a most informative afternoon with David Rosenthal, and when he'd confirmed our worst suspicions, I flew back and went directly to the police station to report to Conrad. We were there going into it for the fifteenth time, it seemed to me, when the call came. Crighton, did you trip that signal or were you saved by the world's thinnest piece of luck?"

She shuddered, looking smaller and more feminine by the moment. Carson leaned across the marble to lay his hand on her arm.

"No, I think that was while I was still functioning—or just before I came completely unglued. I was staggering around in the dark and I thought maybe I could do something to one of those fire things, but it was all protected by some kind of cover. I just grabbed in desperation and tore the wire down. It must have brought it off."

"You cut that much too close," George said solemnly. "I will spare you the I-told-you-so, but consider yourself having been given a stern lecture."

"Yes, sir," she said, looking properly contrite.

Conrad come out of the guards' office, grimmer than ever, followed by a puzzled Nelson Brooks.

"Come on. I want to talk to all of you. Is that Lounge still available?"

"We'll use my office," Brooks said with a note of authority in his voice that had been absent for the past several days. "It is more appropriate."

They trooped off toward the elevator and eventually

followed the Director into his own rooms. They were brilliantly lit, and crisply efficient, and as each took a chair, Crighton thought, I'm back in the real world again—blessedly.

"Uh, Mr. George," Conrad said in a low, somewhat grudging tone, "since it was you that really psyched this thing, maybe you'd better tell the Director what's been going on—or is he up to date?"

Brooks scowled and started to say something, but George forestalled him.

"No, I'm embarrassed but I haven't had a chance to see as much of Nelson as I've wished—and of course, it wasn't until this morning that I thought I was getting the feel of our problem. I want to note at once, Lieutenant, that your initial diagnosis was correct: it was indeed a matter of money, sex, or booze, just as you said it would be."

Conrad permitted the nearest thing to a smile that any of them had seen on him, and said, "Yeah. It always is."

"No, I thought it was much more complex than that, but I was wrong. Nelson, very briefly, this is apparently what happened . . .

"Alan Welles needed the Lieutenant's money because his divorce not only separated him from his wife's bank account and its resultant luxury, but she attacked his own income through some punitive alimony. In order to raise money, he began to sell off the finest volumes of your rare book collection, replacing them with copies that were so marginal that all they were good for was to take up space. In retrospect— and ignoring the damage he has done to you and the Library—it was really an ingenious idea. I must admit that the more I brood on it, the more I am filled with admiration for the man!"

Carson grinned and nodded, and Brooks looked

more irritated by the moment. George hurried on.

"Because of his access to the rare book trade—he was nationally known, he had the Werner-Bok's pedigree behind him, and he'd been appraising their auction stock for years—all he had to do was say something like, 'I've turned up a splendid copy of so-and-so, Bill, would you like it? I'd rather you didn't mention my giving it to you—can't afford to show favoritism among dealers in my position, you know'—and off it'd go! I don't *know* that was his approach, but it seems very likely. I *do* know in Rosenthal's case, he told him that 'someone has brought some things to the Library and though we already have a copy of this one, the donor says that if I broker it separately, we can get the rest of the titles for the collections.' Poor Rosenthal thought he was helping out the institution and never questioned what was going on at all. What we don't know is: Was he selling only to Rosenthal, and if not, how many more dealers were involved? He must have been personally acquainted with half the major houses in the East, wasn't he?"

Brooks clutched at his forehead and nodded.

"In any event, this was going along beautifully for we still don't know how long or how many, when DeVeer started on that poison pen campaign of his. Apparently, all DeVeer wanted to do was cause a bibliographic ruckus. You recall that the three Bibles he was using for bait are absolutely virginal—flawless—they'd stand up to any scrutiny without any damage to the Library. He just wanted to bring the press in to dramatize the 'waste of money' on those 'useless rare books.' This would get you and the Rare Books Division on the defensive and get himself in the catbird seat. I don't believe he had the faintest idea of what Welles had been up to.

"But Speidel found out about the letters from an

evening trip he always made through the wastebaskets—and here was dirt beyond his wildest dreams. The amount of dissension he could stir up with something as spectacular as this must have driven him straight into the hall. He runs over and tells Elsie Brewer that her ideal, Rose, is going to be ruined by DeVeer. Brewer runs to Rose to tell him what DeVeer is up to. Rose, probably in simple innocence, tells Welles, and Welles with a very guilty conscience wonders, 'How much does he know?' Is he just trying to stir things up, or does he really know what's been going on, but thinks it's Rose who's doing it? Probably Speidel didn't know or tell enough of the actual details for Welles to be able to make a rational judgment, and in the absence of truth, Welles decides he can't afford to take a chance. He never liked DeVeer much anyway, and he thinks if he kills him casually, no one will think anything of it, and any threat to him will be eliminated right off the bat. So he decides that the forthcoming concert is the sublime time.

"He urges his old friend, Rosenthal, to come down in late afternoon and he promises to have him on the eight o'clock train so he can have supper aboard and be home by midnight. The good man arrives at National Airport on the shuttle, Welles drives him to the Library, they tape the interview, play it back one time, and Welles drives him over to Union Station. Welles then comes back to the Library, probably comes up the back way and stays out of sight until the orchestra is nearing the intermission. He lifts a phone somewhere—probably one of the pay phones up on the third floor—and garbles his voice slightly to tell Pop Wright to go and get DeVeer. He then watches for Wright to come out and go into the Lounge, he goes into Rare Books behind his back and down to Deck One. He either takes the knife off that paper cutter or has already put it in a file drawer across from the Esterházy material. In any event, he waits till DeVeer appears and kneels down to that bottom drawer that Welles has specifically requested material from; Welles comes up, no doubt DeVeer says I thought you were down in the recording room, he says no I dashed up here to get it, DeVeer looks back down, and that is the last he ever knew.

"Welles let the poor man bleed into that drawer for a bit until the worst was past and then dragged him around to the support at the foot of the stairs. He propped him against the support so the beam edge filled the wound, cleaned up the floor, and went back upstairs . . ."

"Wait a minute," Conrad broke in. "I wanted to ask about the 'cleaned up' part. Why didn't anybody notice anything about that?"

"My guess is, he probably used a bolt of the bookbinder's cheesecloth—there are stacks of it down in that cage—tidied things up and put it in another filing drawer for later disposal."

"Mightn't somebody come on it accidentally?"

"It was like that Esterházy drawer you discovered." George avoided "I sent you to." "The odds were enormously against someone touching either one of those drawers. Probably less than two percent of those files will be opened in any year! Half of the collection of a big research library won't be touched in twenty years! No, he had very little to worry about until he could return and destroy it all at his leisure."

"I still don't see why that cop didn't spot any of this when he was checking it out."

"No, Lieutenant," George replied, "I come to his defense again. I keep telling you, in the peaceful environs of a library, there is simply no reason to look for the unusual. The man had fallen down the stairs, the light was poor, people had trampled the linoleum all around the place. There was no reason to think otherwise."

"How did he get out of there without running into the guard?" Brooks asked.

"Don't you remember? You were used to provide that alibi yourself! Welles simply took the stack elevator to the top floor, walked into one of the offices, and called Wright. He told him to go and find you and tell you that Rosenthal would not be coming to the Lounge. As soon as Pop went out the door, Welles followed him, probably went down the back way, went under the Great Hall and came up by the front door where he joined the crowd like everybody else."

"Wouldn't someone have seen him—the guard in the rear, if no one else?"

"Of course! Someone could have seen him almost all evening. But so long as no one saw him actually standing over DeVeer, who would care? Everybody saw everybody that night. The staff was all over the place —just as they always are. Only the people who were in the Lounge knew that his voice was coming out of the radio, and remember—there was no investigation of who was where, because there was no suspicion that DeVeer had done anything more than fall down the stairs!"

Carson, who had been listening to the whole conversation with a self-satisfied look on his face as if he had devised it all himself, prompted George, "Tell 'em about Schwartz. I think that's the wildest part of all."

"Ah, yes, and possibly the most unnecessary. Schwartz had been upgrading the junk editions, of course, and in view of how long it must have been going on, they seem to have worked together very well. Apparently Welles would hand him a decayed volume he'd picked up in some boondock library and then put the Werner-Bok's copy on top of it and Schwartz would make the used one look as much like your mint copy as possible. Then they'd stuff the repaired job in the hole and Welles would sell the good one.

"We'll never know precisely what gave it away, but while the rest of us were accepting DeVeer's accident at face value, Schwartz must have tied it to Welles at once. I wonder if it may not have been as simple a thing as the borrowing of that cutter blade that did it. Probably Welles didn't much care whether Schwartz knew or not, having gotten used to Schwartz's having something on him, but he seriously misjudged the risk in this one. Apparently Schwartz began to blackmail him at once, and Welles decided to do away with him, too. I think when Welles painted himself as an authentic live-and-let-live Epicurean, he was quite genuine. But when something crossed him, he was so detached about it, he could talk to the three of us in the basement at twelve, eliminate Schwartz at twelve-thirty, and breeze off with Crighton for lunch at one! Terrifying!"

"He tried to pin the Schwartz murder on Speidel, didn't he?" Brooks asked.

"Ah, the *Tamburlaine* confession. I think with his penchant for ironies, he did that as much for a laugh at the system as he did to achieve any real purpose. If he could fool the Lieutenant with it as a suicide note, it would end any further inquiry about Schwartz and put a finial to the whole DeVeer thing. If he could get me to dramatize the Marlovian tie to Speidel, he could hang one if not two murders on him and eliminate him from the scene. And I suspect as much as anything else, he did it to give Speidel the fright of his life through his own brand of scholarship! Actually, I suspect he threw the whole thing off as a gesture to amuse himself. The chance of any of us reading that page was pretty slight, you know, and as it turned out —with the blood all over the page—it was a miracle it was read at all. Remember, if he'd been killed on the morning paper or a copy of *War and Peace*, I doubt if anybody would have thought to look at the page."

"Then why did you?" Conrad asked.

George laughed. "By this time, I was convinced we had a highly intellectual adversary, and there's nothing like the printed word for the intellectual to use as a weapon! When Welles cut that rope over poor Speidel's head . . ."

There was a knock against the opened door, and everyone looked around to see Speidel himself standing there, his eyes sparkling in the little patch of face that appeared between a black, crushed hat and a huge, black overcoat.

"*'When the battle ends, we all will meet and sit in council,*' eh? I understand that the good Mr. Welles has finally resolved our doubts. Yes. And all he ever wanted was to *'live in peace and do what things I would.'*" He turned to Conrad and said, "That's from *Faustus*, Lieutenant."

"No doubt," Conrad rasped.

Brooks stood up furiously, throwing back his chair as he rose.

"Speidel, you can cut the condescension and the holier-than-thou act. I trust it won't come as a surprise to you that you will have your dismissal on your desk Monday morning."

Speidel looked startled. A frightened glance crossed his eyes for only a moment, and then was quickly replaced by one of craft. He smiled.

"No, Dr. Brooks, I don't think so. If you think about it, you'll know I can tell things about your administration that would ruin you forever. I think not, no, no dismissal. You will learn to love the way I run that division in the years ahead."

"Like hell I will! I've had time to test my values in the past few days, mister, and the main thing I learned was I'd put my reputation too goddamned high. Believe me, Speidel, you can say anything you goddamn please, but hear this: If it's true, then I deserve it, and I'll take the consequences. But if you slander me by one goddamned syllable, I'll see you in jail the rest of your natural life. Do you hear me? Then get out of here. Now!"

The terror returned, but he laughed again, and started to speak.

"Get out, I said! I don't want to hear another word!"

The man attempted a look of arch contempt which failed, turned, and was gone.

There was deep silence in the room. Conrad's face twisted into that near-smile a second time, and George said quietly, "That was very well done, Nelson. I congratulate you."

"I suspect I've had it, but I can at least go out of here clean," Brooks said.

"You can never tell about these things. Play it straight. The sight of a librarian riding out something as dramatic as this just may appeal to somebody!" George rose and turned to the young people.

"I do believe we've missed dinner somewhere along the line. Will you be my guests tonight? Let's leave the Director and the Lieutenant for the administrative details. If you need us, I presume tomorrow will do just as well?" he asked the detective.

"Yeah. It's okay with me. I've just got one small thing to ask. Can you tell me how that guy shot a pistol in a library and nobody heard a frigging sound?"

"Of course. You'll find that books are the greatest noise absorbent this side of rock wool. You go fire a blank at one end of Nelson's decks, and you'll find by the time the sound gets to the other it sounds like a wet champagne cork."

"Hmmm. I'll just do that. Uh, George . . . uh, you've been quite a help on this. Yeah. Well, I'll be calling you."

"I'll be in touch, too, Ed," said Brooks. "And Miss Jones, you've proved yourself a very valuable addition to the, uh . . . institution. I . . . thank you."

George waved a hand and led Carson and Crighton from the room. When they reached the hall, Carson said: "Well, sir, that's as close to a testimonial as you're going to get from officialdom, I do believe. I hope you have some deep, inner satisfaction to pay for your labors."

George grinned. "I do indeed. I feel five years younger and twice as sure of myself as I did just last week. I think we all came through this thing ahead. Crighton, how're your nerves?"

"They're coming back fine, sir. It's the premature gray in my hair that worries me."

"I'm particularly fond of gray," said Carson.

"I thought you might be," said George. "And how's your applied historical method?"

"If I may say with pardonable pride, it worked. We collected the evidence. We sorted it into significance and noise. We drew conclusions, generalized them, and took action. I tell you, it flew."

"I quite agree and I congratulate you. Frederick Jackson Turner would be proud."

They had reached the Great Hall and as they neared the door, George turned back and looked up into the shadowy vaults above.

"Strange. I am getting a paternal feeling about the old mausoleum. I wonder how many books they're really missing. You know, Welles was right. There's no way of knowing without looking into every one, and then how can they be sure? Hmmm. And somewhere there's a copy of a first edition *Tamerlane* waiting to be offered to an eager world. I wonder where and when . . . ?"

They looked at each other and smiled the knowing look of conspirators . . . and went out into the night.